A MURDER AT THE MOVIES

ELLIE ALEXANDER

Storm
PUBLISHING

To request permissions, contact the publisher at rights@stormpublishing.co

Ebook ISBN: 978-1-80508-410-5
Paperback ISBN: 978-1-80508-412-9

Cover design: Dawn Adams
Cover images: Dawn Adams

Published by Storm Publishing.
For further information, visit:
www.stormpublishing.co

ALSO BY ELLIE ALEXANDER

The Body in the Bookstore

This book is dedicated to libraries and librarians, most especially my childhood library in Vancouver, Washington, where the summer I turned thirteen, I checked out every single Agatha Christie novel on the shelves, igniting my unending passion for reading and writing mysteries.

ONE

If you had asked me years ago what I would be doing in my early thirties, I never would have imagined that I'd be working at a bookstore in a converted manor house, spending my lunch break sitting outside on the sweeping Terrace, soaking up the golden radiance of the California sunshine, lingering over my chicken salad sandwich and sipping my mint-infused lemonade, listening to the lulling sound of birdsong, and drinking in the view of the meticulously manicured gardens surrounding the Terrace.

Yep, this is my life, and I love every minute of it.

Someone pinch me, please.

My younger self would have scoffed at the idea of working at a family-owned bookshop in a quaint small town. That Annie Murray had been a driven criminology student who had grand plans to move to the big city and take over the world. But there was so much she had to learn and she had no idea what lay ahead.

That's okay. It was part of growing up, and I had done a lot of growing up in the last few years, thanks in a great extent to the Secret Bookcase. I swirled the reusable straw in my lemonade and smiled at the thought. I was proud of what I had accomplished and equally excited about everything we had coming up.

I mean, who could not love this?

Today, I was spoiled because I had the Terrace to myself. I shifted my laptop to the side and closed my eyes for a second, letting the heat from the sun warm my skin. It was rare for the estate to be so quiet, which was all the more reason to take advantage while I could.

By tomorrow, the bookstore would be humming with visitors in town for the long weekend. I liked the balance between busy days and days like this when I didn't have to keep one eye on the clock or scarf down an energy bar behind the cash register because there wasn't a spare minute to take a lunch break.

As if on cue, an email notification dinged on my laptop. I set my drink on the side of my chair and checked my messages. The first email was from a customer in South Carolina searching for a copy of *I Married a Dead Man*, a mystery written by William Irish and originally published in 1948. We received dozens of similar requests. One of the things I loved most about this job was connecting books and readers. Our inventory of new, used, and rare books and collectibles was one of the biggest in the country. It wasn't uncommon for customers as far away as Australia to reach out to us and happily agree to pay exorbitant rates for international shipping when they discovered we had a copy of a book they'd been searching for for years.

I flagged the message to check inventory when I was done with my break.

The second message was from a law firm in Silicon Valley.

I knew immediately what it was regarding. I'd been making inquiries into the death of my best friend, Scarlet, ever since Dr. Caldwell, my former criminology professor and Redwood Grove's current detective, had shared her case notes with me.

Thus far, everything seemed to lead to a dead end, but that wasn't going to stop me.

How do you let go of the past? Is it possible, when trauma haunts you like a ghost lingering in the shadows, its sorrowful whispers echoing through every memory?

I'd spent the better part of a decade trying to figure that out and attempting to piece together who had brutally murdered Scarlet days before graduation to no avail. We had been tasked with trying to solve a cold case for our final assignment. There was no doubt in my mind that whatever Scarlet had uncovered from the case ultimately led to her death, but it wasn't until I reconnected with Dr. Caldwell a few months ago that I had confirmation.

Dr. Caldwell had received a note from Scarlet's presumed killer, warning her to cancel the assignment. She assumed the warning was a prank or had come from a student who wasn't prepared for the final. When Scarlet was found dead, Dr. Caldwell realized her error. She had lived with the crushing guilt ever since.

It was a feeling I was all too familiar with. Scarlet's death was as much my fault. I shouldn't have encouraged her to dive deeper into the investigation. I shouldn't have treated it like an adventure. I should have gone with her to meet her "source."

It should have been me.

I scanned the email, holding on to a tiny glimmer of hope that the message might contain a nugget of news. It didn't. Just more of the same...

We regret to inform you that our latest inquiries have failed to uncover anything new.

I sighed and slammed my laptop shut.
You're torturing yourself, Annie.
And you have a lot of work to do.

I glanced toward the garden. Late summer was in full bloom. Honeybees buzzed between immaculately trimmed rose bushes and rows of rosemary and lavender. Leafy palms stretched toward the sun, the only giveaway I was in Redwood Grove, California, not a royal garden in the English country-side. Pastoral grasses and views of the coastal mountains extended in the distance, drenched in buttery sun. The air was tinged with a hint of salt water and a touch of humidity that made my curls spring and frizz. I smoothed them down and let the midday heat warm my cheeks. It made the freckles on my arms pop and my entire body feel like it was wrapped in a giant hug. I leaned back against the Adirondack chair and soaked it in, taking one last moment to center myself before returning inside.

I needed to get back to work. There were about a million details to cross off my list before tonight. I still couldn't believe we were hosting the official premiere of *Midnight Alibi* in my sweet little town.

Earlier this summer, Redwood Grove hosted our inaugural Mystery Festival. The idea came about because the bookstore where I'd worked since college, the Secret Book-case, was in need of a serious influx of cash and customers to keep our doors open. An Agatha Christie-themed bookstore housed in an old manor house in a remote section of Northern California didn't exactly make us a destination for travel. That changed with the Mystery Fest. The entire community had rallied to invite bookish mystery lovers from all over the region into the village square for a fully immersive weekend of author talks, panels, a mysterious pub crawl, and more.

The event was such a success that we were in the black at the bookstore for the first time in years and already planning for a Halloween reader extravaganza.

I would have been content to focus on our fall festival, but a few weeks ago, I received an unexpected call out of the blue from an independent filmmaker in LA.

"Hey, Annie, there's a call for you," Fletcher, my coworker, had said, waving me over to the cash register on an unusually soggy summer afternoon.

Rain splattered against the original single-pane windows with such violence that I thought they might shatter. I had been in the middle of setting up a new front of store display sent by one of the big publishing houses. "Is it actually for me, Fletcher? Or do you just not want to have to talk on the phone?" I asked, tilting my head to one side and giving him my best half scowl. Fletcher could talk anyone's ear off in person, but for some reason I could never quite figure out, he hated answering the phone. He would gladly handle returns, damaged books, or deal with unsellable stock, all of which could be frustrating and a time suck, in exchange for not having to take customer orders over the phone. I didn't get it.

"No, she's asking for you." He pointed to the phone and then covered it with one hand. "She says she needs to speak with Ms. Murray. Ms. Murray, so fancy."

I scrunched my brow, abandoned the display, and went to answer the phone. No one called me Ms. Murray. In fact, I'd bet that even our most loyal customers didn't know my last name.

"Ms. Murray, this is Heather Hathaway, the film director." She paused, waiting as if I was supposed to know who she was.

"Okay." I glanced at Fletcher and whispered, "Heather Hathaway?"

He shrugged and shook his head.

She cleared her throat, sounding irritated. "As I said, I'm a film director, and I'm calling with very good news for you today."

Was she hoping that we would carry her film? I hated to break it to her, but we didn't have the shelf space for DVDs.

Every inch of the bookstore was devoted to our extensive collection of mysteries. Plus, customers weren't interested in DVDs. Everything was streaming these days.

"I happened to read a review of the Mystery Fest you put on in an online journal while I was waiting at my dentist's office last week," Heather continued. "And this is where you come into the picture. I've decided that Redwood Grove would be the perfect place to hold the premiere of my new thriller, *Midnight Alibi*."

Now it was my turn to give her a pregnant pause. I had no idea what went into hosting a movie premiere.

"You want to hold the movie screening here at the bookstore?" I clarified, making sure I hadn't misheard her.

Fletcher's light blue eyes swelled with excitement. He rubbed his hands together. "Say yes, say yes," he mouthed.

"Our main event space is the Conservatory," I said to Heather. "It can hold a little over a hundred people, depending on how we configure the seating. We do have a projector and screen that we've used for events. I'm guessing you've seen our website and social media. Our bookstore is housed in an English estate, so we have plenty of other smaller spaces inside that could be used, as well as a large outdoor terrace if you wanted to show the movie after dark."

Fletcher gave me a thumbs-up in approval of my response.

"No, no, that won't do. You misunderstand me. I want to hold the screening in your *town*, and I'd like your help coordinating the event." Heather was immediately dismissive. "We need a much larger space. What you need to understand is that this is the *world* premiere. I'll be bringing the cast, crew, producers, all Hollywood types. We can't cram into a ballroom with folding chairs. I need a bigger space for my guests."

"Can I ask why you want to host the screening here? I understand you read about Mystery Fest, but these sound like two very different events."

"The article included pictures of your town, and it's just so utterly adorable. It's like stepping back in time. My movie is a bloody charmer, and I want to capture that spirit. I want guests to feel like they're part of the film. I'm envisioning a traditional showing at a movie theater or somewhere that can accommodate more people, an Italian dinner since the film is set in an Italian restaurant, and I'd like to make a weekend out of it and show some throwback Hitchcock films and do talkbacks."

I didn't know what a talkback was, but I could google it after our call. "I could put you in touch with the Redwood Grove Royal Playhouse. It's a historic movie theater that can accommodate six hundred people," I suggested.

"Six hundred is much better," Heather said with relief. "I would still need your help. I'm in the middle of finalizing post-production, setting up press junkets and screenings, and working on the last distribution details. I need a partner on the ground, so to speak. Someone to coordinate with the theater and set up dinners, that sort of thing. I'd love book sales at the event, especially if you can feature some Hitchcock-style stories. Think old-school detectives and damsels in distress."

The longer we spoke, the more enthused I became about the idea, and before I knew it, I was suddenly thrust into planning a spontaneous mystery film weekend complete with a Hollywood premiere.

Heather was bringing a few members of the cast and some film industry friends to the event. There would be a handful of critics and press in attendance as well. Since the movie was an homage to Hitchcock, Heather asked for my help arranging viewings of classic mysteries throughout the weekend, along with a dinner for her special guests and smaller talks at the bookstore.

When I hung up the phone, I stared at Fletcher in disbelief. "Did you catch the gist of that?"

"Uh, yeah." Fletcher tapped the computer screen. "I googled her while you were talking. She's legit."

"Who's legit?" A voice sounded behind us. It was Hal Christie, my boss and owner of the Secret Bookcase. Hal was in his sixties with white hair, a tightly shaven beard, and kind eyes.

"Annie just got off the phone with a film director who wants to hold her premiere here," Fletcher blurted out. Then he gnawed on his fingernail. "Sorry, Annie, I didn't mean to steal your thunder. I'm just so excited; you know what a movie buff I am. I can't believe that Hollywood is coming to us, but you tell him. She picked us because of Mystery Fest."

I pressed my hands together, my fingers strumming rapidly in eager anticipation. "Me too. I wasn't sure it was real at first, and Heather sounds like she might be a little intense plus the timeline is going to be tight, but if you two are game, I think we can pull this off."

I filled them in on the details.

"We should talk to Rufus Wells," Hal suggested when I finished, licking the tip of his finger and lifting it in the air as if he'd had a bright idea. Usually, he did. Hal had spent his entire life in Redwood Grove and knew everyone in town. "Rufus owns one of the largest collections of vintage film reels around. He might be willing to screen some of his private collection. I'm sure he has a ton of Hitchcock."

We made lists of everything that needed to be done so that we could divide and conquer. Hal agreed to reach out to Rufus, Fletcher would start with ordering books and merch for the weekend, and I agreed to check in with the movie theater and figure out dining options.

Now, just a few weeks later, after extensive planning, everyone was arriving tonight for a celebratory dinner. The film festival would kick off tomorrow with matinees of *The Birds* and

North by Northwest, followed by the premiere of *Midnight Alibi*.

Break's over, Annie, I told myself, pushing to my feet and twisting my neck from side to side. I tucked my laptop under my arm and returned inside. Stepping into the bookstore always made me smile. I headed to the Foyer, a bright and open space at the front of the store where we rang up customer orders and served coffee, tea, and pastries.

Hal greeted me with a broad grin, the creases in his kind eyes deepening with delight. "How was the Terrace? It looks like it's a gorgeous day out there." He peered out the large bay window that looked onto the front grounds.

"Beautiful as always. I might have stayed out there a bit too long, but it was so dreamy and calm. Plus, the sun felt so good." I patted my cheeks. "Am I red?"

"Only your hair." Hal winked. He tidied the front counter, adjusting the rack of stickers and repositioning a stack of signed author copies. "When do the film people arrive?"

I glanced at the clock behind the register. "In a few hours. I told Heather I would be sure to get to the Stag Head earlier to make sure everything is ready."

"I'm sure Liam will appreciate the help." Hal walked around the counter, rolled up the sleeves of his tattered cardigan, and poured himself a cup of hot water at the station in front of the large bay windows.

"Liam Donovan and the word 'help' have probably never been uttered in the same sentence." I scoffed.

Hal leafed through the basket of teas, opting for a citrus lemon. "He sounded genuinely excited about the event. It's the most enthusiastic I've ever heard him."

"Good. Then you can sit by him tonight and be my buffer." Liam Donovan owned the Stag Head, a pub in the village square where he hosted historical trivia nights and liked to expound on the virtue of reading non-fiction. Liam acted like reading mysteries was a crime against humanity. I wasn't sure if he really loathed the genre or if he just enjoyed making me fume. It was probably both. Liam always managed to bring out the worst in me, and I got the sense that that was his end goal. He called it witty banter. Pri, my good friend, called it flirtation. I called it confusion. I never exactly knew where things stood between us, and I couldn't get a handle on my emotions whenever Liam was around.

He was the only business in town that opted not to participate in Mystery Fest, so I was shocked when he volunteered to host dinner for the film crew. I quickly realized it was because of Rufus. Liam was also a film buff. Once a month, he featured historical documentaries on an eight-millimeter projector at the Stag Head. Partnering with Liam wasn't on the top of my list, but as a key sponsor for the premiere, the Secret Bookcase was going to get great exposure. Hosting smaller talks with the actors, director, and filmmaker at the store would mean a boost in foot traffic.

Tickets for the film fest sold out immediately.

We stocked up on Hitchcock's fiction and biographies. Fletcher created a FROM THE PAGE TO THE SCREEN display in the front of the store with bestselling mysteries that had been made into movies, like *Gone Girl* and *Shutter Island*.

I had a feeling that book sales were going to be strong.

"Aside from being your Liam buffer, what else can I do?" Hal asked, plunging his tea bag into his cup of steaming water.

"That's it." I patted my laptop. "I'm going to run upstairs and print out the itineraries for everyone, then I'll head home to change and meet you and Fletcher at the Stag Head for dinner."

"Wonderful." Hal beamed with pride. "Have I told you lately how wonderful you are, Annie Murray?"

I could feel heat creeping up my cheeks. Hal was like a grandfather to me. I knew he was being sincere, but I didn't need his praise. "It's not me. It's a town effort, just like with Mystery Fest."

His smile faded. "Can I give you a piece of advice?"

"Yeah."

"When a compliment is given, take it, my dear."

I started to protest, but he cut me off.

"I know you don't enjoy being the center of attention, and I know that you are humble to a fault." He raised his bushy white eyebrows to prove his point. "I also know how hard you work. Your efforts don't go unnoticed. It's important for you to know that."

A lump formed in my throat. I swallowed hard to force it down. "Thanks, Hal," I managed to squeak out.

His smile returned. "Go take care of your work. I'll see you later this evening."

I knew he was letting me off the hook. Accepting praise has always been hard for me, but after Scarlet's death, it was nearly impossible. How could I go on and live a full, happy life knowing that her life had been cut short?

It wasn't fair.

Maybe, just maybe, if I could bring her killer to justice, it would bring me a sense of relief, but then again, I'd spent my entire lifetime being weighed down by guilt. I couldn't imagine that changing anytime soon.

I took the servants' stairwell up to the second floor. The upper levels of the estate were off-limits to customers. We used them for storage, offices, and Hal's private living quarters.

Fletcher was in our shared office, talking on the phone. I snuck in quietly and pulled up the event schedule for the weekend on my computer.

"No, no, I'm sorry, but like I've mentioned at least five times now, tickets have been sold out for days," Fletcher said with a touch of irritation. "We don't have any extra seats."

I caught his eye.

He covered the phone with one hand and whispered, "It's another filmmaker, Izzy, who claims she's supposed to have a reserved seat. Do you know anything about that?"

"Izzy who?"

"Izzy. Just Izzy." He motioned for me to hang on. "No, I've already explained that. Your name isn't on our list."

I quickly pulled up the ticket reservations and scanned for anyone named Izzy.

"That's fine. Feel free, but you'll have to speak with Heather directly." Fletcher sounded like he was ready to end the call.

I pointed to the list on my laptop. "No Izzy," I mouthed to Fletcher.

He nodded. "Yep. Thanks for that feedback. Good luck with your quest."

"What was that all about?" I asked after he hung up the phone.

He rubbed his temples and cracked his bony jaw. "She claims she's a friend and fellow filmmaker of Heather's, and she was supposed to be on the VIP list. I explained that we don't have a VIP list and that she's not even on the ticket list, but she won't take no for an answer. She's going to call Heather now and wanted to warn me that my surly attitude will be noted."

"To whom?" I chuckled. Fletcher was anything but surly. He was a Sherlockian scholar who had a tendency to drone on about Sir Arthur Conan Doyle, but he loved working at the bookshop and went out of his way to make sure every customer who walked through our doors left with the perfect book. Sure, he could be wordy sometimes, sharing obscure facts about the writer and his famous detective, but Fletcher was harmless and had a natural ability to make book lovers feel welcome. He was always the first person to greet customers when he was working the register, inviting them to make a cup of tea to enjoy while browsing. He had become like a brother to me. I knew he would do anything for me and vice versa. Whenever the bookstore was slow for a stretch, Fletcher and I would break out our secret stash of chocolate-covered marshmallow cookies (a guilty pleasure that he had gotten me hooked on years ago), pour steaming mugs of strong coffee, and conspire about new events we could host or how to convince Hal to transform a couple of the unused bedrooms upstairs into guest suites. Half of the upper level had sat empty for years. Fletcher came up with the idea of transforming long-forgotten rooms as another revenue stream. He sketched out drawings of how the rooms could be themed like Sherlock's study and Jessica Fletcher's Cabot Cove office. Readers could stay overnight in the bookstore for the ultimate book lover's experience.

"She didn't elaborate." Fletcher stood and stretched. He was tall and rail thin with lanky limbs that reminded me of the inflatable wobbly tube man directing customers to a gas station off the highway. "Are you printing the schedule?" He lifted a warm sheet of paper off the printer.

"Yeah. Did something change?" My hand hovered over the button to end the print.

"Nope." He studied the sheet. "It looks good. It's still hard to believe Hollywood is coming to Redwood Grove."

"Well, not exactly Hollywood. Heather is an independent filmmaker, and none of the actors in the movie are household names, at least not yet."

Fletcher snapped his fingers and tapped his forehead. "Now you're thinking, Annie. We could be witnessing stars in the making this weekend. I intend to get autographs and selfies to save for posterity should any of them hit it big."

"Good idea." I grinned and gave him a wink, pointing to his Sherlockian-style murder bulletin board near his desk. Red yarn stretched between playbills, photos, and vintage book cover designs. The corkboard was covered with push pins, sticky notes, and all of Fletcher's treasure. "Because I've been meaning to tell you that I don't think you have enough stuff on the wall. You could really use some more autographs."

"Hey now, you know all too well that each and every item that goes on my murder board has a special place in my heart." He spoke with his index finger pointed at the ceiling and a mock scowl dancing across his lips.

"Fair enough." I extended my palm gracefully to signify my agreement. "I think it's sweet that you display your keepsakes, but seriously, if you put one more tack in that board, I'm pretty sure it's all going to come tumbling down, my friend."

"Don't worry, I can always make space." He pressed one of the tacks deeper into the corkboard to prove his point. Then he handed me the stack of paper and returned to his desk. Our desks spoke volumes about our different personalities and working styles. Clutter makes my head spin. Color-coded tins with pencils, pens, rubber bands, paper clips, and sticky notes each had a specific place on my desk. An Agatha Christie event calendar and my reusable mug were the only other items I kept on hand.

I could barely see Fletcher above the unbalanced stack of advanced reader copies sitting precariously on the edge of his desk. In his spare time, he built miniatures. Nearly every inch of free shelf space in our shared office housed one of Fletcher's builds, like tiny replicas of the Tower of London and Buckingham Palace. Currently, he was constructing a Paddington station set. Tiny plastic pieces, tweezers, and a magnifying light took over his entire desktop. I didn't know how he got anything done in the mess, but I wasn't going to judge. He never missed a deadline and knew where everything was amongst the clutter. It was just one of the many ways we were different.

I peered around the leaning tower of books and waved with two fingers. "You sure about that? Can you see me over here? Hi, I'm Annie; I don't know if we've met because I've been living behind your Leaning Tower of Pisa for the last eight years."

He pursed his lips together and pretended to be upset. "You don't want to go there. Should we talk about your precious Sharpies? What happens if I accidentally misplace them? Or worse yet, what if I mess up your perfectly organized color coding?"

I gasped and cradled my canisters of pens. Each one contained varying shades of the rainbow. Like any rational person, I clumped navy blue and eggplant purple pens in one container and fire-engine red and pumpkin orange pens in another. "You wouldn't dare. Hands off the Sharpies."

He gave me an evil grin before changing the subject. "What's the dress code tonight?" He pointed to his short-sleeve button-up shirt and bow tie. "Is this appropriate, or should I go home and change before dinner?"

"Fletcher, this is Redwood Grove, and dinner is at the Stag Head. You could come in shorts and a T-shirt and be fine."

"Are you wearing that?" Fletcher craned his neck and stared at my Secret Bookcase T-shirt.

"No, I'm going to change, but you're much more dressed up than me."

"What about a costume? I could break out my Sherlock cape from the Mystery Fest."

"I don't think that's necessary." I gathered the papers into a neat stack and tucked them into my book bag. "Wear whatever you feel comfortable in. I'll see you there shortly, okay?"

I ducked out of the office before he had a chance to respond. I knew that if I didn't, I would be there for another twenty minutes discussing Fletcher's potential outfit choices.

Fletcher's insecurities came out in different ways than mine. I wasn't concerned with what I was going to wear to the dinner, but I was worried about everything going smoothly tonight. My body hummed in eager anticipation. In a few hours, an entire contingent of filmmakers would be arriving in Redwood Grove. Here, in my little hometown. I still couldn't quite wrap my head around it. Everything had happened so fast, and now, suddenly, the event was upon us. A not-entirely-unpleasant mixture of nerves and excitement pulsed through me. I was about to host my first movie screening. I was going to be mingling with Hollywood actors and world-renowned film critics. The press would be descending on the village square to cover the event, which would likely be all over social media. This was going to be a once-in-a-lifetime opportunity for the Secret Bookcase and for me. Of course, it was my responsibility to make sure that it was a smashing success. No pressure, right?

TWO

Professor Plum, my cat, must have sensed my nerves because he trotted between the bedroom and bathroom with me as I changed and got ready. As my longest and most faithful companion, he was the other half of many of my conversations and my four-legged confidant.

"What do you think of this green skirt?" I asked him, holding up a knee-length jewel-toned skirt and posing in front of my bathroom mirror.

He meowed in response and nuzzled his soft head against my ankle.

"Thanks, I think so, too. It's cute—a party skirt. Not too fancy, but this is a movie premiere, after all."

I bent over to massage his head, running my fingers beneath his purple collar to scratch his neck. Professor Plum was a tabby cat with silky fur and the personality of a dog. He greeted me at the door every time I returned home. Pri deemed him a "dat," her word for a cat who didn't realize he wasn't a dog. It was a fitting description. I'd never had a pet before Professor Plum, so I didn't have anything to compare him to. My parents owned a small diner that struggled to stay afloat. They spent every waking minute in the restaurant with its aging wallpaper and checkerboard floors. I basically grew up in the kitchen or tucked into one of the empty, faded booths with a book. There was no time for pets or playdates.

I wouldn't say it was exactly a lonely childhood. More singular. Books and puzzles became my escape and companions. Much like they still are today.

I could still remember the smell of grilling burgers and onions and the taste of the Neapolitan shakes I sipped while I scribbled out math problems as quickly as I could so I could get back to reading the latest Dorothy L. Sayers novel I'd checked out from the library.

After a quick change and touching up my makeup, we headed for the kitchen at Professor Plum's insistence. He paced between my dining nook and the fridge while I prepared his dinner. The kitchen was my favorite room in the cottage with its pale yellow walls, generous windows that let in the natural light, and the breakfast nook with bench seating. I added a collection of California-inspired pillows with wildflowers to give it a pop of color. In the mornings, I would often linger with a cup of coffee and a book before heading to work.

"Here you go, sir. Dinner is served." I set Professor Plum's dishes on his cat tray. "Don't wait up for me and keep an eye on the place as always."

I left him with a final pet and cut through Oceanside Park. The park was in the center of the village square. Redwoods and palms flanked the lush green grasses and pathways. Pink and white oleander bloomed in wild bunches. I'd read enough Miss Marple novels to know to stay clear of the pretty yet poisonous flowers that had become synonymous with California gardens thanks to oleander's drought tolerance.

My route to the Stag Head took me in a straight diagonal through the park. I passed kids playing in the splash pad and families spreading out picnics. In the central pavilion, ancient wisteria formed a fragrant canopy of shade. I breathed in the heady scent mingled with the aroma of grills being fired up for barbeques.

Suddenly, I was ravenous. Or maybe it was just my nerves.

I brushed my clammy hands on my skirt, squared my shoulders, and crossed Cedar Avenue. The Stag Head sat on the edge of the town square, right next to the gravel drive that led to the Secret Bookcase. A sign posted on the exterior door announced that the restaurant was closed for a private event. The single-story, intentionally distressed white brick building had large windows that looked out onto the park and town square.

It could have been a cool vibe, if it weren't for Liam.

Why was I so jittery?

I hadn't had that much caffeine, and the Mystery Fest we hosted had been ten times the scale.

"Annie, you coming in, or do you intend to stand outside for the duration of the night?" A deep, husky voice interrupted my thoughts.

That's why I was nervous—Liam Donovan.

Liam propped the door open with one foot and waved me inside. "You're not going to come in? What, do you think I bite?"

His dark eyes twinkled with a devilish mischief. Liam took great pleasure in trying to get under my skin. He brushed a strand of wavy hair out of his face and stepped to the side to make way for me.

I moved past him quickly. "Am I the first one here?"

The inside of the Stag Head was decorated with dozens of craft paper stags, historical photos of Redwood Grove, and moody lighting. Distressed wood floors and a long bar gave the space a rustic feel.

Liam had pushed tables together to create one long shared table in the center of the room. The high-top tables were pressed against the back wall to allow people to move freely throughout the room.

"You said seating for thirty, correct?" Liam shut the door behind us. He tightened his black apron which he wore over a pair of jeans and a short-sleeve shirt.

"Yeah. Thirty." Why was I repeating him?

"Do you want to see the kitchen? Chef is nearly done with prep." Liam pointed to the far end of the bar.

"Uh, I guess. If it's not too much trouble."

"This is your gig, Annie. You tell me."

I wasn't used to Liam being nice to me. Typically, he went out of his way to offend me, belittle mysteries, and make himself seem important.

"Yes, okay. I'd like to speak with the chef." I hoped that I sounded collected and professional. Liam's drastic attitude change had me rattled.

A symphony of delectable flavors enveloped my entire body as I stepped through the swinging door to the kitchen. I'd never been in the Stag Head's commercial kitchen before. It wasn't much to look at—a narrow galley with industrial equipment, a six-burner stove, and so much stainless steel it made my eyes squinty.

The chef glanced up at us, not taking his hands off a sauce pot simmering over an open flame. Trays of deviled eggs, stuffed mushrooms, skewered olives, and pesto puffed pastries sat ready for the starter course.

Heather requested a classic Italian feast since *Midnight Alibi* was set in an Italian diner. She also insisted on food that tied in with the theme of the thriller, hence *deviled* eggs and *skewered* olives.

"How can I help you?" the chef asked, sprinkling chopped basil into his sauce.

"This is Annie Murray, who is organizing the film fest."

Liam introduced me formally like I was some kind of Hollywood celebrity.

What was his ulterior motive?

"Do you want to talk through courses?"

The chef turned the heat to low and wiped his hands on his black apron. "Appetizers are ready to go. We'll have those out while the guests are arriving, assuming that's okay with you?" He waited and looked at me for approval.

"Sure, great." I felt an immediate sense of familiarity with the galley kitchen, having just been reminiscing about my childhood experiences.

"Then we'll do a soup and salad. The minestrone is done." He lifted the lid on a stock pot on the back burner.

The scent of Italian herbs and veggies made my stomach flop with anticipation.

"I'll do a simple salad—greens, sun-dried tomatoes, house-made croutons, with a balsamic vinaigrette," he continued, returning the lid to the soup pot. "For the main course, we have pasta, stuffed meatballs or peppers for vegetarians, and garlic bread. Dessert is tiramisu and espresso."

Silencing the grumbling in my stomach was impossible. Everything sounded and smelled delicious.

"I'll pour wine," Liam added. "We'll do cocktails, sparkling water, whatever people are in the mood for."

"So you'll be behind the bar for dinner?" That was a relief.

"No, I'm joining the table, but I'll jump in if anyone needs a refill." He shot me a challenging stare. "I'm sure Hal mentioned that Rufus and I go way back. I'd like to sit next to him, but I'll let you take care of the rest of the seating chart."

How gracious of him.

I resisted the urge to roll my eyes.

"If that's everything, I need to get back to my sauce," the chef said.

"Of course, thanks for everything," I replied, waiting for Liam before returning to the dining room.

"We're good, then?" Liam asked, but it was more of a statement.

"Yep." I set my bag on the table. "I'm going to set out the place cards."

"Fine. I've got pre-work at the bar."

We worked in silence for the next thirty minutes, which was fine by me. This version of Liam was familiar to me. The strong, gruff, silent treatment was nothing new.

The table setting looked lovely. We created film-reel place cards, menus, and decorations for the event. I borrowed a few items from the bookstore to add to the atmosphere—two Gothic candelabras that I adorned with black tapered candles, a fake prop sword that would serve as the centerpiece for the table, and plastic magnifying glasses.

I stood back to appraise my work.

Not bad, Annie.

As much as I would have preferred to host the dinner some-where—anywhere—other than the Stag Head, I had to admit that the rustic, dimly lit space matched the eerie tone I was going for with the décor.

A knock sounded on the door.

Liam looked up from quartering limes and lemons. "What time are guests supposed to arrive?"

I checked my watch. "Not for another twenty minutes."

"Do you want to let people in early? It's your call."

"I guess. I'm ready."

"Fine. Go for it." He gestured to the heavy oak door.

I took one final walk around the table. I didn't think I had missed anything. Heather would be bringing promotional mate-rials for the film. Now we needed the guests to arrive and the wine to start flowing.

A woman in her mid-to-late forties, I wasn't a good judge of age, with a messy ponytail and an oversized black trench coat, waited at the door. She puffed on a vape pen.

"Can I help you?" I asked.

She pushed me aside and stepped inside, making a beeline for the table. "Is this seating for thirty? It doesn't look like there are enough chairs. I explicitly said thirty guests."

"Are you Heather?" I closed the door behind her and waved away the cloyingly sweet smell of raspberry-scented tobacco.

She stopped and stared at me with newfound interest. "Oh, you recognize me. You must be a fan."

This was awkward.

"I'm Annie Murray from the Secret Bookcase." I extended my hand.

She puffed on the vape pen, inhaling deeply like she was at a yoga retreat doing breathwork.

"Hey, you can't smoke in here," Liam interjected.

For once, I was grateful to have him nearby.

The fake smell of chemical raspberry had taken away my appetite.

"This is my event. I'm paying for this dinner. What do you mean I can't smoke; for your information, it's a vape pen, not a cigarette."

Liam tossed his thumb toward the sign posted next to the tap handles that prohibited smoking of any kind—including vaping and cannabis. "It's my bar, and state law says otherwise."

She glared at him but put her vape pen on the table. "So you're Annie. I don't know what I was expecting, but not you."

A heat spread up my neck. What did she mean by that?

This wasn't how I pictured our first interaction going.

"Sorry, I can see by your face that I offended you. That's not my intention. I'm just so LA." She ran her hand over her black leggings, black shirt, and black ankle boots. "I forget anytime I travel out of Southern California how different this part of the state is."

Her statement wasn't helping the situation.

"Again, sorry. I'm sticking my foot in my mouth. I appreciate your color choices and style. We're all about the black monotone look in SoCal. It's refreshing."

Liam caught my eye across the bar. Heather had her back to him. I stifled a laugh as he mimicked her wild gestures and pretended to vape at the same time.

His show of solidarity made me even more confused. He knew how to wind me up but also how to make me laugh. What did it mean? Was he toying with me? I wanted to believe that our friendship was progressing. We had bonded after a traumatic experience at Mystery Fest, where he had shown up at the right time and been an ally. Something had shifted since that experience, but I didn't trust it. Normally, I prided myself on being able to read people, but Liam Donovan was a bit of an enigma.

My outfit wasn't making a statement about color. I opted for a green jewel-toned skirt and matching short-sleeved blouse with cap sleeves because the shade blended with my red hair and green eyes.

Stop it, Annie.

Just because you're wearing something cute doesn't mean you're not capable.

There was no point in beating myself up for not wearing something more sophisticated or running home to change into a little black dress. This was Redwood Grove, which was the vibe Heather wanted. I could handle this. I'd dealt with plenty of difficult and demanding customers over the years. Even during Mystery Fest, I had my hands full with an author who had a massively inflated ego and his editor who constantly insisted he needed more visibility.

The best way to defuse the situation was not to take Heather's comments personally. This was her premiere, her night. She was the client, and I would treat her with the utmost professionalism and then text Pri all the gory details later. It was good to have a friend like Pri to vent to. I couldn't wait to tell her that Liam and I actually saw eye to eye on Heather. She'd never believe it.

Heather riffled through a black leather bag. "You're sure this is thirty seats?"

"Positive. I double-checked my count while I was placing the name cards and menus." I scooted out the chair at the head of the table. "I thought you could sit here so that everyone can hear you, but I'm happy to rearrange if you have other ideas."

She pulled out a bundle of glossy black file folders secured with a red rubber band. "These need to go at each seat, do you mind?"

"Not at all." I took the stack from her.

"Where did you put Martin?" Heather leaned closer and squinted at the place cards.

I set a file folder with a sticker of a skull and the words *Midnight Alibi* in blood splatter on one of the plates. "He's down at the other end."

"No, no, no. That will not work. I need him right here by me." She tapped her finger on the seat to the right of her.

"That's no problem." I picked up Martin's name card and swapped it.

"He needs VIP treatment tonight. I want a drink in his hands at all times. He should be served first. Don't let any of his food come out cold." She reached for her vape pen like it was a security blanket.

"He must be important." I returned to setting out the movie folders.

"You don't know Martin Parker?" She looked at me like I had said I didn't know who the president was.

Liam scoffed from behind the bar.

Heather swiveled her head toward him. "This is no joke. I'm deadly serious. Everything must be perfect for Martin tonight. He's the most revered critic in the industry. He has the ability to make or break this film. My entire career and livelihood are riding on his review. If Martin doesn't enjoy the film, I'm ruined."

That sounded like a lot of pressure. I felt bad for her. I knew that reviews were an important piece of a movie's release, but if one critic could ruin her career—that was terrible. "Please tell me that you're kidding. That sounds like so much pressure."

She blew out a long sigh. "No, sadly, I'm not. I'm dead if he pans my movie."

"Oh no, don't say that around me. I make a living selling murder." I hoped if I could joke with her and keep it light, it might help relieve some of her stress.

"You and me both, sister. It's kill or be killed in the film world, and I don't intend to make this my last meal tonight."

"Then I'm going to have to talk to the chef and make sure the food is absolutely exquisite tonight." I winked, still trying to bring some levity into the moment.

Heather forced a smile. "Yeah, thanks."

I could tell that she was unsettled. I had a newfound appreciation for her situation, and her words made me even more grateful that I was in the book business. I couldn't fathom Hal putting that kind of pressure on me or anyone else. My first impression of her softened a little. She was clearly consumed with making the weekend a success, and my job was to do everything I could to help her in that endeavor. Heather might be intense, but I had agreed to help her make this weekend a smashing success, and that is exactly what I intended to do. Our small but mighty team at the Secret Bookcase could handle this.

I drew in a deep breath, smiled softly, and silently told myself, *You've got this, Annie. Redwood Grove might not be Hollywood, but you are ready to work your own kind of movie magic.*

THREE

Guests began arriving shortly after I finished setting out Heather's packets. Liam turned on the soundtrack for *Midnight Alibi* and poured glasses of wine.

It didn't take long for me to spot Martin. A painful hush fell over the pub when he strolled inside and immediately cut to the front of the small line at the bar. He reminded me of Hercule Poirot with his short, stout frame and round glasses. He appeared to be in his fifties, with a shock of white hair pressed flat against his forehead with copious amounts of gel. Like Heather, he wore black slacks and a black suit jacket.

"Martini, dry—bone dry," he said to Liam. It wasn't a request. It was a demand.

Liam ignored Martin and focused his attention on the woman in line in front of him. "Would you prefer red or white?"

I recognized the young woman from the movie trailer. She was the lead actress in *Midnight Alibi*—Cora Mitchell.

Cora hesitated and moved to the side to make room for Martin. "It's okay, Martin can go in front of me."

Liam held a wine glass, ready to pour. "The Stag Head is

my pub, and in my pub, I serve in order of who's in line. So, what will it be, red or white?"

A fluttery feeling spread through my chest. There was something about seeing Liam put Martin in his place that made him more attractive. Not that I thought Liam Donovan was attractive. Quite the opposite, but it was nice to witness him standing up to a bully.

"Uh, excuse me, son. Do you know who I am?" Martin scoffed.

"I don't care if you're the King of England," Liam retorted, reaching for a bottle of Merlot. "Like I said, this is my bar, and in my bar, we wait our turn like civilized adults."

Martin sputtered.

I knew I shouldn't stare, but I couldn't tear my eyes away from the bar. Heather hadn't been exaggerating about Martin. Everything about his body language screamed entitlement. This was a man who was clearly used to getting what he wanted. Watching him trying to muscle his way to the front of the line made me feel a new kinship for Heather.

Heather raced over to try and remedy the situation. "Martin, excuse us for a moment, I need to have a word with my young starlet." She yanked Cora out of line. "Go ahead and serve Martin; we'll only be a minute," she said to Liam.

Liam shrugged. "You sure about that?"

She flicked her wrist like she was hoping to cast a spell and make everyone vanish. "Oh yes. Cora and I need just a minute for some girl talk."

Liam met my gaze again. "Girl talk," he mouthed.

I shook my head and then let it flop in disappointment. Obviously, Martin held all of the power in their dynamic, but it was painful to watch Heather become almost submissive around him. Were Liam and I suddenly on the same page? We didn't agree on a lot of things, but it was refreshing to know that he immediately had Martin pegged.

"Martini, dry." Martin folded his arms across his chest. He smiled with smug success as he watched Heather drag Cora to the table.

"What the hell do you think you're doing? I made it crystal clear that your job is to impress Martin this weekend, not piss him off," Heather fumed, and practically threw Cora into an empty chair.

I picked up a perfectly folded napkin and smoothed it flat, trying to look like I wasn't eavesdropping. Although it was impossible not to. Everyone in the pub could see what was happening.

Cora protested. "I didn't do anything. I was just in line to get a drink." She motioned to the bar with one hand.

"Martin Parker is the most influential critic in Hollywood, no, scratch that, in the entire film industry. I gave you your first break; don't blow it, Cora. Do not blow it." Heather spoke in hushed, angry whispers, constantly checking on Martin.

"I know. I get it. I swear, I tried to let him go in front of me, but the bartender stepped in." Cora caught my eye and shrugged with resignation, like she knew this was an argument she couldn't win.

I busied myself with rearranging the already neat place settings and refolding napkins.

"Don't let it happen again. You need to schmooze with the man, not get on his bad side, understood?" Heather didn't wait for Cora to answer. She swept back to the bar and placed her hand on Martin's arm.

I couldn't hear what she was saying, but I could tell from her body language that she was trying to appease him.

Cora slumped deeper into her chair and reached for her nameplate. She flipped it between her fingers and then tapped it on the table repeatedly, like a nervous tic. "Great. I've already gotten the evening off to a banging start."

"What's the deal with the film critic?" I asked, placing a

napkin on the plate next to her. "Does he have that much sway?"

She tossed her shiny platinum locks over her shoulder and pounded her forehead with her middle finger like she was tapping a pressure point to relieve anxiety. "You have no idea. He's legendary in the movie industry and not in a good way."

"I work at the mystery bookstore here in town, so I have no idea how film premieres work, but I will say as a fan of the genre, critic reviews have never swayed me from enjoying a good mystery—in print or on the big screen."

"That's kind of you to say." She smiled, revealing pristine veneers. Her high cheekbones were even more pronounced by the shading of her makeup.

My idea of makeup was putting on some lip gloss and maybe a touch of eyeshadow. Cora's face looked like it had been professionally contoured with velvety blushes and shimmery bronzer. She was truly a stunner, but the sadness behind her beautifully lined eyes gave me pause.

"No, really, it's true," I said with sincerity, wanting to reassure her. She looked like she was on the edge of tears. "I understand that the film industry is different, but I love movies, and so do my friends, and none of us care what one reviewer says. The same is true in the bookstore. Many of our bestselling titles don't have stellar critic reviews. Readers can and should form their own opinions about what they enjoy. I'm sure everyone is going to love your movie. Try not to let it get in your head. This is supposed to be a celebration tonight."

She brushed away a tear and nodded with her head down. Then she put her nameplate back in its spot and traced the outline of the skull on her packet with her index finger. "Yeah, I hope you're right. I really appreciate you being so nice to me. I'm Cora, by the way. I didn't catch your name."

"Annie Murray." I extended her a hand. "The Secret Bookcase, where I work, is arranging and sponsoring the film fest. We're all so excited and thrilled to have you here."

"Thanks, that's sweet. Heather mentioned that a bookstore was going to be part of this." Cora nodded with understanding. "It's like a mystery-themed bookshop, right? That's so cool. I've never heard of something that niche before."

"The largest mystery bookstore on the West Coast," I replied, unable to contain my pride. It was impossible not to gush whenever I described the store. "We're located in an old English manor house with Agatha Christie themes in every room. There's a terrace outside and lovely grounds. You can pour yourself a cup of tea and get lost amongst the books for hours. You should stop in while you're in town."

"That sounds amazing. I'll have to swing by and check it out. It's probably got some great spots for staging pics for social media." She made a clicking sound with her tongue and reached into her clutch. "That reminds me, I'm supposed to be posting tonight. Heather gave us a list of hashtags to use to help promote the film. It's cool if I take some pictures and video, right?"

"Yes, of course." I leaned back to make sure I wasn't in her shot and used the opportunity to shoot Pri a quick text:

> You're never going to believe what's going down. Got outfit shamed by the director. Liam is being bizarrely nice and agreeing with me on everything. And the film critic is a total ass.

She replied immediately:

> Omg! I need all of the tea. This is so cruel. Tell me everything.

I grinned as my fingers flew on the screen.

> So much drama.

She shot back a string of emojis.

> Come by tomorrow. Coffee in exchange for the tea.

I chuckled and put my phone away.

An older gentleman in his late sixties wobbled up to the table, balancing two glasses of wine in one hand and steadying himself with a cane in the other. He was stout with chin-length wavy gray hair and ruddy cheeks. "Cora, I believe this is for you." He offered Cora the glass of red.

"Oh, thanks, Sam. You didn't need to bring me wine."

Sam raised his glass. The wine was a pale, buttery color. "It was the least I could do. I saw that you got caught in the cross-fire with Martin." He tipped his head in the direction of the bar where Heather and Martin were still talking.

"He came out of nowhere," Cora tried to explain. "I didn't mean to cause a scene."

"Don't sweat it, kid." Sam circled the table, looking for his name. His cane rattled against the floor in a steady rhythm. When he found his spot, he pulled out his chair and set his cane next to him. Then he carefully lowered himself into seat and stretched out like he was preparing for a long night, crossing his long legs and leaning his head against the back of the chair.

"Sam, this is Annie; she works at the bookstore sponsoring tonight," Cora said, gesturing to me.

"Wonderful. It's good to meet you." He started to get up.

I stopped him. I didn't want him to have to move. I wasn't about to force someone with a cane to get up on my behalf. "No, no, stay where you are. You look comfortable, which is our goal for tonight."

"Thank you." He lifted his glass in a toast. "It was a cramped flight on a little plane. One of the cons of being tall and getting old is these legs don't bend the way they used to."

"I wouldn't know. I barely pass the height requirements to

ride the rollercoasters at Disneyland," I teased. Although being on the short side had its advantages, too. I could sneak in most places without being noticed, which was fine by me.

"Sam is a major film producer," Cora explained as a way of introduction.

"Did you produce this film?" I asked.

"Heather is quite persuasive. I didn't intend to back a smaller independent film, but she marched into my office with about a dozen reasons why if I didn't fund *Midnight Alibi*, I would be making the biggest mistake of my career. Given that I'm nearing retirement, I appreciated her moxie."

"Moxie?" Cora scowled.

"You're too young for the term. How's spunk?" Sam held his wine glass beneath his nose and inhaled it like a sommelier.

"I'm not that young," Cora protested.

She looked young to me. The makeup made her appear older, but she had to be in her early twenties at most.

Was she even old enough to drink? I felt almost protective of her in a sisterly way. She seemed fragile, especially in comparison with the larger-than-life personalities of Martin and Heather and even Sam. I remembered how out of place I felt when I was assigned to my first crime scene in college. The seasoned detectives had treated me like a kid on a field trip for school instead of a serious student who was intent on learning as much as she could.

Sam tipped his glass. "To youth."

"How does producing work?" I asked, taking my seat, which was conveniently right next to Sam. I wanted to shift the conversation away from Cora, and I was genuinely interested in learning more about the behind-the-scenes of how movies were made. I was also curious about his relationship with Heather. Was he ultimately in charge, or was she?

"Usually, it involves writing big checks." He wiggled his

untamed bushy eyebrows. "And trying to rein in the cast and crew from spending those big checks."

"I thought this was an independent film. In publishing, authors front the cost if they're going indie." I was surprised that Sam's primary role was financing the film.

"It's all semantics for money," Sam replied, rubbing his index finger and thumb together as if he was holding a wad of bills. "Indie films tend to have private funding sources, whereas the studios back the big-budget blockbusters. For most of my career, I worked for the studios, but now I like to fund smaller projects. As a producer, I finance films that are de-risked. It's industry speak, but basically, I'm the lead financier and oversee the entire project."

"That sounds like a big job," I said. I got the sense that he enjoyed controlling the purse strings. It made me wonder even more about his relationship with Heather. Were they true partners or was there animosity between them when it came to budgeting and allocating funds?

"And a fun one when we get a project like *Midnight Alibi*. Don't you agree, Cora? Or are you still having nightmares about being stuck in a cold bathtub filled with fake blood?" He let out a little laugh.

Cora shuddered and shook her body like she was trying to free herself from the memory. "Don't remind me. I've tried to block out those days on set. No amount of Pilates could have prepared me for how grueling those shoots were. I'm still not sleeping well at night. I seriously think I need to get some therapy because I have flashbacks all the time about that bloody bathtub."

That sounded terrible. "A bathtub of fake blood? I didn't realize the movie was going to keep us on the edge of our seats. I might work at a mystery bookstore, but I don't do very well when it comes to gore," I said with a wincing smile to Cora, hoping to keep the tone light since it was clear that the film had left a lasting impression on her. According to the pre-press materials we received and the trailer Heather had sent, the film didn't look like it was going to be gratuitously violent, but maybe it had been edited that way. I knew how excited our tight-knit community was to be hosting the premiere. Things like this didn't happen often in our village, which was way off the beaten path from any major city. I cringed internally, hoping that residents who'd already booked tickets wouldn't be horrified by the film.

"It's not super gory," Cora replied. "The bathtub scene is the scariest part, and if you're squeamish, it's not real blood. It's a mixture of corn syrup, red dye, and cocoa powder with a little hand soap and cornstarch thrown in. It's just that I had to spend hours in that tub while we were shooting. It was cold and gooey and I had to keep my energy and intensity up to film the death scenes over and over again. I think I have PTSD."

"You're giving away our insider secrets." Sam winked.

Cora threw her hand over her lips. "Sorry. I didn't realize—"

Sam cut her off. "I'm teasing you, kid. In this business, you have to learn how to read the room."

"Where do you want me to put this?" A man's voice interrupted us.

I looked up to see a tall guy hovering over us. I'd seen him around town a few times and recognized him right away.

"Are you Rufus Wells?" I stood to greet him. "Is that your film collection? I can help you with it."

He clutched the box he was holding tightly against his chest as if I had just threatened to snatch his newborn baby. "No one touches these except me. I told Liam I would bring them tonight, but these reels are highly valuable. Only these hands touch them." He wiggled his fingers without letting go of his grip on the box.

"There's space on the pub tables," I suggested, pointing to the row of high-top tables pushed against the back wall. "You can set the box down there or spread out the reels however you want to display them."

"These aren't for display. This is some of the rarest footage in the world. I'm not going to spread the film canisters out like this is a garage sale. They need to be in my line of sight at all times. Do I make myself clear?"

I should have sat him and Martin next to each other for dinner. They could spend the meal trying to one-up each other on who was more important.

"It's your call," I said to Rufus. "I think your collection is safe here, but if you prefer, you can certainly keep it next to you at the table. Your seat is right here."

"And sit with it on my lap while eating? I don't think so." He hoisted the box higher and stomped to the pub tables.

It made sense that he and Liam were friends. He shared the same narcissistic tendencies. Why had he brought the vintage films if he didn't want anyone to touch them?

I didn't have time to dwell on it because the chef delivered a platter of appetizers to the table. More guests trickled in as Liam poured drinks, and people munched on stuffed mushrooms and deviled eggs.

When Fletcher and Hal finally strolled in, I felt the muscles in my neck relax.

"Thank goodness you're here." I gave them both a half hug. Hal looked particularly dapper. Instead of his usual holey cardigan and corduroy slacks, he wore a pair of khaki shorts, loafers, and a short-sleeved button-up Gothic library shirt with a pattern of skulls, ravens, typewriters, and vials of poison.

"Is something wrong?" Hal's face etched with concern as he glanced around the restaurant.

"Not exactly wrong," I whispered, motioning for them to huddle closer. "There's already drama with Heather. She's trying to impress Martin Parker tonight." I pointed out the film critic who was guzzling his dry martini at the bar. "Consider this your heads-up that she is insistent that Martin gets served first and never has to wait for anything."

"Isn't it a communal dinner?" Hal asked.

"Yes, but Heather is on a singular mission to make sure that Martin has the best night of his life."

"Trying to buy a good review," Fletcher noted.

"She wasn't even subtle about it. She told me that the film and her entire career are riding on Martin's critique of the film."

Hal whistled. "That's a statement."

Before I could say more, the door burst open as if being blown by a summer windstorm. A woman with spiky neon-pink hair, black leather pants, and six-inch stilettos raised her left hand and wiggled her bejeweled fingers in a wave. "I'm here. The party can start now."

The room went silent.

Heather's icy gaze made me take a step closer to Hal for protection. "Izzy, what the hell are you doing here?"

Izzy plastered on a bright smile. "Oh, didn't you hear, I'm Martin's special guest."

Heather dropped her wine glass, shattering it on the distressed wood floors and sending Merlot splattering like blood.

FOUR

"Is there a problem, Heather?" Martin dabbed wine from his jacket with a bar napkin.

Heather knelt to pick up the shards of broken glass.

"Leave it," Liam cautioned, grabbing a broom and dustpan. "I'll take care of it."

Heather stood and stared at her stained hands like they didn't belong to her.

"Excuse me. You didn't answer me," Martin said, clearing his throat and tossing the wet napkin on the bar. "Is this the way you treat your esteemed guests? Do we have a problem?"

"No, not at all," Heather replied through clenched teeth. "I'm delighted to have Izzy with us. It will be wonderful to have a fellow filmmaker's perspective on our film. Let me run and freshen up for a moment."

Izzy's smug smile told me everything I needed to know about their relationship. One of the things that I learned in my criminology coursework in college was the importance of body language. So much could be imparted from a look, the way a suspect might twirl their hair when nervous, or minuscule eye movements. Observations came naturally to me. It was probably due in part to my upbringing. Spending so much time alone honed my ability to cut through what people were saying and focus on how they were saying it.

In this case, I had a feeling that even a novice body language expert could easily pick up on the friction between the two women.

"That's who called the store twice today, demanding a seat for dinner," Fletcher whispered as Izzy sauntered past us, every pore oozing with confidence.

"It appears she found a workaround," Hal said, catching my eye.

"She's a filmmaker, too, right?" I asked Fletcher since he had been the one who had spoken with her earlier.

"That's what she said. She claimed to be 'tight' with Heather." He used air quotes to prove his point. "But I doubt that's true."

"No, I very much doubt that," Hal agreed. "I believe a drink might be in order. Who's with me?"

"Me." Fletcher raised his hand and wiggled his fingers. "I'm already on edge from the palpable energy in the room. Maybe a stiff drink will help."

"I don't know if a drink will do it. You might need the entire bottle." I stuck out my tongue and made a face. Then I motioned to the bar. "I'm going to check with the chef and make sure we're still on schedule. I think food will be a good distraction for everyone."

I was careful to avoid the wet section of the floor as I approached the bar. Liam had finished cleaning the broken glass and mopping the spilled wine, but a large water stain remained on the intentionally distressed hardwoods.

"What do you need, Ms. Murray?" Liam asked, pouring wine with one hand and shaking a cocktail with the other. A small but manageable line had formed, but Liam didn't appear the least bit fazed.

"I'm going to see if the chef needs help. I know you're busy after that... incident." I scrunched my nose and bit my bottom lip, trying to decide on the right word.

He shook his head and laughed. "That's one way to phrase it."

"Yeah, well. I'm thinking it might be time for some food to accompany the booze. You know, before things get out of hand."

"Yeah, good thinking." He took the lid off the shaker and used a strainer to pour a drink into a cocktail glass. "I can check with the chef if you need to mingle."

"No. I'm good. It's fine." I slipped back into a nervous pattern of speech.

Knock it off, Annie.

I pressed my mouth into a formal smile and tried to take a professional tone. "I'm happy for a minute of reprieve and you have a line of customers waiting."

"Thanks." He raised his eyebrows twice in the direction of Martin. "A minute might be all you get tonight."

I gave him a curt nod and ignored the fact that he seemed to be reluctant to break eye contact. I turned toward the kitchen and pushed the swinging door open.

It hit something and swung back against me.

I pushed it again and nearly knocked over Heather.

"Oh no. I'm so sorry. I didn't expect anyone to be standing here."

She stuffed something I couldn't see into her pocket. "No, it's my fault. On par for how this entire night is going."

"At least you're wearing black. You can't even tell that you spilled wine," I tried to reassure her.

"Wine is the least of my problems." She dug her knuckles into her temples. "I can't believe Martin would invite Izzy to *my* premiere. Why would he do that? He knows I can't kick her out. He's messing with me on purpose. He's trying to torture me."

"Torture you?" That was a loaded statement.

"Martin loves having the power in this dynamic. Inviting Izzy is no mistake. He's intentionally trying to make me crack. He knows that we hate each other. He's just toying with me. He's so cruel. He's enjoying every minute of this. I never should have tried to suck up to him. I should have just left it alone." She clenched her fists and smashed her lips together so hard that every muscle in her neck and face looked like it was about to pop.

I wasn't sure how to respond. "Like I said earlier, I guess I don't understand the industry, but why does Martin have all of the power? He's only one reviewer."

"Because a scathing review of *Midnight Alibi* will tank the movie, especially coming from someone with his kind of credibility. Everything is riding on opening weekend these days. There's no time for a film to find its audience. If we don't have good numbers out of the gate, that's a death sentence."

"A single review from Martin could do that?" I wished I could help her gain some perspective, but then again, maybe she was right. Maybe Martin had the ability to make or break a movie. If that were true, it seemed like the system was broken. Movies, like books or any other form of entertainment, were subjective. It wasn't fair that one person's opinion could completely dictate a film's success or failure. I couldn't think of the equivalent in the book world. A glowing review from the *New York Times* might help bolster sales, but most modern readers tend to follow crowd-sourced reviews on Goodreads or social media.

"Yes. He's killed more careers than I can count." She pressed a towel against her stained shirt, trying to dry it. "He knows it, and he uses that to his every advantage, including letting Izzy crash my party."

"What about Rotten Tomatoes and reviews from moviegoers?" I asked. "That's where I look when I'm trying to decide if I
want to see a movie."

She patted the towel on her chest. "You don't get it.
Martin's review comes out first. Everyone in the industry sees it,
passes on my film, and opening weekend is a bust."

The chef was doing his best to try and ignore our conversation, but I caught him shaking his head in disbelief. I didn't
disagree with him. I was out of arguments. I'd tried my best to
rationalize with her, but I got the sense she wanted to be
miserable.

"This is going to sound terrible, but if Martin Parker died,
that would be fine by me." She blew out a breath like a fighter
preparing for battle. "He's going to ruin me one way or
another."

I couldn't find the right words for a response.

Heather didn't seem to care. She tossed the wine-stained
towel on the counter and pushed past me, stuffing her hand
deeper in her pocket. "I need to get back out there and do whatever damage control I can."

I took a minute to process what had just happened.

"She's intense," the chef said, plating the last tray of
appetizers.

"You picked up on that, too?" I glanced behind us to make
sure she was out of earshot.

"We don't usually have our dinner guests with death wish-
es." He garnished the eggs with freshly chopped herbs.

I sighed and chewed my lip. "Yeah, I think it's going to be an
interesting few hours. Do you need an extra set of hands? I
could just hide out here for the rest of the night."

He made a tsking sound. "Sorry to say health code won't
allow it."

"Can I at least take that out for you?" I asked, motioning to
the tray.

"Sure. Everything's ready." He handed me the first tray of deviled eggs.

I squared my shoulders.

It's only a couple more hours, Annie. Put on a brave face.

The remaining guests had arrived. I circled the pub and the table, offering small bites and making sure everyone had a drink.

Heather clinked her fork against her glass. "If I could have your attention, everyone. Please come find your seats."

The few people still mingling at the bar came to join the table. I set the appetizers in the center and sat between Sam and Hal.

"Buckle up, kid, we're going to be in for a wild ride tonight," Sam said to me, raising his glass in a toast. "Izzy and Heather vying for Martin's attention. You can't script this. I'm tempted to ask what's his name—Rufus—to film this."

"Is Martin's review that important?" I asked, stealing a quick look to the head of the table where Heather waited for people to take their seats. I wanted to hear if his perspective mirrored hers.

"I'm afraid so. Some say he's the most powerful man in Hollywood." He shrugged. "I might have a few other names to add to that list, but his reviews are the gold standard of the industry. We need him to love this film. Really love this film."

"That has to be a lot of pressure for debuting a film. I was talking to Heather, and she made it seem like if Martin gives the movie a bad review, no one will go."

Sam considered my words and reached to grab a pesto pastry. "I'm confident that *Midnight Alibi* will receive a glowing review. Heather has nothing to worry about."

I was taken aback by his response.

This might be one of those times when Heather could benefit from the wisdom of age. Sam was financing the film. He didn't seem to be sweating Martin's review. He was either very sure he had a hit on his hands, or he'd been in the business long enough to have a better perspective.

"Thank you for being here tonight," Heather continued as the last guest took their seat. "Making this film has been the highlight of my career, and I'm touched that you've trekked to Redwood Grove to celebrate premiere weekend with me. First, I'd like to thank everyone who has made tonight possible, starting with the legendary Sam Brudges, our fearless executive producer."

Everyone clapped.

Sam bowed his head in a show of humility. Although I caught him scanning the table, checking to make sure everyone participated in recognizing him.

"We have an absolute banger of a movie to share with you, and some of the cast will be with us this weekend, including Cora Mitchell."

Cora was on her feet, taking in the spotlight, before Heather had finished her introduction.

"I'd also like to extend my thanks to the team at the Secret Bookcase and the staff at the Stag Head for hosting us and organizing the film fest that will accompany tomorrow night's premiere."

Unlike Cora, none of us stood to be recognized.

"And, finally, a special thanks to Rufus Wells, who has generously offered to screen Hitchcock's 1940 debut, *Rebecca*, for us and showcase some of his collection at the theater."

I noticed that Heather made no mention of Izzy being in attendance.

Bowls of minestrone soup and salads were passed around as Heather spent a good five minutes gushing about what an honor it was to have Martin in town.

"Isn't it his job to attend screenings?" I asked Sam.

Sam grinned and dipped his spoon into his soup. "You're witnessing the great art of ass-kissing. Sit back and enjoy."

Heather went over the weekend agenda and our packets while everyone enjoyed soup and salad. When the main course arrived, she finally sat, and conversations shifted to people sitting near one another.

"Your dinner, Ms. Murray," Liam said, placing a steaming plate of pasta in front of me. "Would you like fresh cheese?"

Why the formality?

"Sure."

I leaned to the side to make room for him to grate parmesan on my pasta. It was impossible to ignore the aroma of his woodsy cologne. A spark of electricity ran through my body. Being in near proximity to Liam made my skin tingle and it was only getting worse the more time we spent around each other. I needed to find a way to keep my emotions in check when it came to Liam, but I was finding that to be harder than I expected.

"That's good. Thanks." I held my hand over my plate to signal my pasta had reached peak cheesiness.

"Enjoy." Liam's words brushed against the back of my neck.

I maintained perfect posture, straightening my spine and staring directly across the table at Cora, until he moved away. I hated that he had the ability to rattle me.

"He's hot." Cora blew on her hand like she was trying to put out a fire. "I love a tall, dark, smoldering type."

"Emphasis on smoldering." I twirled pasta around my fork.

"Is he single?" Cora flipped her hair to the side while her eyes followed Liam to the kitchen. "He's kind of old, but I love a broody man and I wouldn't mind getting wrapped up in those burly arms."

Kind of old? Liam was in his mid-thirties.

"I don't keep tabs on Liam's love life," I said to Cora. I didn't want to spend any more time talking about Liam.

Fortunately, Rufus provided me with a distraction.

I hadn't noticed that Martin left the table.

"Put that down immediately," Rufus shouted. He tried to scramble out of his chair but flipped it over and landed on the floor with a thud. Rufus was surprisingly nimble. He leapt over the chair in a fluid acrobatic move and yanked a film canister from Martin's hands.

"Easy, easy." Martin swatted at Rufus but missed. "Don't touch me."

"You should know better." Rufus examined the vintage reel with the intensity of an appraiser from *Antiques Roadshow*. "Do you have any idea how much this film is worth?"

"Do you have any idea who you're talking to? I'm Martin Parker. I know more about film than anyone on the planet."

That was a bold statement.

"Then you should know that these canisters aren't toys." Rufus wiped the edge of the metal tin with a napkin, buffing away Martin's fingerprints.

"Touching the canister isn't going to damage the film," Martin retorted.

He was probably right. It wasn't as if he had yanked out the old film paper, but then again, I couldn't blame Rufus for being upset that Martin was giving little regard to his valuable collection.

Rufus set the film on the table with the others. He lasered his eyes on Martin. "Consider this your warning. If you so much as lay a finger on any of these again, you'll regret it."

Martin tossed his head back and laughed. "How pathetic. You're worried about a minuscule little film collection. You should be asking for me to autograph them, but after this outburst, that won't be happening."

Rufus gazed at Martin with such hate that I instinctively placed my hand over my heart and sucked in a breath.

Was he going to hit him?

"I promise you do not want to cross me." Rufus stood his ground.

"I'm shaking in my boots." Martin shrugged and strolled up to the bar to refresh his drink.

I wasn't sure what we had just witnessed, but if dinner was any indication of how the rest of the weekend was going to go, I had a feeling that I had my work cut out for me.

FIVE

Dinner remained contentious. The tension between Rufus and Martin was thicker than the creamy layers of rum-soaked ladyfingers in the tiramisu. Heather tried to smooth things over between the dueling film aficionados, but neither of them wanted anything to do with her attempts at finding connections between their work.

Cora flirted shamelessly with Liam. Every time he refilled drinks or cleared plates, she would shift in her chair, make sure her shirt was revealing extra cleavage, and giggle as she asked him how many paper stags had been murdered for the décor.

I wanted to tell Cora it wasn't worth the effort. If she thought acting immature, like a young sycophant, was going to impress Liam, it wasn't.

Why was it bothering me this much, though?

I tried to tell myself it was because it was painful to watch a woman make herself less in order to try and attract a man, but there was more with Liam that I wasn't ready to explore.

Limoncello, amaro, and espresso flowed. Izzy stood and lifted her after-dinner digestif. "Let's do another round of toasts." Her words slurred together in time with the circling motion of her hips. "I'm so honored to get to have first eyes on *Midnight Alibi* by my dear, dear friend and fellow filmmaker, Heather Hathaway."

Heather's face said otherwise. She clearly didn't return Izzy's sentiment.

"Being a woman in this industry isn't always easy, and it's so wonderful to have a sisterhood with you, Heather." She blew Heather air kisses, holding her precariously full drink with one hand raised high. "To sisterhood and carving out a new path forward for all the women who come behind us."

Heather didn't bother to fake a response. She clutched her arms over her body in a protective stance.

Izzy continued, grabbing the top of her chair for support as she almost toppled over. How much wine and limoncello had she had?

"You might think that we're rivals. That's partly true, but we share a common enemy, and, as the ancient proverb says, 'the enemy of my enemy is my friend.' Isn't that right, Heather?"

Heather's face went ghostly white. She shook her head repeatedly, pleading for Izzy to stop.

Izzy ignored her. She knocked back the rest of her drink and placed a hand on Martin's shoulder, digging her fingers into his skin like a massage therapist trying to work out a knot of tight muscles. "And to think we have public enemy number one here. Martin Parker—the person every producer, director, and actor fears more than any monster lurking in the shadows."

Martin belted out a throaty laugh and reached for Izzy's hand. He clapped his large palm over her fingers and turned to meet her eyes. "I wouldn't go that far, Izzy."

"But, Martin, it's true." She yanked her hand away and patted his other shoulder. "Why don't you share with the table what you told me earlier?"

Heather jumped to her feet. "Uh, thank you for the toast,

Izzy. We've got a long day ahead of us tomorrow, so I'd like Rufus to start your presentation now."

"I'm not done. I have more to say," Izzy said, tilting her glass back and taking a long drink.

Martin reached for her waist in a show of strength. He nudged her in the direction of her seat. "Go sit down, Izzy. You're embarrassing yourself."

"Me? It's you, you're the problem." She rocked in motion with her cocktail glass, like she was deep out in the middle of the sea, trying to regain her balance. "*You* want to ruin all of us."

"I would agree with that," Rufus replied in a throaty tone as he opened one of the film canisters. "Anyone who doesn't respect the greats who came before him and set the tone for today's movies shouldn't be trusted."

Izzy took her seat with a heavy sigh, plopping down on her chair and finishing her drink in one swig. "Fine, but I have more to say. I won't be silenced. It's time for the rise of the matriarchy, right, Heather?"

Heather rolled her eyes and muttered something unintelligible under her breath. She pointedly turned her body away from Izzy. "Go ahead, Rufus, please proceed."

Rufus spent the next forty-five minutes lecturing on the history of horror films. The content of his talk was interesting. While showing us snippets of uncut Hitchcock footage, he discussed the master of suspense's legacy in the film industry.

"Hitchcock made the MacGuffin popular. For those of you unfamiliar with the term, it's using an object or goal as a plot device to move the story forward, even though it's actually not important. In this way, Hitchcock revolutionized storytelling, letting him narrow in on characters and building tension without worrying about specific plot details," Rufus explained as he paced back and forth on the far side of the table.

He shared examples of Hitchcock's innovative editing style —quick cuts, long takes, and montage scenes. We listened to clips of music that accompanied the films while Rufus discussed the director's many collaborators, including Bernard Herrmann, whose iconic scores were still recognizable today.

I enjoyed learning more about Hitchcock and his contribution to suspense and thrillers. There was no denying that Rufus was extremely knowledgeable on the subject, but his delivery left something to be desired. He spoke in one flat tone, with little to no inflection.

Hal nodded off a couple of times.

I didn't blame him.

After an hour, Heather finally cut Rufus off. "Thank you for that fascinating background. I know that I've derived great inspiration from Hitchcock and am looking forward to hearing more tomorrow."

"Is that it? Am I done for tonight?" Rufus sounded flustered. He gestured to a box of films. "I haven't even begun to touch upon the filmmakers Hitchcock inspired. We have at least a dozen examples, from Steven Spielberg to M. Night Shyamalan. I've put together sequences from modern films that mimic his style and tone."

"That sounds enthralling. Really, it does, but I'm going to need to stop you here." Heather tapped her watch. "I'm afraid we need to call it a night, as much as I'm sure we'd all love to hear more."

Martin coughed intentionally loud, placing one hand on his stomach and heaving his shoulders. "Ha! Speak for yourself, Heather. I can't believe you've made us sit through this."

Heather stood and brushed her hands together like she was trying to cleanse herself of the evening. "In any event, you're slotted for an hour-long presentation before tomorrow's viewing of *Rebecca*," she said to Rufus in a tone that made it clear he was being dismissed. "It would be wonderful if you could talk for forty minutes, but please do leave at least fifteen to twenty minutes for audience questions."

"With this windbag, good luck," Martin whispered to Izzy, intentionally keeping his voice loud enough to be heard.

Heather looked like she wanted to collapse on the table. I felt bad for her. I was sure this wasn't how she had expected the evening to turn out. I wished there was something I could do to help end the evening on a brighter note. It was hard not to feel partially responsible. Not that it was my fault that this dysfunctional group was at each other's throats, but we had opened up our tranquil hometown to invite these people in and put in an inordinate amount of time and effort planning for the weekend. I hated the thought of the cast and crew bickering. It was like everyone had lost sight of why they were here. Heather had specifically reached out to us because she was charmed and captivated by the sweet spirit of our village. If our friendly and welcoming community of Redwood Grove was going to have newcomers descend for the weekend, I wanted the event to be fun, enjoyable, and memorable for everyone involved.

On a whim, I stood up and clinked my fork on my empty wine glass. "Before everyone leaves, I'd like to take a minute to welcome you all to Redwood Grove; I know I speak not only for us at the Secret Bookcase"—I paused and nodded to Hal and Fletcher—"but also for the entire community. We're a small town with a lot of heart. We're thrilled to have you here and we have a fantastic lineup of events taking place throughout the village square all weekend. If there's anything we can do to help make your stay better, please don't hesitate to ask. We're so excited to be part of the premiere tomorrow."

Heather gave me a look of profound gratitude.

Hal gave me a thumbs-up when I sat back down.

I wasn't sure what came over me. It wasn't typical Annie Murray behavior, but I didn't want to lose sight of the excitement. We were hosting the first screening of a new movie tomorrow. That was a big deal and should be celebrated.

"Well said, Annie, and thanks to the Stag Head for this

wonderful dinner. It perfectly captured the mood of the film."
Heather pressed her hands together in thanks then she returned
to business mode. "I need everyone at the theater by four p.m.
tomorrow afternoon. We'll do an audience Q&A at five p.m.
before the screening of *Midnight Alibi* and then a talkback after
the show. Rufus, you'll start after that. I checked, and it looks
like the run-time for *Rebecca* is a little over two hours, so my
goal is to wrap by nine to give you time for your presentation
and to show the movie. The theater would like to have guests
out by shortly after midnight, but they're flexible if we go a bit
longer."

"I'm glad she's calling it now," Hal said, stifling a yawn. "It's
going to be a long day tomorrow."

"I was thinking the same thing."

Redwood Grove wasn't known for its bustling nightlife. A
typical evening for me would be meeting my best friend, Pri, for
a burger and a pint at State of Mind Public House and then
heading to my cottage for an evening of reading with a cup of
tea and my cat, Professor Plum, curled up on my lap. I couldn't
remember the last time I'd been up past midnight.

"We might have to rotate naps," Hal said with a twinkle in
his wise eyes. "Take turns curling up in the Sitting Room in
between customers."

"That, and lots of coffee," I agreed with a sleepy grin.

Heather finished making sure we each had our assignments
for the weekend. Hal got swept up in a conversation with
Fletcher, Rufus, and Liam. I gathered my things and made a
quick exit, longing for my warm bed.

"Annie, can I talk to you for a minute?" Heather reached
out an arm to stop me just as I was about to head for the door.

"Sure, what do you need?"

She glanced around us like she was worried someone was
eavesdropping. Her eyes drifted around the table, momentarily
landing on Izzy. They shared a hard look. Heather gave her

shoulders a little shake and swiveled her head toward the kitchen. "Maybe we can chat in private for a minute?"

"No problem." I followed her to the kitchen, wondering why the need for secrecy.

The chef and a dishwasher were scrubbing pots and stacking dishes in the industrial dishwasher at the far end of the galley kitchen.

"Don't mind us," Heather said with authority. "We'll stay out of your hair over here."

The chef muttered something in acknowledgment.

"Is something wrong?" I asked, studying her face for any clue as to why she dragged me into the kitchen.

"What isn't wrong? That was a complete disaster. You have to see that. Thanks for jumping in at the end there. I think Rufus would have kept talking all night. I don't know what to do." She ran her finger over her eyebrow in an effort to soothe herself. "I don't think it could have gone worse, and I can't believe that Martin invited Izzy. Plus, Rufus—what a bore. I'm tempted to cancel his talk before the screening of *Rebecca*, but it's too late for that, right? Tickets have already been sold. People are going to show up expecting to hear him speak before the movie. It would be bad to cancel, don't you think?"

I took a moment before I responded. If that's what Heather really wanted, I could make it happen, but I knew locals were excited about the screening and I badly didn't want to let everybody down. And as long as Rufus stayed within the time frame she had given him, it should be fine. I understood her stress, and I empathized with her, but this weekend was a big deal for Redwood Grove. "It's your event. You make the call. If you want to cancel the talk, I can help coordinate with the theater to inform guests. I do want to say, though, that everyone in town is so excited. I know tonight didn't go exactly as you expected, but I'm confident that the rest of the weekend is going to be great and I'm here to help."

"No, no. You're right. It's true. Martin is just in my head." She dug her fingers into her temples. "It's too late to cancel. I wish Rufus was more dynamic, that's all."

I agreed, but I felt like there was another reason she had dragged me into the kitchen. I didn't want to make small talk, so I decided my best bet was to ask her directly. "Was there something else?"

She started to respond, but Sam burst into the kitchen, the door swinging on its hinges. He used the tip of his cane to stop it.

"Oh, good, you're here," he said to Heather. "Keep me away from the knives because otherwise I might kill him."

"Who?" I asked, looking behind him.

"Martin," they both replied in unison, like they had scripted it.

Had I missed something? Before dinner, Sam sounded extremely confident that Martin was going to write a glowing review of their movie. He had assured Cora that she didn't have anything to worry about. Was he saying that because of the way Martin treated Rufus and Cora? It couldn't be new behavior, though. They both had been in the industry long enough to have had plenty of interaction with Martin. What had they expected?

And was there anyone in this group who didn't want Martin dead?

SIX

The following morning, I was sluggish, finding it impossible to drag myself out from under my fluffy down comforter. My bed was like my own personal spa. I'm not prone to overindulgent spending except for my luxurious super-soft sheets, collection of pretty pastel pillows, and matching duvet cover. I'm a firm believer that having a beautiful and comfortable bed lends itself to more blissful sleep. I refuse to skimp on cheap bedding.

Professor Plum nuzzled my chin to rouse me. I'd inherited him from Scarlet. She'd been so excited to get a kitten before graduation, never imagining that her life would be cut dramatically short.

Who could have predicted that?

Not me.

The memory was etched in my brain like a tattoo. It was a movie I had replayed thousands of times. Unlike Rufus's fear that someone might touch his precious vintage reels, I wished that someone would rip the images from my head.

Campus was abuzz with spring color and activity on the day that Scarlet died. Our classmates posed in front of the fountain in graduation caps and gowns. Finals were complete. The last thing we had to do before convocation was turn in our senior projects for our criminology class and meet at the football stadium to walk through the ceremony.

"Can you take this to Dr. Caldwell?" Scarlet asked, shoving a large manila envelope in my hands. She decorated the folder to resemble an FBI case file with the word CONFIDENTIAL stamped on the front.

"Yeah, but why? What are you doing?"

Our friends teased us that we were glued at the hip. Deep down I knew that was because of me. I latched on to Scarlet from our third day in class. She could flit in and out of social groups in ways that I couldn't. I'm better as a best friend or in small groups. Scarlet could light up any room and make small talk with strangers. She had a way of making everyone feel seen, especially me.

"I'm going to follow up on one more lead. A source agreed to meet me, Annie. This is legit. I think we're close to actually solving the case."

"I'll come with you."

She shook her head. "No, you can't. The source is already skittish. They told me to come alone. It's non-negotiable."

"But what if it's dangerous?"

"Annie, this case is years old. We're college students. My source isn't the killer, anyway. They're just as nervous and cautious as me. I'll be fine. Don't worry. I'll see you at the rehearsal later tonight. Tell Dr. Caldwell hi for me."

At the time, I ignored the churning worry in my stomach and the prickling tingling running up my spine. I was young. I hadn't learned to fully trust my intuition yet.

If I had, Scarlet would be here today.

I hadn't solved her murder or the original cold case we'd been assigned.

Dr. Caldwell's classroom was designed for dialogue and discussion. She never stood behind a podium and lectured. She worked the room, walking between the aisles to ask questions or encourage us to follow a thread of an idea further. Usually, our classes turned into lively debates and even reenactments when students would work through the physicality of a crime. However, on the day she assigned the cold case, the mood was different. She observed us filing into the lecture hall, laughing and chatting about weekend plans, in an almost stoic silence. I sensed the difference right away.

She didn't speak until everyone was seated and quiet. Then she handed stacks of file folders to students seated in the front row. "Please pass these around. Do not open your files until you're directed to do so."

I nudged Scarlet and whispered. "What's this about?"

"No idea." She shrugged.

Dr. Caldwell walked to the front of the podium and removed her reading glasses. She let her intelligent eyes focus on one section of seating and then the next, making sure she made eye contact briefly with every student in the room. "As you're well aware, graduation is mere months away, which means it's time for your final project. I need to warn you that this isn't any project. You're being assigned a cold case."

A hush of whispers broke out.

She held her hand to signal us to stop. "This will be your most involved and your most serious assignment to date. Unlike previous hypotheticals and cases that have been solved, this is an active cold case. That means that as we speak, detectives and police officers are still interviewing witnesses and tracking down new leads. You have the oppor-tunity to assist them in that process. One of you in this very room could see something in these files with new eyes that ends up being the break we so desperately need. We've discussed this previously, but let me take this moment to remind you how frustrating cases like can be. We feel a deep sense of responsibility to the victims and their families to bring closure and justice to a case that has long gone cold. Cases like this carry a different emotional weight. We feel a bond and intimacy with the families after spending years getting to know them and their stories. This is where you come in. There is real value in bringing in a fresh perspective. It's possible that one of you might spot something previously overlooked. It's an opportunity for learning, and one I do not want you to take lightly."

She went on to explain that the case involved a missing young woman, Natalie Thompson. Dr. Caldwell and the authorities believed that Natalie had stumbled upon a corruption scheme involving a number of powerful and high-profile businesses, which ultimately led to her abduction and presumed murder, although her body had never been found.

Scarlet and I spent the bulk of our last semester tracking Natalie's movements. Scarlet kept notes and photos of our research in her brightly colored journals that were filled with doodles, poems, and sketches. I documented the places she'd been in photos, videos, and spreadsheets. Our methods were different, but our commitment to cracking the case was unwavering. That was one of the many things that made us a great team. I guess opposites really do attract because Scarlet and I were polar opposites in so many ways. She was tall, self-assured, creative, a peacemaker, and a spiritual seeker. Whereas I tend to be more analytical, in my head, watchful, and diligent. I noticed the small details, while Scarlet could always see the big picture.

We shared one key thing in common—our need for justice, the desire to right a wrong, and make the world a tiny bit safer.

Natalie Thompson had risked her life to bring a truth to light, and Scarlet and I agreed that we owed her our due diligence.

Professor Plum's insistent purring brought me back to reality. It was strange to reflect back on those days now because we were so sure that we were going to actually solve the case.

I tossed off the covers and padded into the kitchen, grateful for the butterscotch morning light spilling in through the windows and the first puffy pink blooms budding on my succulents. Last night seemed like a bad dream. I still couldn't get over how much animosity there was between pretty much everyone in the group. Maybe it was par for the course in the movie business. I thanked my lucky stars for working in the book industry. As I scooped fresh ground coffee beans and drank in their nutty cocoa aroma, I promised myself that today would be a great day for the store and for my friends in the village who'd worked so hard to make the event a success. Redwood Grove was quintessentially cozy and I couldn't wait to highlight that to all of the Hollywood types in town for the weekend. Maybe a bit of our hospitality and kindness would rub off on Heather and her entourage.

While my coffee brewed, I fed Professor Plum and checked my event spreadsheet. Everything was in order. I intended to arrive at the Royal Playhouse at least an hour early. We were setting up a display in the historic theater's lobby and would sell books during intermission and between films. It was great visibility for the store.

After a leisurely cup of coffee and a bowl of oatmeal with Professor Plum curled up beside me in the dining nook, I went upstairs to shower and get ready. My shoulder-length hair is naturally wavy, and summer's humidity reinforced my curls. I decided to wear it in a loose ponytail. I decided on a black skirt, sandals, and a simple, bookish T-shirt for the day. The shirt was cream-colored with retro orange, yellow, and green block lettering and an image of a T. rex that read: PUNCTUATION SAVES LIVES. LET'S EAT KIDS. LET'S EAT, KIDS.

I knew Hal would get a kick out of the joke.

"All right, Professor Plum, hold down the fort while I'm gone." I gave him a handful of treats and left for the bookstore.

As expected, Hal greeted me with a hug and a hearty laugh. "Punctuation does indeed save lives. Let's hope we don't have to wield any commas at the premiere tonight."

"After last night, who knows what to expect? We might want to come armed with commas and semicolons." I winked.

"On that note, we received an urgent message from Heather. She needs one of us to be at the theater when it opens at four to help her with the logistics of seating." Hal scratched his head. "Seats are seats as far as I know, but I told her one of us would be there."

"I'll go," I said, already dreading having to deal with Heather again. "She's probably talking about the VIP seats that we reserved in the first two rows."

"I hate tossing you to the wolves. You could fill me in, and I'll go."

"No, it's fine." I patted his arm. As usual, he was wearing his normal bookstore "uniform"—a cardigan and slacks.

"Let us know if Fletcher and I can help." Hal lifted the sandwich board sign.

I opened the front door for him.

He set out the sign and welcomed in three eager customers. The morning breezed by. Thanks to the film fest and movie premiere, we had a steady stream of readers throughout the day. Books, candles, stickers, socks, and teas flew off the shelves.

Fletcher and I constantly ran upstairs to restock our front-of-store displays and check to see if we had extra copies of popular titles.

At least the drama with Heather was generating book sales.

Before I knew it, it was time to go to the theater. Fletcher helped me prep boxes of special orders for the event and load them on a dolly. Heather had asked us to set up a display table in the lobby for books and merch.

"Are you sure you don't want these guns to roll that over to the Royal Playhouse?" Fletcher asked, flexing his nonexistent muscles. "Can you tell I've been working out?"

"Does working out mean reading heavy hardcovers of Sherlock?" I said with one eye narrowed.

"That counts. That counts." He used a strap to secure the boxes to the dolly.

"I appreciate the offer, but I think I can handle it. I've only been reading trade paperbacks lately, but fortunately, the dolly has wheels, and I don't have far to go." I grinned, grabbing the handle and then flexing with my free hand.

"Okay, see you there later. We've got things under control." He opened the door for me and helped me maneuver the dolly down the front steps.

I waved goodbye and dragged the cart down the gravel path, leaving a trail of tire marks behind me.

The late summer sun warmed my skin. Jasmine bloomed in wild bunches along the driveway. Blackberry vines heavy with the last of summer's fruit twisted along the gate. Colorful bunting and strings of light bowed in the slight breeze. I loved that I lived in a place where nature was all around me. Cottontail bunnies hopped between the well-groomed boxwoods. Hummingbirds and bees flitted between candy-apple-red geraniums and yellow hibiscus flowers.

The pathway spilled out onto Cedar Avenue, the hub of the village square. More people than normal were out and about, soaking in the gorgeous weather at outdoor bistro tables and lingering over happy hour drinks and snacks.

I had a few extra minutes, so I decided to pop into Cryptic Coffee for an iced latte and to say hi to Pri, my best friend, as promised. I had so much to fill her in on about last night.

The coffee shop was in a renovated garage with roll-up doors attached to a large patio. The interior was modern and clean. Succulents and greenery hung from the exposed wood beams and rotating artists' work formed a gallery wall next to the espresso bar. I parked the cart next to the front doors, confident that no one would touch it. This was Redwood Grove after all.

Pri caught my eye and waved me over to the counter. "Annie, what's up?" Her bright golden-brown eyes sparkled with delight.

Pri, or Priya Kapoor, was my age and a true coffee genius. Her espresso drinks were like a religious experience. She loved pushing boundaries when it came to flavor combinations and introducing customers to interesting mash-ups.

"I'm on my way to the theater, but I was promised coffee in exchange for gossip, and I could use a little hit of Pri before I go."

"That sounds ominous." She wiggled her eyebrows. "Although I have a feeling I already know what you're up against. I thought you would never get here, so I've had to take matters in my own hands and do my best eavesdropping. Let me tell you the rumor mill has been on fire today about last night's dinner, and I had the lucky fortune to meet a few of the film people early, and damn—they're all movie industry. So much lip filler, vaping, and, my God, the eyeliner." She ran a finger beneath her eye in a sweeping motion.

"It makes me well aware of the differences between the Bay and LA."

"Look, I love artistic expression. You know that more than anyone. Look at me." She tapped her latest temporary tattoo on her forearm. "But the level of self-absorption is a bit much. They all seem cutthroat and out to tear each other down. I'm glad that's not our vibe here."

In her spare time, Pri dabbled in tattoo design. She had notebooks filled with pages and pages of sketches. Nearly every other week, she ordered temporary versions of her creations, but she had yet to commit to any of them permanently.

I'd encouraged her to turn her art into stickers and sell them at the Cryptic. Seeing the display of vinyl cutouts of Pri's images next to the pastry case made me smile.

"I couldn't agree more. Did you meet Heather Hathaway, the director?" I studied the specials board. A PSYCHOANALYSIS OF MILK—THE SUSPICION LATTE. Dark espresso roast, ginger and blood orange syrup, dark chocolate sauce, whole milk, and a secret surprise.

"No, let me see if I can get all of their names right... Izzy, just Izzy, because why not. Cora Mitchell, the actress, and Sam Brudges, the producer." Pri poured espresso beans into the industrial grinder.

"I'm impressed." The aroma made me appreciate the word *swoon*. "And I have to try your special. I can't wait to see what the surprise is."

"Oh, you'll love it." Pri shot me a devilish grin.

"How were Izzy, Cora, and Sam? What did you hear?" I stared longingly at the pastry case, wondering if I should grab a shortbread layered with blood-red pomegranate jam for later.

"They were all going off about a film critic."

"Martin," I offered.

"Yes, Martin." Pri paused to grind the beans. "He sounds like a gem."

"You have no idea." I shook my head. "He's a beast."

Pri tamped coffee and dialed up the steaming temperature for the milk. "The three of them were plotting—conspiring, I don't know the right term, but none of them sounded thrilled to be here for the movie. It's almost like they were trying to figure out a way to make sure it tanks."

"Really? All three of them?" I wasn't exactly surprised, given the cutthroat nature of last night, especially with Izzy, but Sam and Cora were both connected to the movie and I assumed had motivation for it to be a smashing success.

"You wouldn't believe the things people say standing where

you are now." She looked up at me and moved her hand back and forth between us. "They assume we're not listening because we're mere baristas, but trust me, I'm always listening. Also I'm standing in arm's length of you. What, you think I can't hear everything you're saying? *Please.* Is my hearing supposed to be that bad?"

"I don't know. Do we need to get you fitted for hearing aids?" I laughed. "That's why I love you. And why some people are the worst."

"Yeah, well, they're the worst. I feel bad for Heather. These are the people she *invited* to come to celebrate the film's release. Yikes." Pri scowled, steaming thick creamy milk.

"Not only that, but Cora's starring in the movie and Sam produced it. It seems like they both have a big financial and professional stake in the film doing well. If your producer and your leading actress are trying to sabotage opening night, what does that say about you as a director?" What could they be plotting? Was Izzy trying to steal Cora and Sam away from Heather?

"Ouch, that's cold. Getting taken down internally. It's like a movie coup." Pri shivered. She used a miniature whisk to blend the syrups and chocolate sauce before pouring the shots into the cup and swirling in the milk. "What went down last night?"

I told her about the dinner. She finished my drink by placing a little syringe filled with red liquid on the side of the cup.

"What is this?"

"It's the special surprise. Inject it into your drink if you dare." She threw her head back in a mock evil laugh.

"Of course I dare." I squeezed the liquid into the frothy foam, red oozing over the coffee like a gushing wound. "This is suspicious."

"And delicious. It's my cherry and raspberry house-made syrup."

"You are too clever." I took a drink of her Hitchcockian inspiration. The coffee was beautifully balanced with a touch of sweetness paired with a spicy finish from the ginger. "Also this is your best yet."

"Annie, you say that every time." Pri scowled and squinted her amber-flecked eyes at me.

"But this time it's true." I took a long, luxurious sip to prove my point.

"Did you hear about the altercation earlier?"

"What altercation?" I cradled the earthenware mug in my hands, letting the heat from the coffee warm them. Even in the heat of summer, my hands are always cold. Scarlet used to tease me that I couldn't live anywhere other than California with my cold-blooded tendencies. She was right. I was diagnosed with Raynaud's disease when I was younger. The condition causes my fingers and toes to be perpetually chilly and turn ghostly white when exposed to the cold. Winters in Minnesota or Alaska were out of the question.

"Apparently, someone tried to attack that film critic who's in town for the fest." Pri adjusted the temperature dial on the espresso machine. She had mastered the art of pulling strong, rich espresso shots and balancing them with assorted kinds of milk and spices. I was in awe that she knew what of each of the buttons on the machine were for. The machine's interface looked like it belonged on a SpaceX rocket.

"What?" I didn't mean to respond quite so loudly. I checked around us to make sure no one was paying attention. Then I rested my coffee on the counter and leaned closer. "Okay, now you have to dish on the details. I haven't heard anything about that."

She wiped the steam wand with a wet dish towel. "Yeah, I mean I heard this secondhand, but it's right in line with every-thing you've said. It happened right before lunch. They got into it at State of Mind. According to gossip around here, the critic got knocked off his feet and is going to have a nice bruise on his face to show for it."

"Do you know who?"

She tossed the towel in the sink and shook her head. "I didn't hear officially, but from the way Cora, Izzy, and Sam were talking, I think it might have been Sam."

Sam punched Martin in broad daylight?

I studied the artwork hanging behind the espresso bar. It was a mix of modern abstract paintings and seaside landscapes.

If that were true, why would Sam have taken a swing at Martin?

I couldn't quite wrap my head around Sam. Last night he seemed nonchalant about money and funding the film as well as nonplussed about Martin's potential negative review. But then he'd also claimed to want to kill the guy.

I had a bad feeling that there might be more drama off-screen than on this evening, and unfortunately I was going to be smack-dab in the middle of it.

SEVEN

I finished my coffee while Pri steamed almond milk for a new order. If things had gotten physical between Sam and Martin, I wondered if Heather was going to be able to defuse the situation.

"My shift is over in an hour. Should I meet you at the theater?" Pri asked, handing a customer a rose-infused latte.

"Sure. You might have to grab us seats, but just find me when you get there. I'll be in the lobby."

I thanked her for the coffee and found the dolly waiting where I'd left it by the front door. The Royal Playhouse Theater was on the opposite side of Oceanside Park, but I decided to take the long way around the square; since the park pathways were primarily bark, it would be much harder to pull the cart.

The park wasn't exactly oceanside. The coast was thirty miles away, but that didn't stop the town council and chamber of commerce from claiming that we were a coastal community. I assumed that their goal was to draw in more visitors, but we had plenty of charm to tout, like the towering redwoods that flanked the park and the eclectic mix of buildings that made up downtown. Spanish-style red-tile roofs mingled with California mid-century modern designs, giving the village square a sweet, funky vibe. The architecture matched the mindset of those of us who were lucky enough to call Redwood Grove home. We tended to be independent thinkers and free spirits. There was a deep sense of community spirit and support, especially amongst the small business owners in town.

I passed State of Mind Public House. The patio was packed with people enjoying afternoon pints and early happy hour snacks. Then I continued past the library and historical museum until the Royal Playhouse came into view.

Heather was pacing back and forth in front of the marquee when I arrived at the theater. The old-fashioned marquee extended from the center of the building, lit up by retro neon lights. A ticket booth adjacent to the entrance featured original brass and glass and matched the building's nostalgic façade. Framed posters advertised the premiere, film fest, and upcoming movie releases.

Heather puffed on her vape pen. "You're here, finally. They won't let me in. I can't get ahold of anyone from the theater. I've been pounding on the doors for ten minutes."

I waved saccharine smoke from my face. "That's probably because staff aren't expected to be here yet."

She sucked in her cheeks and took a long drag. "I need in there now. Do you have a key? Can you do anything?"

I glanced at the decorative archway to the large wooden front doors with brass handles and curved windows. "No, I don't have a key. I can text the manager and see if someone is on their way."

"Do that. Do that." She waved her vape pen.

Before I could pull my phone out, a theater staff member appeared, dressed in a red-and-white-striped attendant's vest. "Are you the filmmaker? My boss called and said you need access to the theater."

"I needed access an hour ago," Heather snapped.

The attendant shrugged. "Sorry, we don't open until four, but I can let you in now."

"Yes, please do." Heather marched to the doors.

I sympathized with her nerves. Premiering a film had to be stressful, but she didn't need to take it out on the theater staff. And she was the one who arranged to meet at four. If she needed more prep time, she should have said that earlier.

"Sorry," Heather said to the attendant as if reading my mind. "I know it's not your fault. This is a big night for me, though."

The teenager unlocked the door. "It's cool. Good luck with the movie." They turned on the lights, illuminating vintage movie posters from bygone eras and the concession stands in the lobby.

I lugged the dolly over the threshold, immediately catching a whiff of buttery popcorn that wafted through the high decorative ceilings.

"This is charming," Heather said, taking another puff on her vape pen.

"You can't smoke in here," the teen said.

"What is it with this town?" She looked at me like I was supposed to agree with her.

"It's state law," I replied.

"Which way is the theater?" she asked the attendant, ignoring me.

"Right there. It's kind of hard to miss. It's the only theater we have." They pointed to the left.

"Let me take a look at what we're dealing with first, and then I need to get up into the booth. I'm assuming that's upstairs in the balcony?"

"Yep. Stairs are on both sides of the auditorium." They left us to fire up the popcorn machine.

I left the dolly by the ticket booth and followed Heather toward the auditorium.

"This is quite elegant. Dated but elegant. Much more dated than I expected. The photos online are generous to say the least. But, hey, it's vibes for my movie for sure," Heather said as we stepped inside the auditorium. Carpet ran down each aisle. Plush red velvet chairs with padded armrests awaited movie lovers. A grand crystal chandelier was suspended from the ceiling, a stunning centerpiece harking back to the theater's heyday. Gilded moldings and fixtures gave the space a touch of luxury. Soft dim lighting created an inviting ambiance.

Red velvet drapes secured with gold tassels framed the screen.

Heather strolled down the center aisle, taking it all in. When she reached the front near the screen, she spun around to get a view of the balcony. "What a charmer. This is straight out of a Cary Grant movie. Of course, in my film, Cary would end up gutted."

"Is the film really gory?" I wouldn't choose a particularly graphic or gory novel or movie on my own, but I wasn't opposed to a good jump scare and some blood and guts. I just wanted to know what I was getting before going into a movie.

"Yeah, it's a modern spin on Hitchcock. You have to expect that there's going to be some blood." Heather snapped a couple of selfies.

"Heather, is that you?" A voice boomed above us.

I looked up to see Martin leaning over the gold-and-brass balcony railing.

"Martin, what are you doing here?" Heather's body language shifted. Instead of angling her head at just the right position for a pose, she stiffened her back and bared her teeth like a dog ready to attack.

"I need a word—now." He thrust his thumb down. "Meet me in the lobby."

"One minute. Be right there," she responded in a singsong

voice to Martin. "Go ahead and do whatever you need to do for setup. I'll come find you shortly."

I watched her hurry away like a student about to get sent to detention.

Why did I need to be here?

Heather easily could have called the theater owner herself. Something else was amiss. The question was, what?

I couldn't place my finger on it, but there had to be another reason Heather wanted me here hours before the doors would open. Moral support?

Or was it that she didn't want to be alone with Martin?

I waited for a minute and then returned to the lobby.

They were huddled near the stairs that led up to the balcony, so I tried to make myself scarce. I had work to do anyway. The theater staff had left a folding table next to my cart of books, so I did my best to ignore their conversation while I set up the table and draped it with a long, black tablecloth. We don't do many events outside of the store, but I made a blue-print sketch of how I wanted to arrange book sales. Blame it on my analytical mind. I needed to know exactly how much space the books and merchandise would take up, and then I could calculate an area for our point-of-sale iPad, a small cash drawer, and bags.

"I'm begging you, Martin." Heather sounded like she was on the brink of tears. "You have to stay. The film is drastically different. We cut so much. We went back to the editing room and looked at every shot with fresh eyes because of your feedback."

It was impossible not to eavesdrop. I didn't want to be obvious and stare in their direction, but I guessed that if I did, Heather was probably on her knees begging.

"My feedback?" Martin laughed, but nothing about his tone was funny. "That's how you're spinning it? As I already told you, *Midnight Alibi* is a cinematic catastrophe. You have managed to make an incoherent mess of characters and plot that had me ready to sell my firstborn child in exchange for rolling the end credits. *Midnight Alibi* is uninspired storytelling and lackluster performances. It's a crime against filmmaking, and no amount of lipstick is going to fix this pig."

"Why did you even bother to come? Are you trying to torture me?" Heather banged her head against the wall as she spoke. "You wanted me to get my hopes up that you were going to write a new review just to mess with me?"

Martin threw his arms over his chest and stood taller. "My review has been written for weeks. This isn't up for debate." His eyes drifted in my direction.

I didn't want to be caught in the crossfire, so I pretended to study the back cover of one of the Hitchcock autobiographies for our display.

I snuck another glance in their direction just in time to see Martin unfolding a piece of paper that I assumed must be his review.

He dangled it in front of Heather's face. "Do want to hear my headline suggestions? I'm vacillating between the two. What do you think of this? '*Midnight Alibi*—A Horrifying Ride to Cinematic Hell.'"

"Why are you doing this?" she wailed. "It's like you're enjoying this. This is my life's work that you're ripping to shreds for no reason."

Martin cleared his throat and lifted the paper higher. "I'm not done; don't you want to hear my other headline?"

"No." Heather stuffed her fingers in her ears.

That only encouraged Martin. "I also want something that captures the idea that audiences will leave with a lingering sense of regret for the time they'll never get back. How about '*Midnight Alibi*—The Alibi for a Sleepless Night Filled with Regret.'"

"You can't do this to me, Martin."

"Yeah, you're right. That's too wordy. I'll work on it." He folded the paper in half, put it in his shirt pocket, and patted it for safety. "I'll keep it tucked right here."

Heather pounded her forehead with the palm of her hand. "I don't understand why you won't at least give the film another chance. At least gauge the audience's reaction. You're all the way out here in the middle of nowhere."

"Don't worry your pretty head, darling. I'll watch your film again tonight, but it would take a miracle of epic proportions for me to change a single word in this review. Off it goes to my editor tonight. I suggest you enjoy this evening while you can because once this goes to print, you're going to have a hard time finding many friends in Hollywood."

Heather's intense behavior seemed more justified by the moment. It was one thing for Martin not to like the film, but his words were like a personal assault.

Heather wouldn't have any friends in Hollywood?

What did that mean?

"Just give it a chance, okay?" Heather pleaded one last time.

"You had your chance, and you blew it. You know what I'm talking about." Martin pressed his hand over the pocket with the review and walked toward me with an air of arrogance. His steps were measured, almost in time, like he was leading a parade. It was obvious that he was taking great pleasure in the moment.

I busied myself stacking books and arranging posters and stickers. Martin didn't bother to acknowledge me as he pushed open the doors, letting the afternoon sunlight flood inside.

After he was gone, Heather keeled over and clutched her knees.

I left my display and went to console her. "Are you okay?"

She rocked her body forward like she had just finished a yoga class and was trying to keep her limbs loose. "No, kill me now. My life is over."

I placed a hand on her shoulder. "I overheard some of that. I wasn't trying to, but Martin made it pretty impossible not to listen. I get it. Everything he said was rough, but it's going to be okay. You can't let one person's opinion ruin your entire night. We have a packed house for your premiere. There will be hundreds of excited movie fans here shortly. Don't listen to Martin's skewed perspective. That sounded personal anyway. He was really cruel and awful to you." Heather had been curt and demanding last night, but no one deserved to be treated this way.

She rolled up to standing one vertebra at a time. "It is personal."

"Why?"

"I have no idea. This is what he does to people. He destroys lives with his exacting pen."

"That's the old saying." I nodded in solidarity.

She gave me a sharp look. "What?"

"The pen is mightier than the sword."

"Then I guess I need to find a bigger sword."

I chuckled, trying to break the tension.

Heather's face remained stony. "I'm not kidding. Like Sam and I discussed last night, Martin can't get away with this. He's not going to turn in that review if I have anything to say about it."

I didn't have the heart to tell her that there was no chance Martin was changing his tune. I had no idea what was going on between them, but I had zero doubts that Martin was eager and ready to eviscerate *Midnight Alibi*. I didn't have time to dwell on Heather and Martin's exchange because people began streaming through the doors. Soon the lobby was buzzing with anticipation and the aroma of freshly popped popcorn.

Movie lovers mingled with frothy sodas and flutes of champagne.

I was glad that Fletcher doubled our order because there

was a steady line for book sales. The Hitchcock biographies were the most popular, followed by collections of books to film. By the time we were ready to take our seats, my fingers were sore from typing so many orders into the iPad. I felt bad for Heather and the rest of the cast, but the show of support and genuine excitement from the community was exactly the point I'd been trying to make. No one in Redwood Grove cared about Martin Parker's review. Everyone was thrilled to get to be a part of something like this, myself included.

If book sales were any indication, I had a good feeling that *Midnight Alibi* was going to be an instant hit, at least here in Redwood Grove.

The lights flickered and a tone dinged to warn us that the movie would be starting in ten minutes. Fletcher agreed to watch the table until the intermission, so I went to find a seat. Fortunately, Pri had saved one for me near the back of the theater. I squeezed into my seat next to Pri and nearly spilled buttery popcorn on the floor when I realized that Liam Donovan was on my other side.

"You ready for this?" she asked, handing me a box of Junior Mints. "I bought tons of candy and the extra-large tub of popcorn just in case."

"In case of what?"

"In case it's too scary." She hunched her shoulders. "Candy is the antidote to any good horror film, didn't you know that?"

"No, but it makes sense."

"Let me know if you need reinforcements." She pointed to the collection of movie snacks on her lap.

"Why is Liam sitting here?" I whispered to Pri, sinking into the plush velvet chair, happy for the dim lighting so that Liam couldn't see the tinge of red creeping up my cheeks.

"Sorry, there were no other open seats."

"Trade me. You can have all my popcorn." I rested my wine glass in the cup holder and offered her the tub.

"Hmmm, buttery popcorn or watching you squirm." Pri scrunched her face in thought. "I'll take watching you squirm."

"What are you two whispering about?" Liam leaned closer.

"Nothing." I positioned my arms strategically around the popcorn tub to avoid accidentally making contact with Liam's armrest.

Heather tapped on a microphone. "Welcome, everyone, to the world premiere of *Midnight Alibi*. I'm the director, Heather Hathaway, and I assure you that you are in for an evening of thrilling, heart-thumping entertainment. I'll be answering questions after the film, but for now, enjoy." She swept her hand in front of the red velvet curtains that opened on cue as the lights completely dimmed.

Sound rumbled through the speakers, shaking the floor. My eyes refused to adjust to the dizzying display of flashes in the opening scene.

Like any good thriller, *Midnight Alibi* didn't waste any time getting to the murder.

Pri let out a little scream as the killer attacked his unsuspecting victim with the edge of a golf club.

I didn't mean to, but I startled, too, accidentally elbowing Liam's arm and sending popcorn out of the top of the bucket.

He chuckled. "And here I thought Annie Murray was completely unflappable."

"Not during a jump scare."

He patted my forearm, letting his hand linger for a minute. "Get it together, Murray. We're counting on you to save us."

I rolled my eyes.

Another choppy sequence flashed on the screen. Followed by a bloodcurdling scream.

It took a second to realize that the sound didn't line up with the action or dialogue in the movie.

At that moment, something heavy fell from the balcony and

landed with a thud on the floor a few feet in front of us. Something that looked like a body.

No, it couldn't be a body.

Had someone fallen?

Was it part of the show?

People jumped from their seats and joined in the screaming. "Oh my God! Get help! Call 911."

EIGHT

Pandemonium broke out in the theater. People raced from their seats and rushed for the exits. Some guests froze in place, glancing around as if they were trying to figure out whether this was part of the premiere. Could Heather have staged this to up the tension? Was it a last-ditch attempt to try and impress Martin?

I knew immediately that the fall wasn't part of the evening's agenda.

Pri froze and clutched my arm. "Annie, that sounded bad."

I shuddered and instinctually stuffed my fingers in my ears, trying to block the sound of the thud.

Liam shifted his body into a protective stance, blocking our view like a bodyguard. "You don't want to see this."

"Did someone fall from the balcony?" I asked, already knowing the answer. The smell of butter and popcorn suddenly made me want to vomit.

"Yeah, it looks that way." Liam leaned to the side and lifted his arm to shroud our perspective as the main lights came on.

My eyes stung from the brightness, or maybe because I was

trying to hold in my emotions. A fall off the balcony couldn't be good. Was it survivable?

My criminology training kicked in.

I silenced the repetitive thuds and nudged Liam to the side. "Has anyone called 911? Is anyone trying CPR?"

Liam shot Pri a look like he had missed part of the conversation.

"She's in pure Annie mode now," Pri replied, holding out one hand to signal him to stop. "Let her do her thing."

Liam turned so I could squeeze past him.

There was something morbid about the abandoned popcorn buckets, sodas, wine, and candy boxes left at every seat.

People huddled around the scene of the fall. Someone was on the floor assessing the victim. I pushed my way to the front.

The first thing I couldn't figure out was the angle of the fall. I glanced up at the balcony.

How had they landed in the aisle and not on any of the rows? It was a godsend because someone else might have been injured, but it couldn't have been a natural fall.

As I got closer, I recognized Cora's signature hair. She knelt next to the victim, holding their limp wrist in her hand and sobbing uncontrollably.

The second I saw Martin Parker's face, I knew that he was dead. He hadn't survived the fall. Not to mention that his limbs were contorted in ways that weren't humanly possible.

"Cora." I put my hand on her shoulder.

She flinched and dropped Martin's wrist. Her eyes were the size of giant film canisters. "I was checking for a pulse, but I can't find one."

I bent next to her. "Has someone called 911?"

She pointed a shaky finger to a woman standing nearby with her phone pressed to her ear. "They told us to look for a pulse, but I can't feel anything."

"Let me try." I knew it was futile, but it was also procedure.

I went through first aid protocol, checking for a pulse, making sure Martin's airway was clear, and assessing his body for any visible sign of external bleeding.

"Should we do CRP?" Cora asked.

"Yes. It's been more than ten seconds. He's not breathing, and he doesn't have a pulse, so I'll start chest compressions." I didn't have the heart to tell her that I doubted it would matter, but from my first aid and CPR courses, I knew that, regardless of my unprofessional opinion that Martin was already dead, when a patient was not responsive and unconscious, CPR should be administered immediately. The first few minutes were the most crucial; without CPR to manually circulate oxygenated blood to the brain and vital organs, irreversible damage could occur.

I lost track of everything around me while I concentrated on trying to revive Martin or at least keep his blood pumping.

How had he fallen?

Why was he up in the balcony anyway?

Heather had reserved two rows for her VIP guests in the front of the theater. Martin should have had a seat with the rest of the film entourage. The balcony was packed. Someone must have seen what happened. Part of me wanted to abandon CPR and run upstairs to begin interviewing eyewitnesses.

Had Martin had too much to drink? Could he have fallen over the railing?

That seemed like a stretch.

But how could someone have been pushed off in front of at least fifty people? And at an angle that made him land perfectly in the aisle?

It didn't make sense.

Unless the killer had timed their act to coincide with the flashing sequences on the screen. If that was the case, then the killer had to be someone who had already seen the film.

It was still far-fetched, but one thing I had learned in my

criminology coursework was that no theory was off the table in the early stages of an investigation.

The paramedics arrived and I stood up to let them take over.

Pri, Liam, Fletcher, and Hal were gathered by the side theater doors. I headed in their direction after assuring the first responders I would stay close by to share my account with the police.

"Is it bad?" Pri winced in anticipation of my response.

I nodded and stared at my hands, which started to tremble. "Yeah. It's bad."

In a crisis, I'm usually fairly levelheaded. It's only afterward, when reality begins to sink in, that I tend to fall apart.

Hal must have picked up on that because he tugged off his cardigan and wrapped it around my shoulders. "Fletcher, I think a ginger ale is appropriate at this moment. Do you mind?"

"Huh? Ginger ale?" Fletcher shot me a quick glance and then returned his gaze to Hal. "Oh, yeah. Got it. I'm on it. Back in a flash." He darted for the concession stands.

"How are you holding up, Annie?" Hal studied me with concern. His light eyes clouded with worry.

I was glad for his sweater. It suddenly felt as if the theater had turned the air conditioning on high. Little shivers erupted from my body.

Liam put his hand on the small of my back.

I looked at him in surprise.

"I'm not making a move." He rolled his eyes but tightened his grasp on me. "You're just swaying."

Was I?

"Yeah, maybe you should sit down." Pri pointed to a row of empty seats along the back wall.

"Good idea." Liam didn't wait for me to respond. He guided me to a chair and helped me sit.

"I'm okay," I protested.

"None of us are okay," Hal retorted. "And you administered CPR."

"I don't think it did any good."

"That looked like a fatal fall." Liam's gaze drifted to the balcony.

Fletcher returned with two cups of ginger ale. "I wasn't sure if you wanted ice or no ice." He lifted the cup in his left hand first. "Ice?"

"Sure." I took the drink from him.

"Anyone want a no-ice ginger ale? Or perhaps I could scrounge up something stronger, given the circumstances." Fletcher looked around like a waiter, taking orders.

I knew that everyone reacted differently to stress and trauma. Fletcher was no exception. He was flustered and in shock, too, but his way to deal with it was to keep things light.

A little glow of warmth spread through my body. It was wonderful to know that Hal, Fletcher, Pri, and even Liam were looking out for me. One of the stories I'd told myself after Scarlet died was that she was the reason I had friends. She was more outgoing and social than me, and for some reason I convinced myself that making friends was a struggle. That was a lie. I'd built long-lasting and connected friendships since moving to Redwood Grove. Seeing everyone rally around me literally and figuratively made me realize how much I had grown.

"No thanks. I don't think I can drink or eat anything. My stomach feels queasy." Pri rested her hand on her waist.

"Mine too." I took a small sip of the fizzy drink.

Dr. Caldwell entered the theater, followed by two uniformed police officers. She was petite with short-cropped silver hair and blue eyes that didn't miss a single detail. Her watchful gaze scanned the auditorium. I could tell that she was dividing the space into quadrants and assessing the angle of the fall all in the blink of an eye.

Her neat gray skirt, short heels, and white blouse made her stand out from the other uniformed officers in blue. She took immediate control, directing the few straggling onlookers to await further instructions in the lobby.

She started down the aisle with a black leather notebook tucked under one arm but came to a stop when she caught my eye. "Annie, you're here." She acknowledged Hal, Fletcher, Pri, and Liam with a brisk nod. "You all can stay, but please don't move from this spot until I'm ready to take your statements."

She walked with authority to the paramedics, pulled out her notebook, and waited for them to deliver their report. Then she appraised Martin's body from multiple views, directing one of the officers to take photos. Another placed caution tape around the seats to rope off the area. Dr. Caldwell was methodical in her approach.

"Small details matter," she used to repeat to our class. "Small details matter the most."

I could tell that she was taking in the small details now. She had a habit of raising one eyebrow whenever she was skeptical, which must have been now because I watched as she sighed and pursed her lips while looking from the balcony to the ground.

"How did he fall like that?" Fletcher asked, as if reading my mind.

"I believe that's what Dr. Caldwell is attempting to suss out," Hal noted.

"I've been running through different scenarios," I said, taking another timid sip of ginger ale. Like Pri, I wasn't sure I trusted my stomach to keep it down. "Is it possible he could have been trying to get to his seat? Maybe he was walking between the railing and the front row of the balcony and tripped. It's an old theater. Is the railing still up to code?"

"It has to be up to code," Liam replied. "Tripping wouldn't have launched him over the railing anyway. It might have landed him in someone's lap."

He cut me off before I had gotten to that part of my theory. I agreed with him, but he didn't need to mansplain anything to me.

"As I was saying," I continued with a scowl, "I don't think it's very likely that he tripped, which leaves us with him being pushed over the railing. But how? He's not a particularly large man, but still, someone would have needed to get him in exactly the right spot and push him at the right time, which means that if Dr. Caldwell believes this is a murder scene, it was probably premeditated."

"Spoken like Agatha Christie herself," Hal said with a touch of pride.

Before we could expand any of our theories, Dr. Caldwell approached us. Her measured steps and downturned lips confirmed what I already knew.

"The victim is deceased," she said with a solemn frown. "And I'm declaring this a homicide."

NINE

"Homicide?" Hal sucked in a breath. "You're sure?"

"Positive." She used her pen to point above and then to Martin's body a few feet away. "I'm sure Annie likely explained this to you, but the angle of the fall is not natural, and there are marks and scratches on his neck that show he was likely involved in some sort of scuffle before his fall. The coroner will need to confirm this, but it appears there could be a chance that he was already dead when he went over the railing."

I hadn't noticed any marks on his neck. I should have paid closer attention, but then again, my focus had been on keeping his heart pumping until the paramedics arrived. Everything had happened so fast, and once I was locked into a task like providing CPR, my vision tunneled.

Seeing Dr. Caldwell in action brought a swell of emotions to the surface. Not only because of Martin but because of Scarlet. We had spoken a few times since she shared Scarlet's case file and the warning note she received right before Scarlet was killed.

We'd met for a drink two weeks after she handed off the

files. Our conversation still replayed in my head, and I hadn't fully been able to dismiss her offer.

* * *

I'd arrived at State of Mind Public House first that day. It was a typical midsummer evening in Northern California. The warm evening air was infused with the scent of honeysuckle and jasmine. I ordered a glass of white wine and found a table on the front patio next to a trellis of snaking hop vines. I brought Scarlet's case files along with my laptop because I assumed Dr. Caldwell wanted to go over what (if anything) I had learned, but I assumed wrong.

She breezed in, wearing a pair of flowing linen pants and a tank top rather than her usual silk blouses and slacks. There was no sign of her signature leather notebook or any case files. "Sorry I'm late. I got held up with paperwork. You know that drill. Let me order a drink, and I'll be right with you. Do you have a tab open? Because this is on me tonight."

"It's okay." I didn't need her to buy me a drink.

She firmed her thin lips together and gave me a look that made it clear it wasn't up for debate. "I invited you for a drink. That means I'm buying your drink."

"Fine, if you insist," I said with a smile. "I did start a tab. Justin, the bartender, has my card."

"Excellent. I'll settle that and be back momentarily."

I sipped the tart, crisp wine. It had notes of apples and citrus, but I could barely concentrate on the taste because my entire body burned with cold anticipation of what Dr. Caldwell might reveal next. She had told me to take things slow and sit with the case files first. I hadn't been able to follow that advice, regardless of how well it was intended.

It was like the instant I touched the original police notes on Scarlet's murder, I was sucked back in time. I went straight to my cottage, brewed an entire pot of coffee, and curled up on the couch with Professor Plum tucked next to my hip. I scanned pages and pages of documents, including the incident report, the autopsy, crime scene photos, forensic evidence, witness statements, lab and media reports, and the log of investigative actions taken.

My coffee went cold as a flood of grief that I'd tried to bury gushed to the surface. I sobbed until my cheeks were stained with tears and my eyes stung. Professor Plum sat solidly by my side. He didn't so much as move a paw. It was like he knew that I needed the release. Seeing images of Scarlet and reading through interviews with her family was brutal and maybe necessary.

There was a release that came with the bitter ache of loss.

That night, I didn't sleep at all, but the next day, I felt oddly equipped and ready to do a deep dive into what I already knew about Scarlet's murder and what might be hiding in plain sight in the files.

"You look like you're in deep thought," Dr. Caldwell said, pulling out the chair across from me and setting her hot toddy on the table. "How have you been holding up? I've been worried about you. I'm sure reviewing Scarlet's case files has brought a lot of emotion back to the surface."

My bottom lip quivered. I blinked back tears.

Don't cry in front of Dr. Caldwell.

I reached for my drink and stared at the table. "I'm trying not to be emotional about it."

"Annie, listen to me." Dr. Caldwell took off her glasses and softened her gaze. "I've been working professionally in the field for nearly as long as you've been alive, and I can assure you that our personal attachment to a case is our superpower. Don't listen to the experts who tell you to put your emotions in a box. Of course, we want to be professional and neutral when interviewing suspects and taking eyewitness statements, but good detectives understand that it's our connection to the victims and their families that pushes us forward and keeps us invested in seeking truth and justice. Don't shut out your emotions; harness them."

"I'm trying." I gulped, trying to force the lump in my throat to subside. "I've reviewed every interview with her family members and witnesses, all of the correspondence, interdepartmental memos, and property inventory, and I know there's something I'm missing. It's close. It's right on the edge of my brain but I can't quite grasp it."

Dr. Caldwell swirled her drink with the cinnamon stick garnish. "You'll get there. Give it time. My best advice is to take a break. You've had a chance to look through everything thoroughly. Now is the time to let it rest. I've found every time I give myself space, that's when the breakthrough happens."

"But isn't that what you wanted to talk about tonight?"

"Not exactly." She plunged the cinnamon into her drink and lifted the glass to her lips. "I'm hoping you'll consider coming back into criminology. You were invaluable in helping close our last case. Watching you interact with the community reinforced for me why you stood out as a student. You have a real talent, Annie, and I could use you."

My jaw slackened. I wondered if I had heard her wrong.

She wanted me to work for her?

"You don't have to answer immediately. I can see that you weren't expecting that."

I swallowed again, feeling my heart beat faster.

Work for Dr. Caldwell?

Return to criminology?

The thought was exhilarating. Assisting her had reawakened a part of myself that I had closed off long ago, but I wasn't sure I was ready for such a big move. Not yet. Not until I had time to process what I learned about Scarlet and think about the ramifications of leaving the Secret Bookcase and pursuing a dream I thought was long dead.

I was honored and flattered by her offer, but I wasn't ready to commit.

* * *

Dr. Caldwell's voice pulled me back into the moment. "I'll need to speak with each of you individually as well as everyone in attendance this evening," she said in an authoritative tone to Hal, Pri, Fletcher, and Liam. Then she adjusted her glasses, pushing them up on the bridge of her nose and addressed me. "Annie, I'd like to start with you."

I followed her to an empty row of seats on the opposite side of the theater.

She held her notebook and pen at the ready and peered at me through her oversized black frame. "First, let me express my thanks for you stepping in to help in the middle of a crisis. As I mentioned, Martin was likely already deceased, but that doesn't take away from your heroic effort to try and revive him."

"I wouldn't call it heroic."

"I would." She raised one eyebrow and gave me her signature appraisal. "I wanted to begin with your statement first since you performed CPR and also because, if it's not too much to ask, I would appreciate any observations and insights you may be able to provide. You've spent time with the filmmakers and actors, I presume?"

"Yeah." My eyes landed on Heather, who was pacing in front of the screen, clutching her vape pen with a tight fist and pounding it on the side of her mouth like she was doing everything in her power to resist lighting up. "Unfortunately."

"Any insight you can offer?"

I filled her in on the dinner last night as well as the argument

I'd witnessed between Martin and Heather before the show. "I'm aware that she's the most obvious suspect at the moment, and she does have a very viable motive for wanting Martin dead. I overheard them fighting earlier; he had already written his review of the movie and it was brutal. He was planning to send it to his editor tonight. Heather begged him not to send it, but he refused."

"That is certainly a solid motive." She made a note and then surveyed the empty auditorium. "Do you happen to recall where Heather was sitting?"

"She was sitting in the front row." I motioned in that direction. "The first two rows were reserved for her VIP guests, but right before Martin was killed, she left her seat."

Dr. Caldwell stopped writing and held her pen up like my words had inspired an aha moment. "She left her seat?"

I nodded. "There was a terrible flashing sequence in the movie. It was hard to watch because it was so painful on the eyes. The film needs a seizure warning. I noticed Heather get out of her seat and run up the aisle, right there during the middle of the scene." I pointed to my left.

"Did you see where she went?"

"No. The movie was going, and the flashing was so intense that I had to close my eyes a couple of times."

"Interesting." Dr. Caldwell made another note. "Anything else you can add?"

"The only other thing I would say is that Heather wasn't the only person who had a motive for killing Martin. It was clear at the opening dinner last night that he wasn't well-liked at all. Sam, the producer, stormed into the kitchen, threatening to kill him."

"Hmmm." Dr. Caldwell scribbled in her notebook, keeping her sharp blue eyes focused on me.

"Martin and Rufus got into a physical altercation at the party. Martin touched some of Rufus's rare film reels and Rufus totally lost it. He exploded. If we weren't there, I think he would have knocked Martin out."

"Continue." She tapped the edge of her paper with the tip of her pen.

"Cora, the young actress, mentioned something about Martin ruining careers. I don't know if she was making a blanket statement or referring to her own career, but they had strange energy. The same is true for Izzy, the filmmaker. She and Heather aren't close to say the very least, and yet, Martin invited her. That's weird, right?"

"Quite odd." Dr. Caldwell studied her notebook. "Annie, thank you for your astute input. I knew I could count on you. Please continue to observe. I'd appreciate it if you'd continue to be willing to share any additional information."

"Of course."

She hesitated. "We're due for a catch-up. I'm sorry it took circumstances like this to bring us back together, but I figured you might need more time to process my offer and everything we discussed. Let's get coffee when you're ready."

"Okay, yeah. Thanks." My throat swelled like I'd been stung by a bee. I didn't trust myself not to break down.

"Thank you, Annie." Dr. Caldwell reached for my arm but then pulled her hand away at the last minute like she was overstepping a boundary. "One of my officers will take your official statement, so please stay close by."

"Of course."

She motioned Hal over to be interviewed next. I returned to our little group.

"Did she say anything else?" Pri asked, handing me a box of Junior Mints. "Eat some of these because, you know, chocolate. When in doubt, always turn to chocolate."

"I won't argue with that." I shook a few into my hand. "She didn't say much. I told her about Heather. Did you all see her leave the theater right before Martin was killed, too?"

Pri squished two Junior Mints together and popped them in her mouth. "No. I missed that."

"I saw her," Liam said, pointing to the front row. "She looked like she was fleeing a crime scene. At the time, I thought it was ironic, given the vibe of the movie. Now I guess she could have been going to the crime scene."

"It was during that flashing sequence, right?" The minty candy made my mouth tingle.

Liam nodded. "Yep, she ran right up the aisle."

I wasn't used to him agreeing with me on anything. It was unnerving.

"Be sure you tell Dr. Caldwell that you saw her, too."

"Why wouldn't I?" He practically snarled.

That was more like the Liam Donovan I was used to.

"I just mean that it will be good for her to have multiple eyewitnesses who saw the same thing. It will help her case."

I knew from my coursework that multiple eyewitnesses provided corroborating accounts of an event. If their descriptions aligned and matched, it lent even more credibility to the accuracy of the information.

Fletcher wrung his hands together like he was trying to wash away the murder scene. "This feels like a Golden Age locked-room mystery. How could someone have thrown Martin off the balcony in the middle of a film premiere without being seen?"

"Locked-room mystery?" Liam asked, furrowing his brow.

"It's a style of mystery made popular by the Golden Age writers," Fletcher explained, shifting into his professorial mode. "A seemingly impossible crime, like a room locked from the inside. How did the killer get in and out, or in this instance, how did they toss an adult man over the ledge with hundreds of people watching?"

"It had to be the timing," I said out loud. "That strobing scene. I'm so mad at myself for closing my eyes through it because I don't remember all of the details, but I swear there was a body falling off a cliff. Am I remembering that right?"

Pri jumped in, talking through a mouthful of Junior Mints. "Oh my God, yes! Annie, you're too good. I blanked that out, but now that you say that, I remember seeing a falling corpse."

"It had to be Heather, the director and filmmaker," Fletcher theorized. "She knew exactly when that scene took place, and she left the theater right then."

"Maybe." I wasn't ready to commit yet. That's another important piece of a criminal investigation that I learned in college. At this stage, it was too early to rule anything out or narrow the suspect list. It was critical to remain open to every possibility. Otherwise, if a detective locked on to one suspect or theory, they might inadvertently steer their investigation in that direction, minimizing or overlooking evidence or witness accounts that didn't line up with their hypothesis. "Heather did mention something about doing a new cut and edit. That was part of her plea to Martin to get him to wait to send in his review. She told him that the film had changed dramatically. This is far-fetched, but what if she edited that sequence to be brutal on viewers' eyes on purpose? None of us could even watch. That has to say something."

Pri's mouth hung open. "You mean like she planned the murder? It was premeditated?"

"I don't know, but it's a possibility. I can't imagine a film-maker not wanting their audience to be able to watch important scenes. That sequence felt very different than the rest of the movie. I mean, I get the strobe light effect to build tension, but it went on too long."

Fletcher cracked his knuckles. "It's a good premise, Annie. Heather realized that Martin was going to submit his review. She knew there was nothing she could do to get him to change his mind, so she hatched a new plan—kill him. She pieced together a new version of the film. One that would send the entire audience into seizures. She made the flashing so distracting that we would all cover our eyes, and then she struck."

Hearing him repeat my theory made it seem even less plausible.

I sighed. "I don't know. That sounds like a lot of work."

"But you said that she was desperate," Pri added, shaking more Junior Mints into her hand. "If she believed that Martin's review would really destroy her career, she could have done something that drastic."

To my surprise, Liam agreed. "I heard her talking last night, and she hates the guy. I wouldn't be shocked to hear that she planned and executed his murder. She does make gory thrillers. Is it that much of a stretch to believe that she could have plotted her own revenge?"

I wished I could get my hands on a copy of Martin's review. I wondered where the printout went. Had he already sent it before he was killed? Was the paper or his phone on him at the time of death? If our outlandish theory was correct, then I would expect that Heather would have taken his phone, laptop, or any other device that might contain a copy of his review. She would need to delete the evidence.

Hopefully, Dr. Caldwell's technical team would be able to determine whether files had been deleted.

"Hey, speaking of dinner last night, did you happen to hear Sam and Heather talking?" I asked Liam.

"You mean plotting to kill him?" Liam wiggled his eyebrows.

"Did you hear that, too?" I declined Pri's offer of more candy.

Liam ran his fingers through his hair, brushing a strand from his eye. His hair naturally fell that way, shielding his left eye like a pirate. He constantly tossed his head to the side to try and stop it from obscuring his vision. Part of me wanted to suggest that he get a trim, but it would be a shame to see him cut off his unruly locks. "I went into the kitchen right after you left, and they were fuming. They didn't even bother trying to be discreet. They were raging about Martin."

"Could Sam have been her accomplice?" Pri asked.

"Ohhhh, that's a good theory," Fletcher said, snapping his finger and thumb together. "Sam could have strangled him first and been waiting for Heather upstairs."

"Did anyone see Sam in the front before the movie started?" I asked. "I came in late."

"I didn't." Pri shook her head.

"Me neither," Liam agreed.

"Nope. That makes three of us," Fletcher said.

"So if Martin was strangled, Sam could have done it, and then he and/or Heather waited for the flashing scene to toss him off the balcony." I tried to think through how long it would have taken Heather to run from her seat in the front row upstairs. Not long. Less than a minute. And she would have known exactly how long the strobe light scene would last. As much as I wanted to keep an open mind, it was hard not to believe that we were on the right track. Heather had a strong motive and the opportunity to kill Martin. How much more proof did we need?

TEN

The officer who took my official statement was tight-lipped in comparison with Dr. Caldwell. Not that I expected otherwise. They didn't know my history or personal relationship with her. I answered each question with as much detail as I could, knowing that even the most minute observation could be important to cracking the case.

After each of us had a chance to report what we'd seen, we reconvened in the lobby. The police were allowing people to go, but no one wanted to leave. The tone shifted from earlier in the evening. Guests chatted in hushed conversations. Even though the front doors were propped open, the lobby felt humid and stifling. I wasn't sure whether it was from so many bodies crowded into the space or if it had more to do with mood.

People clumped together in small groups, drinking sodas and eating hot dogs and not even attempting to be discreet about keeping a steady gaze on the police activity. It was surreal, almost like we were spectators on a movie set watching a dramatic scene play out in front of us. Only this was very real.

I couldn't believe Martin was dead. Given my short interactions with him, there were plenty of potential suspects. He hadn't done much to endear himself to anyone. Not that that justified his murder, but it did give me plenty of people to keep a close eye on.

"How are you holding up, my dear?" A familiar voice sounded next to me.

I turned to see Hal approaching. His eyes were typically bright and filled with an almost childlike wonder. It was one of the things I loved most about him. Hal never failed to take notice of life's little delights. He was always the first to point out iridescent hummingbirds flitting through the gardens or the family of quail that would parade along the gravel pathway. But today I could see the pain in his flat eyes and how he cupped his hand over his chin like he was trying to hold in his emotions.

"Okay, I guess," I answered truthfully. "I mean, all things considered."

He reached out to touch my arm in a grandfatherly way. "It's heartbreaking for everyone, but I'm especially concerned about you."

My chin quivered. "Thank you. I appreciate that, and the feeling is mutual. How are you?"

He moved closer and offered a deep sigh. "I suppose I'm like everyone here." His shaky hand swept toward the clusters of people nearby. "Things like this don't happen in our beloved Redwood Grove, do they? You would think that an old Christie-ophile like me would be seasoned to death, but to witness it in the flesh is another story."

I squeezed his cardigan. "If we weren't disturbed by Martin's death, I think there would be a serious problem. Even Dr. Caldwell and trained detectives struggle with their own emotional response to death."

"Wise words, Annie. Wise words." His lips thinned into a small smile. "You know Agatha once said, 'Every murderer is probably somebody's old friend.' I can't help but ruminate on that thought as we're surrounded by friends here. What is it that makes someone take the terrible leap to end another's life?"

"I wish I knew." I sighed, feeling the weight of his worries. "I suppose that's one of the reasons I was drawn to study criminology in college—trying to understand the murder mindset and use that to bring justice for the victims and families."

"It's a noble calling, Annie." Hal pressed his hands together in gratitude.

A commotion broke out near the far doors on the opposite side of the concessions booth. I peered around Hal to get a better look.

Rufus was trying to push past a police officer blocking the entrance to the balcony. "Out of my way. I have to get up to the booth. My films are up there."

I couldn't hear the officer's response, but it was clear from their body language that they weren't budging.

"Do you understand how valuable those reels are? Escort me if you need to, but I'm not leaving the theater until I have my reels back in my hands." Rufus's voice echoed through the historic lobby. Was he intentionally trying to cause a scene?

The officer tried to appease him to no avail.

"Let me speak to your boss—now!" Rufus lunged forward.

The officer forced him back and raised his voice. "Stay right there, sir. If you approach me again, I will arrest you."

Rufus threw his hands in the air and practically spat. "Someone better get me access to the booth, or I'll be calling my lawyer."

Pri and Fletcher scooted over to us. "What is happening?" Pri said, intentionally bulging her eyes and jutting out her chin. "Are we in some kind of a weird documentary? This is all too bizarre."

"Maybe it's a new reality show," Fletcher added. "Fake a murder during a murder movie and see how we react. Very meta."

I wished that were true, but, unfortunately, I had no doubt that Martin's death was anything but fake.

"I realize I quote the one and only Sherlock Holmes too often for some of your taste, but I keep hearing his words. 'My mind rebels at stagnation. Give me problems. Give me work.'" He waved his hands in broad circles as if hoping to speed up the investigation.

"Yeah, I'm with Sherlock on that one," I said, lacing my fingers together. "There's nothing worse than waiting idly when we could be doing something—anything—to help."

As if reading my mind, Dr. Caldwell breezed past us on her way at that moment to defuse the situation. She noticed me. "Oh, Annie. Excellent. Why don't you come with me? I could use another set of eyes and this will be a good teaching opportunity."

What did she mean by a teaching opportunity?

Technically I had a degree in criminology, but she knew I hadn't practiced in years. Was this her subtle way of trying to persuade me to take the job? It was a nice confidence boost, and I wanted to be involved in the investigation. But I still wasn't sure that returning to criminology was the right choice. I loved working at the Secret Bookstore, and organizing events like Mystery Fest and this weekend made my work even more rewarding. In theory.

"Care to elaborate on what she means by *teaching*?" Pri wrinkled her forehead in confusion.

I shrugged, hoping that I sounded casual. "No idea."

The crowd parted to make room for Dr. Caldwell to pass. I followed after her like a lost puppy dog. I understood her request for insight and any observations, but I was shocked that she was inviting me to take part in the actual investigation. I wasn't sure what my role should be. I figured my best bet was to follow her lead.

"What's the problem?" she asked the officer, intentionally ignoring Rufus.

"I need to get into the booth—now," Rufus interrupted, trying to push past the officer again.

Dr. Caldwell lifted her index finger and swiveled her head toward Rufus. She gave him a look that left no room for interpretation as to who was in charge. "You will not speak until spoken to, understood?"

Rufus cowered and hung his head.

"That is your one warning. If you so much as whisper another word, we will have you handcuffed immediately and taken to the station for interfering with a criminal investigation."

Damn. She put Rufus in his place like no one else had been able to all weekend.

"As you were saying," she prompted the officer.

Her colleague explained that the balcony was closed off and how Rufus wanted his films returned. She took her time responding to Rufus, which I was convinced was only to make it crystal clear that she had all of the power in their dynamic.

"Give me your full name, sir." She opened her notebook and clicked her pen.

"Rufus Wells."

"Where do you reside, Mr. Wells?"

"Here in Redwood Grove." He rocked on his heels and cracked his knuckles as he spoke. "I'm a film historian and collector. You've likely seen some of my collection on display at the museum."

"I have not." She tapped her pen to the page. "I need your address, phone number, and email."

I had to stifle a laugh. His karma had caught up with him.

Rufus proceeded to give her the information she requested. He squirmed like a little kid who needed to use the bathroom as Dr. Caldwell peppered him with more questions, completely ignoring his demands to get upstairs. "When was the last time you were in the booth?"

"During the movie. I was in charge of making sure there were no issues with the film." He tried to make himself look important by arching his neck.

"You were inside the booth for the duration of the film?" she asked, sounding skeptical.

"Until the accident, yes. Why would I leave? I had to be there to run everything." He sounded incensed that she had asked. "Heather asked me to stay in the booth in case there were any technical difficulties."

"Technical difficulties, such as?" Dr. Caldwell caught the police officer's eye. I couldn't decipher their unspoken exchange, but the officer must have picked up on their code because they scrolled through notes or photos on an iPad, holding the screen for Dr. Caldwell to see.

"Anything can go wrong during a screening, even with new technology. *Midnight Alibi* is digital, but that doesn't mean there can't be glitches. Heather asked me to run the booth and watch out for any problems. She gave me a copy of the film on a hard drive. I was responsible for making sure the aspect ratio and resolution were correct, adjusting and calibrating the audio system to provide an immersive audio experience, and then being on hand in case there were any technical issues or glitches during the screening."

"That sounds very technical." Dr. Caldwell circled a section on her notes. "Yet you mentioned that you're a film historian. The reels you're hoping to obtain are vintage, is that correct?"

"Yes." Rufus sighed with annoyance. "I'm a film expert. Look me up. You'll see that my resume is extensive. I've followed the art from its infancy in the silent film years to today."

Dr. Caldwell wasn't impressed. "Why wasn't Heather in the booth if this is her movie?"

"She wanted to be in the audience. A director wouldn't be in the booth. They need to be with the audience. She said it gives her a better sense of how the film is screening if she's seated amongst everyone."

"And she left it to you to fix any issues?"

"That's right." Rufus looked like he was trying to maintain his composure, but at any minute he might break out into a sprint and run up to the balcony.

"That's a lot of trust to put in you. How long have you and Ms. Hathaway been acquainted?"

"Not long at all. We communicated via email prior to the premiere to coordinate which vintage films to show. We obviously discussed my qualifications. Even with digital films, it's a specialized skill set. The theater really needs to do a software upgrade. There's barely sufficient storage for high-def films. I told Heather I would calibrate the projector for optimal picture quality in addition to screening my personal film collection. Aside from our email exchanges, I met her for the first time last night at dinner."

"You must have made an impression for her to give you such a huge responsibility."

"Not really. The odds of any issues with a digital film are small. I offered to keep an eye on the booth so that I could make sure there were always eyes on my films."

"Ah, I see." Dr. Caldwell nodded and made a quick note.

Was that the breakthrough she'd been waiting for?

It was incredible to watch her work. Her consistent, unyielding questions had caused Rufus to admit that he had volunteered to stay in the booth. It might not seem like a significant detail, but it was a different story than what he had told Dr. Caldwell to begin with.

"You volunteered, and you were alone in the booth for the duration of the film?" Dr. Caldwell continued.

Rufus nodded. "The film hadn't been on that long. Martin fell about twenty minutes in, but yes, I was in the booth the entire time. I wasn't alone, though."

"Who was with you?"

He craned his neck toward the ceiling like he was trying to paint a mental picture. "Sam the producer came by briefly with Cora and Izzy. He wanted to show them the original eight-millimeter projector. There aren't many theaters that still have working projectors. Then Heather came up right before the accident."

"Heather was in the booth when Martin fell?" Dr. Caldwell clarified.

"No, she ran in just a minute or two before the accident. She was very flustered. She said the film shouldn't have been strobing the way it was, and she was angry that I hadn't fixed it."

"Why didn't you fix it?"

"I thought it was part of the film. It's not my job. It's not my film. I was just there to run the equipment." Rufus sounded defensive. "How was I supposed to know?"

Dr. Caldwell didn't react. "How long was she in the booth?"

"I don't know. A minute. Maybe less."

"Did she fix the issue?"

"No. And if you want to make note of anything, you should take this down." Rufus pointed to her notebook. "I found it quite odd that she didn't shut the movie down. I had the flash drive. I asked her if we should pause the movie and swap it out, but she refused. She muttered something about sabotage and then ran out of the booth. The next thing I knew, people were screaming and pandemonium broke out. People were running down the aisles, rushing out of the balcony, and I heard people saying that someone was dead."

"Heather used the word *sabotage*?" Dr. Caldwell clarified. I knew she was making sure that she had an exact account of Heather's language because sabotage would suggest that someone else was involved.

"I'm sure of that, yes." Rufus pinched the bridge of his nose and nodded, keeping his steely eyes on the officer guarding the door.

"Did you see where she went after she left the booth?"

"No. Everything happened so fast. I was focused on the screen, trying to figure out what was going wrong with the film and whether I should stop it, and then I heard that terrible thud. I was confused temporarily because I thought it was part of the movie or maybe Heather had hired actors to give the audience a real jump scare, but then I realized that someone had actually gone over the balcony."

"What did you do next?"

"I stopped the film as soon as the lights came on."

"Did you see anyone else?" Dr. Caldwell pressed. "Think carefully before you answer."

"The balcony was full, but Cora, Izzy, and Sam were all up there. Everyone was stunned. No one moved until the police arrived and escorted us downstairs."

"And after that?"

"I've been down here with the masses, trying to get upstairs to make sure my films are okay," Rufus said, sounding like a worried parent.

Dr. Caldwell clicked her pen. Her lips pulled down as she studied him. "You seem quite concerned with the films. More so than a death."

"No." Rufus shook his head repeatedly. "I'm devastated that Martin is dead. I was looking forward to discussing *Midnight Alibi* with him. What you need to understand is that my film collection is extremely rare and extremely valuable. There's a killer running around. What's to stop them from taking my collection?"

"Are you implying that the killer threw Martin off of the balcony as a distraction to steal your films?"

"Yes. Thank you. Finally, you get it." Rufus threw his arms out. "These aren't films you can acquire at your local store. These are Hitchcock originals. I never should have agreed to screen them. They should be locked up in glass cases at home. If you won't let me up there, can you at least check to make sure they're safe?"

"I will do that as soon as time permits," Dr. Caldwell replied in a scolding tone. "My priority is the murder victim."

"Murder?" Rufus took a step back and recoiled. "Martin was murdered? You said something about a killer, but I suppose I brushed over that. I thought it was an accident, that whoever pushed him wanted to injure him, not kill him."

"It was not an accident." Dr. Caldwell tucked her notebook under her arm. "My deputy may have additional questions for you. Do not leave the premises until you've been cleared to do so."

"You'll let me know about the films, right? They're worth a considerable amount of money and I want them back in my possession as soon as possible."

"Annie, this way," Dr. Caldwell said, pointing toward the door that led upstairs. She waited until we were out of earshot to speak. "Tell me, what did we learn from that exchange?"

"Well, he lied. He said that Heather asked him to stay in the booth, but then he changed his story and said that he volunteered to be in the booth."

"Excellent." She took short steps on the carpeted stairs. "Anything else?"

"He didn't go into detail about Sam, Cora, and Izzy stopping by the booth to check out the vintage projector, but that means all three of them were upstairs when Martin was killed. I assumed they were in the front row with Heather, but that changes the scenario. Any of them could have pushed Martin, including Heather."

"Which matches eyewitness statements. Multiple people, including yourself, saw Heather running out of the theater."

I wondered what else she might have learned from the witness statements. Firsthand accounts often serve as starting points for an investigation. These initial leads provide detectives with next steps, like identifying potential suspects, locating additional witnesses, and directing a team where to gather physical evidence.

"But what about the sabotage comment? The strobing wasn't part of the movie. I wondered if it was intentional. Heather could have cut it like that to distract people while she killed Martin—if the murder was premeditated. But now it seems more like she was really upset that something had gone wrong with the film and ran upstairs to try and fix it."

"Also a viable possibility."

We made it to the top of the stairs. Yellow crime scene tape stretched from the railing to the first row.

"I'm not sure what it means for the case," I admitted.

"It's information, which is the most valuable asset we have for the time being. It also reiterates to me that we're nowhere near making an arrest. Any of the aforementioned people could have killed Martin. And all of them are on my 'persons of interest' list."

ELEVEN

"Tell me, Annie, what do you observe from this angle?" Dr. Caldwell asked, lifting the caution tape for us to duck under. "I'm not pressuring you to make a decision on your career path. I genuinely want your input. However, should you decide you want to return to the field, this case provides us with an excellent opportunity to revisit what you learned in your coursework and put some of that into practical application."

A fluttery feeling spread through my chest. I remembered the thrill of dissecting mock crime scenes in college. This was real life. I didn't want to get it wrong.

"Can you infer how the killer might have planned and executed their mission?"

I took a minute to study the railing and the aisle and walkways below. Nothing jumped out at me. "Would Martin's body need to be upright?" I asked, bending my arm at a ninety-degree angle to demonstrate.

"Go on." She gestured with her hand, making the gold and silver bracelets on her wrist cling together.

I wasn't sure I even understood what I was attempting to

prove, but part of a working theory was to work through it. "Okay, if Martin was standing here with his back to the screen, the killer could have pushed his shoulders and then helped his feet go over the railing. Although that only works if Martin was really inebriated. Otherwise, you would think Martin would have fought back or held on to the railing. Is there also an outside chance that he could have already been dead, and the killer simply pushed his body over?"

"We will have to wait for the autopsy and toxicology reports. It's possible that the killer overwhelmed Martin and was able to force him over the railing. It's equally possible that Martin was under the influence of drugs or alcohol. As for him already being dead, I've considered that as well and it's certainly on the table. But that theory poses other issues, such as how the killer managed to keep him upright. The reports will tell us more, so we'll proceed without forming any official judgments for the time being."

"I'm stumped as to how the killer managed not to be seen. Have you heard anything from the eyewitnesses seated up here yet?"

She held the tape again and motioned to the chairs at the end of the row. "Let's take a seat for a moment."

I waited for her to speak.

She opened her notebook and showed me a page of notes. "There are dozens of eyewitness accounts. They have a consistent theme."

"That's good, right?"

"Yes, except there's one problem. Each person reported observing someone wearing a black trench coat attempting to assist a 'drunk person,' their words, not mine, out of the balcony. When asked for further details, each report is fuzzy. Witnesses claim that the theater was too dark to make out hair color, height, etc., and that the strobe lights on the screen were blinding so they only caught flashes of what happened but assumed that the person was under the influence of drugs or alcohol because of the way they staggered and appeared to be..." She stopped to consult her notes for a minute. "Ah yes, the exact quote is 'it appeared that he was being dragged or held up by the person in the trench coat.'"

I took a minute to process this new piece of information. Having witness statements match and line up was key in a murder investigation. The fact that everyone reported the same thing was a good sign. Consistency among different witness statements could strengthen a case, although the fuzzy details didn't give us much new insight into specifics.

"So you believe there's also a possibility that Martin wasn't drunk—he was already dead?" I played out the scenario in my mind. If Martin was killed prior to being thrown off the balcony, his assailant had to be quite strong. Lugging the weight of a dead body would have taken a significant amount of muscle. Did that rule out Sam? He used his cane for balance and walking. I couldn't imagine him having the physicality to pull off the murder. Cora and Izzy were both shorter than Martin, but I heard them talking about their Pilates class. It wasn't out of the realm of possibility that if one of them had killed him in a fit of rage, they might have had a sudden surge of strength. There were plenty of instances of people displaying extraordinary feats during a crisis, like being able to lift a car after an accident or moving heavy debris like a concrete slab after an earthquake.

"That's correct." She pointed behind us. "Let's step into the booth because my team recovered something of interest."

I couldn't believe how much she already knew, given that Martin had died less than an hour ago. It gave me even more appreciation for her talent and exacting approach. My mind latched on to the puzzle, playing out a variety of potential scenarios and how each of the suspects could have been involved in Martin's demise. It was a reminder of how exhilarating this stage of an investigation could be when it was our job to explore every possible thread. Nothing was too outlandish in this phase of examining a crime scene, which meant our role was to pursue any and every line of thought.

More caution tape sealed the booth door. Dr. Caldwell untacked one side of the tape and waited for me to enter first. Yellow evidence markers flagged points of interest in the small room. Large plastic bags were piled on a small table. The space wasn't big, probably about six feet wide by eight feet long. A large glass window provided a view of the theater and screen.

She picked up the first bag and showed it to me. "This will be sent to forensics for analysis."

"Is that a black trench coat?" I picked up on a musty smell in the room. The shag mustard yellow carpet looked like it had been installed in the 1970s and never updated since.

"It is. My team found it hidden under the first row of seats." She gestured out the window to the balcony section of seating where Martin had potentially been killed.

"Could the killer be that naïve? Won't you be able to match DNA? Without washing the coat, they probably left skin cells or a stray hair behind."

She returned the bag to the stack. The other items her team had collected were smaller—pens, pieces of paper, a DVD, and hairs and fibers. "That's the question I keep asking. The killer staged an elaborate plan—strangling Martin, timing the fall with the flashing sequences, and pushing Martin over the railing at the precise angle. Now why would they work through every detail and discard their disguise under the seats? It doesn't add up."

"Unless they wanted you to find the coat," I said out loud before I'd even realized that I was speaking.

"Mmm." She lifted her head and gave me a half nod. Her eyes twinkled. "Tell me more."

"What if it's not the killer's coat? They planted it on

purpose to implicate someone else. They could have worn a similar coat and made sure they were seen when they pushed Martin over the balcony. They left wearing that coat and planted this coat as evidence."

"Have you noticed anyone wearing a similar coat?"

My mind had already gone to the same place, which gave me another boost of confidence. A vision of Heather walking into the Stag Head wearing a long black trench coat flashed in my mind. "Yeah, Heather," I said to Dr. Caldwell. "Every piece of evidence is pointing to Heather."

"It is, isn't it?" She pursed her lips, letting her eyes land on the stack of evidence. Then she removed her glasses and cleaned them on the edge of her sleeve. "It's almost too convenient. Not that I wouldn't appreciate closing this case and having it wrapped up with a neat little bow. But everything is too easy at the moment. If you recall, that's not usually a good sign. It's a magical unicorn of a case and that has my radar up."

I chuckled. "I remember you talking about your first magical unicorn case."

She returned her glasses to the bridge of her nose. "The case I thought I had closed in less than three hours." She cringed and covered half of her face with her hand. "I was so young and ridiculously overconfident. I called my boss and told him that I'd solved the case. I honestly believed they were going to give me an award or at least recognition for setting the record of being the fastest newly minted detective to solve a murder, only to learn that I was on a completely wrong track and had given the killer ample time to flee the state. That's not a mistake I will make again."

"But there are instances where a case can be straightforward." I tried to make her feel better. It was an honest mistake. I could see myself doing the same thing.

"Absolutely. More often than not." A relaxed smile crossed

her face. "Most criminals aren't masterminds, but that's what bothers me about this. Heather could be our killer, but I believe it's equally as likely that someone is setting her up to take the fall."

"Everyone at dinner last night saw her wearing the black trench coat," I said. "Actually, come to think of it, Cora mentioned that it was all she ever saw Heather wearing. It would have been easy for the killer to pick up on that, and it's not as if a black coat would be hard to come by. We were joking that the attire for dinner last night felt like a funeral."

"We'll send it to forensics and see what comes back. If we find Heather's DNA, then we'll have some decisions to make."

"I don't envy your position. What do you do if the evidence points to Heather, but your gut says otherwise?" I quickly surveyed the booth. Could the killer have left a tangible piece of evidence behind here, too? Nothing immediately jumped out at me, but Rufus's behavior and demeanor sparked my curiosity. Why had he immediately assumed his films were missing? And why had Heather put him in charge?

"We'll have to cross that bridge when we come to it." She sighed. "There's one other interesting development I'd like you to know about."

"What's that?"

She moved closer to the projector. "I intentionally did not mention this to Rufus during our exchange. His reels are missing."

"His Hitchcock collection is actually missing?" I was stunned that she and I continued to be on the same wavelength. "I assumed that Rufus was overreacting about his film collection. Did someone steal them? All of them?"

"It appears that way."

"Why?" I asked out loud, glancing around again in hopes that something obvious would appear out of thin air. I knew it didn't work like that, but I couldn't come up with a clear link between the two. "Do you think it's connected to Martin's murder?"

"It's quite a coincidence if it's not." She cleared her throat, her head flinching slightly as she studied the soundboard. "I would put my money on the two being connected. As to why, I have no idea at this point."

"Rufus is going to flip out." My neck felt tense from strained attentiveness.

"That's an understatement," she agreed. "Although gauging his reaction will certainly tell us more."

I was glad she felt confident about that, but I was still baffled as to how the two could be connected. I understood the value of Rufus's historic films, but how did that tie in with Martin's death? Rufus had been upset that Martin had touched the vintage reels. "Could Martin have stolen them?" I asked Dr. Caldwell. "That would give Rufus a solid motive for killing him. Rufus treats the reels like they're living beings."

"It would give him a motive, but another question we should consider is how did Rufus know that Martin stole them?"

I liked that she was using "we." It made me feel like I was providing her with some kind of value. "True. He seemed pretty agitated earlier about getting in here so he could recover them. Maybe he's a good actor, but he didn't appear to know that the films are missing."

"I agree with that assessment."

"Could it be misdirection on the killer's part? Do you think they took the reels to distract from the murder?"

She made a clicking sound with her tongue. "I intend to pursue that line of thought for sure."

"Is there anything else I can do?"

"More of the same." She moved to the door. "I'm going to allow everyone to leave for the evening. Those who have been lingering will be encouraged to make their exits. We've already made it clear that no one is to leave Redwood Grove."

"What about tomorrow? We're supposed to show four films with talkbacks and Q&A sessions. Should we cancel those?"

"No. In fact, I'd like those to continue. It will be an excellent opportunity to observe the suspects. Please stay in touch. I'll do the same. We'll have a strong presence at the theater throughout the remainder of the weekend."

"Sounds good." I started to move toward the stairs, but Dr. Caldwell stopped me.

"Annie, be careful, though. While the crime seems centered around the film crew, that doesn't negate the fact that there is a killer on the loose in Redwood Grove."

"I will. I promise." I headed downstairs with a prickly feeling running up my spine. Dr. Caldwell was right. My thoughts drifted back to the Mystery Fest when another murder had occurred in our sweet village. That experience had rattled me and the entire community. I supposed, in many ways, before that, I had taken my safety and well-being for granted. I wasn't going to do that again. Martin had been killed and I didn't want to be next.

Pri was waiting at the bottom of the stairs. We shared a look, but I didn't have time to relay what I'd discussed with Dr. Caldwell because she hollered to get everyone's attention.

"All right, folks, we're going to need you to clear out. We have each of your contact information and will be in touch if we need more from you. In the meantime, no one is to leave Redwood Grove without permission by yours truly."

People began milling toward the exit.

"Did you learn anything new?" Pri asked, holding a box of Skittles in one hand and red licorice ropes in the other.

I told her about the coat and the missing films.

"Rufus is going to go nuclear," Pri said, chomping on a piece of licorice. "They basically had to keep an officer on him the entire time you were gone with Dr. Caldwell to keep him from running upstairs."

"It doesn't make sense. Unless Martin stole the reels, but then why would Rufus kill him?"

"Revenge?" Pri suggested. "By the way, if you can't tell, I'm stress-eating sugar. This is my third box of candy. Take some, please. Take it all. I can't stop myself."

"I'm good." I declined her offer. "But I'll hold it for you if you need me to."

Pri started to hand over her stash and then clutched it to her chest like a security blanket. "Nope. On second thought, never mind. I'm not ready. We're witnesses to murder. More sugar might be necessary."

"Fair enough. You keep it."

She tore off another bite of licorice. "What do you think about revenge? It's a classic motive, isn't it?"

"Yeah, I like the revenge angle. The only thing is that would mean that Rufus has his films; otherwise, if he killed Martin, he would have no idea where they are."

"Oh, you're good." Pri gnawed on the licorice, holding it on one side of her mouth.

"The one theory that makes the most sense is that the killer is using the vintage reels as a distraction."

"That would work."

We funneled in with the crowd. Liam, Fletcher, and Hal were a little way behind us.

"Let's wait for them to catch up," Pri suggested.

Familiar faces breezed past us and then people scattered in different directions, spreading out across the village square.

"You ready?" Liam asked.

"Me?" I pointed to my chest. "Ready for what?"

"I'm walking you home."

"I'm not a twelve-year-old. I can walk myself home."

"No one is debating that you're a strong, independent

woman, Annie," Hal chimed in. "But while you were with Dr. Caldwell, we decided that we'll head home in groups. A murder has occurred and we can't be too careful. Liam agreed to go with you. Fletcher, Pri, and I will make sure we all get home safe and sound."

"I'm fine," I protested. I wasn't about to admit that having an escort home sounded nice.

Hal gave me his most serious grandfather face. "This one isn't open to debate, my dear."

It was rare that Hal put up a fight on anything, but when he did, he didn't back down.

"Okay, fine. I'll see you all bright and early tomorrow." I power walked toward the park, hoping that if my pace was fast enough, Liam wouldn't be able to keep up.

"Where's the fire, Murray?" Liam easily fell into step with me, his long strides easily outpacing mine.

"I said okay to appease Hal, but I really don't need an escort," I lied. The truth was I felt a bit lightheaded, and my breath was rushed and rapid. The reality of Martin's death was fully starting to sink in.

"Too bad. You're stuck with me." He reached out his hand. "I can hold your hand if you prefer."

I wrapped my arms around my chest. "Uh, no thanks."

"You want my opinion on the murder?"

"Do you have a theory? I thought you were above mysteries."

"In book form, yes, but in reality, no." He held a branch out of the way so it wouldn't hit me on the shoulder. "I think they all did it. Isn't that one of Agatha Christie's tropes?"

I scrunched my forehead and gave him a suspicious look. He seemed well informed for someone who was so down on mysteries as a genre. Had Liam secretly been reading up on all things Miss Marple and Hercule Poirot? What if he'd been a closet mystery fan all along? Doubtful, but I chuckled internally at the thought. "Not a trope, but an extremely popular plot from one of her novels, yes."

"Everyone hated him. I think they teamed up together and killed him."

Could Liam be right? Was there a chance that everyone connected to *Midnight Alibi* had scripted Martin's murder?

TWELVE

We made it to my cottage: a sight for sore eyes with its climbing pink and white peppermint roses trailing around the front door, fragrant bunches of potted rosemary, and a platter of fresh baked raspberry almond cookies waiting at my doorstep. Being one of the youngest residents in my complex meant that my retired neighbors spoiled me with homemade treats and clippings from their abundant backyard gardens.

Professor Plum peered out the dining room window, eagerly awaiting my arrival home. Liam waited uncomfortably while I dug around for my keys, which had fallen to the bottom of my book bag.

"You don't need to wait for me. I've got it from here."

He folded his arms across his chest. "I told Hal that I would make sure you got home safely, and that's what I'm going to do."

"What about you? Who's going to make sure you get home safely?" I challenged.

He glanced away, looking like he was stifling a smile, before turning and meeting my eyes with a heated intensity that sent a flush of heat screaming up my neck. "Look, you don't need to make this a thing." He shifted his body weight like he couldn't decide if he should just leave.

"It's not a thing. I don't prescribe to outdated gender roles, that's all." I found my keys and pulled them out of the tote. "Here they are. Thanks for the chaperone."

"Annie, wait." Liam reached for my arm but then stopped himself.

"What?" I held my keys at the ready.

"Nothing. Never mind." He stepped off the porch. "Lock your door, though."

"Will do." I gave him a half wave as I went inside. No one in Redwood Grove locked their doors. There was usually no need. Our small, tight-knit community looked out for one another, but tonight I would follow Liam's advice. Until Martin's killer was behind bars, I intended to remain vigilant.

He lingered on the porch a moment longer before turning and returning toward the village square.

Professor Plum greeted me at the door with a hungry meow. I dropped my tote on the entryway table and reached down to pet him. His regal purple breakaway collar was a bit loose. It was probably time to upgrade his collar. I hadn't changed it since Scarlet died.

He swatted at it with his paw.

"Is it itchy, Professor Plum?" I scratched the area under-neath his chin. "Let's get you a new collar tomorrow, what do you say?"

His meow sounded like a yes.

Sometimes I could almost swear that he understood me. Maybe it was because I tended to have conversations with him about Scarlet. Aside from Dr. Caldwell, Professor Plum was the only other living soul on the planet who connected me to Scar-let. He was my tether to keeping her memory alive.

I gave him his favorite flaked salmon and made myself a cup of tea. We curled up on the couch and watched reruns of

Murder, She Wrote until we both dozed off. I slept for the remainder of the night on the couch, not bothering to change into my pajamas or crawl into my bed.

The next morning, I woke up wondering if Martin's death had been a bad dream. It didn't take long for me to plant myself firmly in reality. My phone buzzed with texts from Heather.

> At the police station.

> Can't get a hold of Sam or Cora.

> Come bail me out.

Dr. Caldwell had arrested Heather?

What changed overnight?

And why was Heather texting me to help her?

I took a quick shower and tugged on a pair of capris and a bookish T-shirt. I pulled my hair into a ponytail and dusted my cheeks with a little blush. Then I fed Professor Plum and went straight to the police station.

The police station was located near the library. Like most of Redwood Grove, it didn't look like a typical police station. The brick exterior was reminiscent of a vintage cottage. A well-maintained front garden with a white picket fence, fragrant blooms, and an old oak tree shaded the entrance. The wooden shutters on the windows were painted a calming seafoam blue.

The station was more than a place for law enforcement; it was a hub for community engagement and support. Posters advertising the film festival and screening of *Midnight Alibi* flanked the doors. It was ironic to think that what had started as a fun and exciting event had taken such a dark turn.

A friendly receptionist greeted me from behind an antique desk. "Good morning. Can I help you?"

"Is Dr. Caldwell in?" I asked. The atmosphere inside was relaxed. A pot of coffee brewed on a side table next to bookshelves with mysteries, local histories, and stacks of free community newsletters. A bulletin board displayed upcoming events and lost pet fliers, which only reinforced the sense of togetherness that made Redwood Grove such a special place.

"She's at the theater. Is there something I can assist with?"

"No, that's okay. I'll swing by the theater on my way to work and talk to her there." I knew that no one other than Dr. Caldwell would be able to grant me permission to speak with Heather, but I wanted to confirm that she was actually in one of the holding cells in the back of the building. "I got a text about posting bail for Heather Hathaway. Is she here?"

"Are you posting bail for her?" The receptionist sounded surprised. "The amount is five hundred thousand dollars."

I knew that bail amounts were based on the criminal offense. If Heather's bail was a half million dollars, that had to mean she was being held for the highest crime—murder.

"No. I don't have that kind of money."

"Does anyone in Redwood Grove?" She shrugged and rolled her eyes. "I don't know what's going on. I just answer the phones."

I thanked the receptionist for the information and returned outside. Poppies, cosmos, sunflowers, and black-eyed Susans stretched to the sun. Swaths of colorful bougainvillea and creeping ivy stretched along the buildings. The park and town square were quiet at this early hour. A handful of locals gathered at Cryptic and the café for coffee and breakfast, but otherwise it would be a few hours before the village was bustling with activity.

A uniformed officer was posted at the front door.

"Is Dr. Caldwell here?" I asked.

"She is, but she gave me strict orders not to allow anyone inside." He planted his feet on the sidewalk like he was preparing to hold me back if necessary.

"Could you tell her it's Annie Murray? She knows me."

The officer considered my request. "Is she expecting you?"

"No, but I think she'll let me in. I'm a former criminology student and I've been assisting with the case." I have no idea why I blurted that out. Saying it made me want to stand taller. It was true, I was helping the lead detective with a murder investigation. I didn't have that on this year's bingo card. I must have sounded confident to the officer because he clicked on his walkie-talkie and told Dr. Caldwell I was waiting to see her.

"Go ahead." The officer stepped to the side to let me pass. "She's in the balcony."

"Thanks." I resisted the urge to give him a salute before laughing at myself.

Annie, you're not joining the military. You're loosely helping with your former professor's case.

The lightness of the moment quickly evaporated. A cold chill came over me as I stepped inside. Last night had started with such anticipatory energy and excitement and ended with Martin's death. A pall hung in the air.

I tried to shake off the visions of Martin's body sprawled out on the red carpet.

Could Heather have really done it?

Dr. Caldwell had seemed skeptical last night.

I wondered if she received new irrefutable evidence.

"Annie, I'm glad you stopped by," Dr. Caldwell said when I crested the stairs. She knelt next to the railing studying the floor below through her glasses. "There have been some developments overnight."

"That's why I came by. I got a text from Heather asking to bail her out."

"Interesting." Dr. Caldwell pushed her glasses up the bridge of her nose and stood.

"I can't believe her bail is set so high. Is there new evidence?"

She brushed her hands on her gray slacks, smoothing them down. "I would say that bail is merely a formality at this point."

"There's no way you already received the forensic report on the trench coat. That would be record-breaking fast, right?"

"No. I wish. There's a backlog in forensic labs. Do you remember what I taught you about the typical turnaround timeframe?"

"At least two weeks, but it can fluctuate dramatically based on numerous factors." I remembered discussions from our class about how movies and television greatly exaggerated how fast forensic evidence was turned around.

"Such as?"

"The type of analysis, whether you're using a public or private lab, the type of case, the number of items, availability of crime lab staff, and whether there are problems with the samples." I rattled off the list from memory.

"Excellent." She nodded with approval. "And, yes, you are correct. I don't expect results anytime soon."

"What changed to make you detain Heather?"

She motioned for me to sit, then she turned on her phone and handed it to me. "Give this a read."

I scanned the document.

Midnight Alibi is a mind-numbing example of incompetent storytelling. To call it a film is generous; it's an insufferable endurance test for any moviegoer with the misfortune of being subjected to its abysmal excuse for a plot. Its characters are insipid caricatures, utterly devoid of depth or emotional resonance. I've seen better acting in preschool pageants. The cast delivered lines with the passion of automated customer service agents. Heather Hathaway's direction is as uninspired as a beige wall, making the entire viewing experience akin to watching paint dry in slow motion. To call this movie forgettable would be a mercy; it is more accurately a monument to cinematic ineptitude, a blight on the very concept of storytelling, and an unforgivable waste of time that even a black hole of entertainment value would find difficult to match.

"This is Martin's review?" I said to Dr. Caldwell, handing her back her phone. "Ouch."

"Ouch is an understatement," she agreed.

"No wonder Heather didn't want this to get out. I can't imagine a review like this will sell many tickets." My stomach felt sluggish. How terrible for Heather and everyone else involved in the film.

"Not unless someone is hoping to torture themselves, according to Martin." She tapped the screen.

"This is a draft, though, right? Did it get published?"

"Not to my knowledge, but that is the reason we have detained Heather until further notice. We discovered the files on her laptop. She deleted them, but they were still in the cloud."

"That's not very savvy of her," I said, considering my inter-actions with Heather. In our planning conversations, she was meticulous and focused on each and every detail, from the appetizers that were served at the opening dinner to the speaker lineup for the talkback sessions. She didn't strike me as the type who would overlook deleting every trace of Martin's review.

"The file has been completely erased from all of Martin's devices—his phone, tablet, laptop."

"So you think that she killed him in order to gain access to his devices and then deleted the review?"

She stretched her neck to one side and considered my words. "It's a viable theory."

"But why send it to herself? Why would she want to risk having a copy floating out in the ether?"

"An excellent question. One I've been trying to work through myself," Dr. Caldwell said with a small sigh. "Much like our discussion last night, everything about this is too neat. Too clean."

"How did you recover the files?"

"She gave our team permission to go through her digital

footprint. Now, tell me why would someone who had the review saved do that?" She put her phone back into her black leather satchel. Her entire look was polished, from her matching satchel and leather notebook to her trim slacks and black blouse.

"You think she is being set up."

"I don't have proof, but my instincts tell me when something is wrapped up like a shiny package with a neat red bow that there's a good chance it's a red herring."

"But you arrested Heather."

"I prefer 'detained.' This is a murder investigation. I can't take any chances, and it's imperative I follow protocol. Heather will remain in custody, but this case is far from closed, I can tell you that much." She crossed her legs and looked out at the auditorium.

"Do you have any thoughts on who might be setting her up?"

"Take your pick. Each of the other suspects could be responsible." Her eyes remained focused on the screen.

I looked in that direction. The theater was empty and cold. Maybe it was because I knew what had happened here, but there was a morbidity that seemed to mingle with the dust particles floating in the air. "What were you looking at when I arrived? I noticed you seemed to be studying the angle of the fall again?"

"Correct." She frowned. "Unfortunately, I've yet to put my finger on what's bothering me about the crime scene. Maybe your set of young, fresh eyes will lend a new perspective."

"You want me to have a look?"

"Please." She uncrossed her legs, making room for me to get by.

I stood and walked to the railing, feeling my knees buckle slightly. My stomach felt queasy as I followed in Dr. Caldwell's footsteps and knelt down. The room began to spin slightly. I thought I might pass out.

I'm normally more composed, but bending over from this height sent my head swirling.

I forced my nerves away by letting my hands make contact with the carpet to ground myself.

If I was going to seriously consider a job change, studying crime scenes would be part of my work life. I needed to shift into a logical mindset.

Think, Annie.

How had the killer succeeded?

We knew that they were disguised by a black trench coat and used the cloak of flashing lights on the screen, but how had they flung Martin's body over the railing with precision?

The more I stared at the scene, the more impossible it seemed.

Suddenly, I was struck with a revelation. I stood up too fast, causing tiny bright white spots to cloud my vision.

I steadied myself on the railing. "Dr. Caldwell, I don't think Martin fell."

"Come again?"

"I don't think he fell."

"Tell me more."

"What if Martin was already on the main floor? What if he was dead, perhaps sitting in one of those seats." I pointed below us. "What if the killer faked the balcony fall?"

"Why would they do that?"

"To throw off the timing? To distract us from what really happened."

"What about the thud? What about witnesses seeing something fall? What about the screams?"

"Maybe the thud was a sound effect? Maybe it was all staged." I felt like I was close to forming a theory, but it was like trying to unravel a spider's web with my bare hands.

"Annie, I do believe you might be on to something. Give it time. It will come."

I hoped she was right. In college, she frequently lectured on the fact that any criminal investigation requires patience and precision to fully comprehend. It was like tugging at one thread on an intricate web that sent vibrations throughout the entire structure of my understanding.

THIRTEEN

Dr. Caldwell's phone dinged. "I need to return to the station, but let's keep communication open. This has been quite insightful. I hope it has been for you as well." She gathered her things. "In case it comes up again, you should know that Heather will remain in custody for the short term. I'm not sure why she's attempting to post bail. I was very clear with her about the reasons for detaining her."

"Thanks for letting me get a glimpse behind the scenes. I'll keep thinking on theories and I'll let you know if I hear anything. The festival is good to go for the remainder of the day?"

"Yes." She hoisted her satchel over her shoulder. "We've given the green light to the theater to open as soon as the crime scene cleaners have finished. We preserved as much as possible of the site layout. As you know, we had to make sure the area was preserved down to the tiniest detail in order to compile a rigorous accounting of evidence. Now that that is complete, the area will need to be cleaned, but then the event can proceed as planned."

"Right." I followed her downstairs.

She gave the officer on duty further instructions. I checked my watch. I didn't need to be at the Secret Bookcase for another thirty minutes. Plenty of time to stop into Cryptic for a coffee. I left the theater and took my time walking along Cedar Avenue, intentionally stopping to smell blooming clumps of wisteria and to pet a shaggy Goldendoodle on its way to the park. It was good to see people out and about enjoying the dreamy weather. This was the Redwood Grove I knew and loved. Couples strolled hand in hand, peering in shop windows and pausing to admire window displays.

Many of the shops and restaurants in town had gotten in the spirit of the festival weekend, decking out their storefronts. The grocer featured movie night essentials with popcorn tubs and themed snacks like nuts, cheeses, imported chocolates, and cocktail mixing sets. Artifacts, one of my favorite local boutiques, had embraced Hitchcock classics. Caroline, the owner, procured a collection of shower curtains printed with dainty floral designs for *Psycho*, bird jewelry, art, and scarves for *The Birds*, and assorted binoculars for *Rear Window*. It was a clever way to pay homage to the filmmaker.

Seeing the kind of time and effort the small business community had put into making the weekend a success only fueled me more to want to bring Martin's killer to justice.

The line was short at Cryptic. Pri deftly kept it moving. She chatted easily with customers while pulling creamy shots of espresso and steaming oat milk. The high school student running the cash register and pastry case struggled to keep up with her pace.

"I was hoping you might stop by," she said when it was my turn to place my order. She held a large spoon over the edge of the steaming pitcher to keep the foam back. "Did you see who's here?"

I glanced around the coffee shop. I recognized a few faces, but no one stood out.

"No, outside." Pri tilted her head toward the exterior patio.

My eyes drifted in that direction. Sure enough, Sam, Cora, and Izzy were gathered at one of the picnic tables, sharing a plate of breakfast pastries and coffee.

"When did they come in?"

"Not long ago. Maybe ten or fifteen minutes." She swirled a foam flower onto the top of my latte. "But something is going down with them?"

"Why do you say that?" I tried to be subtle as I stole another peek at the table. Nothing seemed off other than that they were huddled close together like they were discussing something important and didn't want to be interrupted.

Pri passed me my drink. "I overheard snippets of their conversation while they were waiting for their order. I could have misunderstood because I was steaming milk, and the espresso machine isn't exactly quiet, but I swear I heard Cora say something about Martin leaking information that couldn't get out. The other two rallied around her and promised they would make sure it didn't."

"Information that couldn't get out," I repeated, tasting the latte. It was a new special—the Rear Window Sunset: two strong shots of espresso with oat milk, orange zest, and a pinch of cardamom for extra flavor. As usual, the drink was beautifully balanced and layered. "Could they be talking about Martin's review?" I didn't tell her about my conversation with Dr. Caldwell, but it was no secret that Heather hadn't wanted the review to be released.

"I have no idea." She rinsed the pitcher and reached for the next order ticket. "If you can find a way to worm yourself into their conversation, maybe you can find out. All I know is that..." Pri trailed off. Her doe-like eyes doubled in size as she stared behind me.

I froze. "What? What's wrong?"

She pressed her lips together tight and shook her head. "Do not turn around, Annie. Act casual."

"Okay, why? Is the killer behind me? Am I in danger?" My heart thudded in my chest. My hands felt clammy. I kept my gaze focused on Pri, willing myself not to turn around.

"It's Double Americano. Double Americano is in the building. What do I do?"

Relief flooded my body. I threw my hand on my chest and exhaled. "First of all, don't do that to me again. I thought someone wielding a bloody knife was standing behind me. A man died yesterday, remember?"

"Sorry about that. It's just that Double Americano hasn't been here for weeks. I can't believe it. Why didn't I dress up today?" She smoothed her apron and brushed a strand of hair from her face.

"You look amazing." I tried to reassure her. For nearly a year now Pri had a crush on a customer she had nicknamed Double Americano, though her crush's infrequent visits to Redwood Grove only heightened the obsession. I had often teased her that "DA" was a figment of her imagination since none of the rest of us had ever set eyes on the coffee client who made Pri's cheeks flush crimson.

"Oh my God, Annie, it's happening," Pri said, clapping her hand over her mouth and then fanning her face like she was in the middle of a heat wave. "What do I say? What I do?"

It was bizarre to see Pri squirm. She was normally so composed and easygoing. Pri could talk to anyone. She made small talk with strangers and had an innate ability to make everyone feel like her best friend. I envied her. I wished I could blend seamlessly into any social situation, but I'd always been better as a one and only friend. That's why Scarlet and I were so close.

"Annie, help." Pri bit her bottom lip and waved her fingers

like she'd burned herself on the steaming wand. "What do I say?"

"How about if you start with *hello*? That seems easy and reasonable."

Pri grunted under her breath but didn't have a chance to say more.

"Priya, it's so good to see you again," a soft lilting voice said behind me. "I've been dreaming about your coffee."

I turned to see a woman about our age, dressed immaculately in cream linen pants, a silky tank top, and a teal sweater. She was tall with striking features and a broad, inviting smile.

"Hey, yeah. Hi." Pri stumbled over her words. "Hi. Hey."

I noticed her hands shaking as she tried to tamp down ground espresso beans. I needed to do something to rescue her. All kidding aside, she obviously hadn't been exaggerating about finding herself at a loss for words when Double Americano was around and I wasn't going to let her flounder.

"I don't think we've met yet," I said, introducing myself and extending my hand. "I'm Annie Murray. One of Pri's biggest fans. You're not wrong about her coffee. It's so good." I took another taste to prove my point.

Double Americano extended a slim hand in return. I checked to make sure she wasn't wearing a ring. She wasn't. That was a good sign.

"I'm Penny Shurr. How wonderful to meet a friend of Priya's. I rave about Cryptic to everyone I meet." She pronounced "Priya" with the slightest hint of a Southern accent. Her voice was smooth, effortlessly fluid like spreading soft butter on toast. There was a soothing quality about her tone and her entire aura. No wonder Pri was attracted to her; their energies had a symbiotic balance.

A deep shade of maroon spread from Pri's neck all the way up to her forehead. She picked up a frothing pitcher, but it slipped out of her hand as she put it in the sink. "Oh no." Pri quickly reached for a towel to wipe up milk splatter.

"Do you live in the area, Penny?" I asked since I could tell Pri was a mess. Seeing her speechless and unnaturally clumsy made me adore her even more.

"Sadly, no. Although, I've been pitching my boss to work remotely. Every time I visit Redwood Grove, I'm captivated. It's so charming and calming. Maybe it's all of the redwood trees and the fresh air, but I would love to find a way to live here." She smiled at Pri, which made Pri's cheeks turn even brighter. "When I was here last time, I took a drive through the outskirts of town and stumbled upon a small vineyard and orchard for sale. I've made about thirty manifestation boards ever since."

"I know that farm." Pri finally spoke. "That's the old Wentworth property."

"Really? I thought they owned the library and a few of the buildings along the square," I said. The Wentworth family name was notorious in town. Their original estate, which now housed the historical society and a small museum, was destroyed in a mysterious fire in the early 1900s. The family disappeared without a trace after the fire, leaving behind unanswered questions as to what had happened to them and their rumored fortune.

"Yeah, they owned almost all of Redwood Grove. They gifted the winery and orchard to their daughter as a wedding present." Pri recovered a bit of her confidence as she poured espresso into a large ceramic mug and offered it to Penny. "Your double Americano."

Penny cradled the mug in her hands like it was a rare, valuable treasure. She closed her eyes and inhaled deeply as she breathed in the heady aroma. "This is the coffee of my dreams. Seriously. No one does coffee better than you. Will you marry me?"

I might not be the best conversationalist, especially when it came to making small talk, but I was confident in my ability to read people and body language, and this seemed a pretty strong cue. Penny was definitely flirting with Pri.

Pri laughed easily. "You're not the first coffee proposal I've received."

"Oh no, I'm going to have to up my game." Penny sipped her coffee. "Hey, do either of you know of any good real estate agents in town? I'd love to tour the property. I've been wanting to get my hands in the dirt and do something new and adventurous. I'm clueless about what it takes to run an orchard and vineyard and I know it's a long shot, but depending on the price and whether or not my boss will agree to remote work, I'm serious about putting in an offer. Why not?"

"Really? Cool." Pri tried to sound casual, but I could tell that she was freaking out internally. "That property has been sitting empty for decades. If you want, I can call my friend Marcus. He's a real estate agent. He could probably get us in to see it this afternoon."

"Would you come along?" Penny asked with enthusiasm.

"Uh, no. Sorry, I didn't mean to imply that. I wouldn't want to barge in." Pri fidgeted with the straps on her apron.

"If you're free, it would be great to have you tag along and get your opinion," Penny said, sounding hopeful. "You know Redwood Grove better than me, and having an insider's perspective would be extremely helpful."

I concealed a smile. They were both going out of their way to sound casual and nonchalant. Part of me wanted to jump in and set up a date for them, but I followed Pri's lead.

She brushed her hands on her apron. "Sure, yeah. Let me text Marcus and see if he's free later."

I took that as my cue to make an exit. "Great meeting you, Penny. I'll be eager to hear what you think of the Wentworth farm. Thanks for the coffee, Pri."

The initial awkwardness had worn off. I had a feeling that we might be seeing a lot more of Penny around town.

Since I still had a few minutes before I was due at the bookstore, I took Pri's advice and headed over to the table where Sam, Cora, and Izzy were seated. As was typical the patio at Cryptic was one of the most popular spots in town. Large coral and teal sun umbrellas shaded each table. Strings of lights stretched from the roll-up garage doors to potted lemon and orange trees on the far side of the patio. Music wafted from inside.

I passed the dog-watering station complete with a knee-level faucet, large silver bowls, and a canister with coffee-shaped dog treats. The Hollywood crew had taken over one of the long wooden tables near the back.

"Hi, everyone. Sorry to interrupt, but I noticed you were here and I thought I would check to confirm that you're still planning on being part of the film fest later today," I said, intentionally interrupting their conversation.

Cora startled and threw one hand in the air. "Oh, it's you. You scared me." She ran her hands through her platinum hair and then twisted it into a messy ponytail.

Sam lifted his index finger and waved it back and forth in a warning. "Cora, I don't want to have to tell you this again. You need to calm down."

"I'm sorry. I'm just so jumpy." She let her hair fall to her shoulders again but continued to swirl the ends with her finger. "What if the killer is coming after each of us? I could be next."

Sam scowled. "There's not a serial killer on the loose. What happened to Martin was planned and premeditated."

How did he know that?

He gave Cora a frustrated shake of the head, then he turned in his seat to face me. He moved his cane to the side to make room for me to sit down. "Apologies. Cora is prone to overacting."

"There was a murder last night, so I don't think it's overacting," I defended Cora. I didn't like his dismissal of her feelings. It was completely valid for her to be on edge.

He frowned. "My point is simply that it's broad daylight. I don't think any of us are in danger."

"What are you thinking about this afternoon?" I asked, remaining standing. I didn't want to get caught up in a long conversation with them.

"The show must go on," Izzy responded, curling her fingers and brushing the top of her black, glossy nail polish. "Martin would want it that way. He was a true professional. We were just discussing which one of us will say a few words to honor his memory and legacy before the first film."

Cora cleared her throat. "But what about—the—the—"

"No." Sam cut her off. He reached for his cane and tapped it on the ground twice. "That topic is closed. We're not going over it again."

What were they not going over again?

Cora looked like she wanted to say something more but hung her head and stared at the plate of untouched pastries sitting in the middle of the table.

"We'll meet you there at the agreed-upon time this afternoon," Sam said to me, closing the conversation.

"Okay." He'd left me no room to continue to ask questions, so I took my coffee and walked away.

Why had he cut Cora off like that?

What had she wanted to say?

As I was about to leave through the front door, I felt a tap on my shoulder.

It was Cora. Her eyes were wide and bulging. She jammed her hands into her armpits like she was trying to soothe herself with a tight hug.

She glanced behind us quickly. "Can we go, like now? Sam's going to be pissed if he sees me talking to you. I really need to talk to you, though. Can I walk with you for a minute? There's something important I need to tell you. It's about Martin and his murder."

FOURTEEN

Cora looked much younger without layers of heavy makeup and black eyeliner. Her skin was flawless and fresh with a dewy quality, but her eyes were bloodshot and puffy. I wondered if she'd had too much to drink last night or if it was the stress of Martin's murder.

"Is there somewhere we can talk in private?" She looked toward the pizzeria and the Stag Head. Both were closed. Her gait was stiff and rigid.

"What about the park?" I pointed across the street to Oceanside Park. A few moms huddled in the play area sipping coffees while their toddlers scrambled up the fake volcano and a group of early-morning yoga enthusiasts stretched in a sunny section of grass near the fountain. Otherwise, the park was all ours.

"Okay, uh, yeah." She hesitated. "It's kind of out in the open."

"There are a few secluded benches tucked in amongst the redwoods if we take the path over there." I motioned in the direction of the bark pathway that snaked through the park.

"That's good, yeah. Let's hurry." She darted across the street without looking.

Was she worried about being seen with me? Why?

I jogged to keep up with her.

"This way?" She reached the Y in the pathway first, barely stopping before picking the route to the left.

What was her hurry?

Was she worried that we were being followed?

"This is good. No one will see bother us here." She slid onto the bench like she was auditioning for a role in a Jane Austen period drama. Her head flopped against the back of the bench. She fanned her face with one hand and whistled. "I'm going to have to up my Pilates sessions. I don't know why I'm so winded from that. Nerves, I guess."

It wasn't as if she had gone for a five-mile hike, and she'd set the pace, not me.

I decided against saying anything that might antagonize her.

"You seem worried; is everything okay?"

"No, nothing is okay." Her voice tremored slightly. She banged her head gently against the bench. "I don't know what I'm going to do. I'm in big trouble."

Allowing a suspect space to speak and feel comfortable was often the key to getting them to reveal information. I wasn't sure why Cora had decided to confide in me, but I was grateful that she trusted me. "Is there something I can do to help?"

"Probably not. I'm sorry to drag you into my personal drama, but you're the only one I know who's not mixed up with our dysfunctional group of misfits. I guess I'm sort of hoping that you can give me some advice." She inhaled deeply and sat up. "I already know what you're probably going to say."

"I don't know what I'm going to say." I was surprised she thought she could guess my reaction. I prided myself on not having a tell. Whereas Pri and Scarlet were enthusiastic and effusive, I tended to be observant and more internal. How could she know what I was thinking?

"You're going to tell me to go to the police, but if I admit everything to the police, they're not going to believe my story, and they'll arrest me, and my career will be over, and I'll spend the rest of my life behind bars for murder."

That was not what I was expecting, although she wasn't entirely wrong. If she told me anything pertinent to Dr. Caldwell's investigation, I would encourage her to share that directly.

"Why would they arrest you?" I decided we needed a reset. Before I made any decisions about whether or not to involve Dr. Caldwell, I needed the whole story.

She massaged her scalp and twisted different sections of her hair. "Because they're going to find out the truth about me."

I wanted to place my hand on her knee in an effort to encourage her to connect with the dirt beneath our feet. She was so skittish that I felt my blood pressure rising.

"I'm not sure I follow." For someone who dragged me away for a private chat, she wasn't being very forthcoming.

"I know." She sighed and blinked rapidly. "Can this stay between us?"

I couldn't promise her that. My loyalty lay with Dr. Caldwell and her investigation. If whatever Cora intended to share was connected, even loosely, to Martin's murder, I didn't have any other choice but to loop Dr. Caldwell in.

"I'm willing to listen to whatever you have to say, and I'll keep our conversation in confidence, but not if it involves information about Martin's death that impacts the case."

She twirled her hair around her finger. "I get that."

"Listen, no pressure. If you'd rather not talk, I understand. I just want to be clear up front."

"No, it's good." She cracked her knuckles and stretched her neck from side to side like she was working up the courage to continue. "The problem is it does involve Martin. He learned something about me. About my past. He was going to write an article about it. I convinced him not to, but if the police find out, they're going to think I killed him to keep him quiet, and I swear I didn't."

Her interaction with Martin flashed through my head. He had said something about when the truth about her came out.

"Why would they think that?"

"Because what he found out about me could end my acting career." She brushed away a fly that landed on her rail-thin arm. "Martin wasn't a great guy. He liked having all of the power in a relationship. I'm sure you know the type. It's standard Holly-wood. We think there's been progress, but it's still a bunch of old white men running the show. Anyway, when I first met him, I was so young and stupid. I honestly thought he might be able to help advance my career. He seemed like an ally. He promised that he would put me in touch with the right people. But that changed when I refused to date him."

Date him?

Gross. Martin had to be at least thirty years older than Cora.

She pressed her elbows tightly into her sides, making her body appear even smaller. "He used his influence to manipulate people and get them to do whatever he wanted. It must have worked. I've heard a ton of rumors about women who are now megastars, pulling in millions for every film, who Martin had a hand in 'advancing' their careers. But once I learned what code for 'advance' meant, I refused. I want a long-term career in film. I really do. I know this is what I'm supposed to do, but not like that. Not with Martin."

I felt a new level of empathy for her. "When you refused, he threatened to reveal whatever he discovered about your past, is that right?" I asked, choosing my words carefully.

"Exactly." She twisted her hair tighter. At this rate I didn't know how she was going to have a hair left on her head. "*Midnight Alibi* is supposed to be my official debut, but the truth is I did a few films prior to this. Films that I'm not proud of, if you know what I mean."

I had a feeling I knew exactly what she meant.

"Martin knew about my previous work in the adult-film industry. He tried to use that to force me to date him." She rocked slightly at the memory. "I still can't figure out how he knew. I changed my name. I dyed my hair. I thought I had left it behind, but he told me that he was going to include that in his review. He hated the movie, and he had a zinger of a line—his words, not mine—about how the acting in my adult films was better."

"That's terrible." I felt for her, and her story made me like Martin Parker even less. "You should tell Dr. Caldwell. She's very practical. I can't imagine she would arrest you just because of this."

"But that's the problem. I threatened him in front of people. I begged him not to include that piece in his review. He was bitter because I rejected him. He wanted to get back at me. It was a revenge move. It had nothing to do with his actual review. I didn't care if he panned the movie. I just didn't want him to tell the entire world about my past. *Midnight Alibi* is my big break. If other casting directors and producers find out how I got my start, they'll never cast me again. My career in Hollywood will be over." She let out a deep, heavy sigh. "That's a motive. That's a clear, solid motive for killing him, and what's even worse is that I was right there when it happened."

I took a second before I responded. I wanted to believe her. She sounded sincere, but she was also a professional actor. She could be playing me. I didn't know what her motivation for that might be, but I wasn't ready to trust her either.

FIFTEEN

"Did you see Martin fall at the theater?" I asked Cora.

She glanced up at the sky and then squeezed her eyes tight as if the sun was too bright. "I'm not sure. I think so. I saw a flash, but the movie was going bonkers at that point."

"The strobing sequence wasn't supposed to be part of the film?"

"No." She shook her head vehemently. "The digital file must have been corrupted. That wasn't supposed to happen. It was blinding. I couldn't even look at the screen. I don't know what went wrong. Heather was pissed."

It was good to have Cora confirm what I'd already suspected. I made a mental note to ask Heather the same question and see if her answer differed.

"Actually, now that I think about it, I did hear scuffles, though, like someone was fighting. I thought it was bad sound effects in the movie, but later, I realized it must have been Martin struggling to fend off his killer."

"Did you tell the police that?"

"No." She made little circles with her neck like she was

warming up for a performance. "I didn't want to draw extra attention to myself."

Her behavior didn't line up with what she was saying. That was a glaring red flag. It could mean a lot of things. She might be uncomfortable admitting everything she had told me to a practical stranger, or she might be lying. I felt almost sisterly toward her, like I wanted to protect her. If she was being honest, Martin had put her in a terrible situation, one that, unfortunately, many women had faced in the workplace. However, I needed to approach this information methodically and set my emotional connections aside. She could be playing me. I wasn't sure what her motivation for spinning a story might be, but the burden of proof was on me. Until I could look into her account of their relationship, I had to treat everything she was saying with caution.

"Was anyone else nearby when Martin fell?"

"Oh, you mean when Martin was pushed?" She nodded her head in rapid bobs. "Yes. All of us. Everyone attached to the movie was in the balcony. That's one of the reasons I wanted to talk to you alone. They're going to try and pin it on me. I know it. I'm going to be the easy scapegoat. You know the detective. What's her name? Dr. Callwell?"

"Caldwell," I corrected.

"Do you think she'll have any leniency if I talk to her first? Should that be my move?" Her knee bounced as she spoke, firing questions in rapid succession. "Do I risk her assuming that I killed him to stop him from publishing the review? Will she lock me up immediately?"

"I can't answer any of those questions with authority. The only thing I will repeat is that Dr. Caldwell is professional and thoughtful. Her approach to criminal investigations is methodical. I think it's imperative that you share everything you've told me with her. Your information could be instrumental in the case."

"But what if she thinks I did it?" Cora kicked off one of her platform flip-flops.

"It's a possibility. It also seems much worse for you if she learns that later from someone else, versus you being honest and up-front."

"Yeah. That's what I keep coming back to." She bent down to pick up her shoe. "I just wish that I had never met Martin. He's the cause of all of this. I wouldn't be in this position. I completely reinvented myself. No one would have ever known if it weren't for him. My secret could have stayed buried in the past forever. If this gets out my name will be in headlines for all the wrong reasons. They say that any press is good press, but that's *not* true."

I considered pointing out that nothing was ever permanently deleted on the internet. If not Martin, someone else likely would have stumbled upon Cora's secret. In some ways maybe it was better if it was leaked now. She could deal with it and move forward, but then again, I didn't know how things worked in Hollywood. Maybe working in the adult entertainment industry was a career killer.

"You're right," Cora continued before I could respond. "I know you're right. I wish there was another way, though."

"I think you'll find Dr. Caldwell to be quite pragmatic." A new thought came into my mind. "Does anyone else know about your past? Heather? Sam?"

"No, no, no." She waved her hands like she expected I was going to stand up on the bench and announce it to the park. "No one knows. Only Martin and me. Now that he's dead, there's no reason that anyone in the industry ever needs to hear about this. That's why I wanted to speak with you. I can't trust Heather, or Sam, or anyone in LA. This has to stay quiet. I can trust Dr. Caldwell to keep it quiet, can't I?"

"Yes. I'm sure of that much," I replied with certainty. "She is a vault and a consummate professional."

Cora stood and twisted from side to side like she was limbering up. "I'm going to do it now. If I don't, I'll lose confidence and then never go. Thanks for letting me vent and listening." She took off toward the fountain. Then she stopped and turned around. "Which way is the police station?"

I pointed her in the right direction. Cora scurried away like a little mouse. Her movements were quick and jerky. She darted forward, stumbling on her clunky flip-flops and nearly face-planting on the ground. Once she caught her balance, she shot a fearful glance over her left shoulder like she was trying to gauge whether anyone was following her.

Once she was out of sight, I took a minute to catalog our conversation. If she was lying, she could have dropped the act. Her skittish sense of urgency and paranoia tended to make me think she was telling the truth and was genuinely fearful that her secret was going to get out.

I didn't have time to dwell on it, so I stood and headed in the opposite direction for the bookstore. I was going to be late. Hal wouldn't mind, but I wanted time to rehash everything with him and Fletcher before the store got busy. If the festival was going to continue later this afternoon, I also had more prep work to do, and we needed to get in touch with Rufus. If his films were still missing, then we were going to have to pivot and quickly come up with a backup plan.

I was relieved that Cora was going to talk to Dr. Caldwell, but I couldn't get a good read on her. I wouldn't share her secret either, but I did have dozens of new questions. The first was why there was no mention of her acting history in Martin's review. If she knew that Martin was going to reveal her secret, that could have led her to take measures into her own hands. She could have killed Martin in order to delete any mention of her previous career from his write-up.

I considered the theory on my walk to the bookstore. Not wanting anyone in the industry to find out how she got her start was a powerful motive for murder. Her almost manic behavior could also point to her being the killer, or it could be due to genuine stress and worry.

I walked along the pressed gravel drive that led to the Secret Bookcase. Hal and Fletcher had already set out the chalkboard sign with our hours and a rotating quote. Today's was from *Psycho*: WE ALL GO A LITTLE MAD SOMETIMES.

Is that what happened to Cora? Had her desire and determination for stardom caused her to snap?

I wasn't naïve enough to take her word at face value, and I had to remind myself that she was a professional actress. She got paid to lie. It wasn't a stretch to imagine that she tapped into the acting tools she used on-screen to plead her case to me. I just couldn't figure out why. The only plausible explanation was that she believed that my relationship with Dr. Caldwell would offer her protection. I made a mental note to talk it through with Dr. Caldwell later.

"Annie, good morning. We were about to call out a search party," Hal said, greeting me with a wave and playful wink.

"Sorry, I got caught up talking to a few of the movie people." I walked around the register and tucked my book bag under the counter. "Where's Fletcher?"

"He's bringing another box of Hitchcock biographies downstairs. We sold through most of our inventory last night. Although, after what happened, I'm not sure how I feel about proceeding with the event." He tugged at his cardigan sleeve. "It seems in poor taste in some ways, don't you agree?"

"Yeah." I turned on the point-of-sale system and organized the stickers and bookmarks. "I spoke with Dr. Caldwell about it this morning. She was at the theater, and her perspective is that they'll use it as an opportunity to observe the suspects and potentially gain new insight into the investigation."

"That makes me feel slightly better." Hal sighed. "It's still hard to comprehend that a man was killed, here, in our beloved

Redwood Grove. It makes me think of my Agatha. This is the feeling she captured in the pages of her novels when something nefarious would happen in St. Mary Mead."

Hal was referring to *the* Agatha, as in Agatha Christie. He was convinced he was the long-lost descendant of the famous author. He'd never been able to prove his theory, but there were threads that lined up like the fact that the great dame of mysteries went missing for eleven days in the 1920s. She vanished from her home in Sunningdale, Berkshire, and her car was later found abandoned by a quarry.

As if that weren't enough of a mystery, she was discovered at a hotel in Harrogate, Yorkshire, registered under a fictitious name. Multiple theories arose as to the nature of her disappearance, from it being a publicity stunt to her attempting to get back at her husband for having an affair. Hal's theory was more unique and potentially less plausible—although certainly not out of the realm of possibilities. He believed that Agatha spent those unaccounted-for days giving birth to a baby—his mother.

The math worked. Agatha was thirty-six years old when she went missing. Hal's mother had been adopted as a newborn infant. She'd never learned any information about her birth parents, only that they'd arranged for her adoption with a small private agency in Yorkshire.

Hal had spent the bulk of his adult life trying to prove his bloodline connection to the late great Ms. Christie. Thus far, without success.

"Have you made a decision about attending the Harrogate Festival?" I asked.

Hal cleared his throat. "I'm going next year and I want you to come with me."

"You are?" I couldn't believe it. Hal had been talking about the festival for years but always found an excuse not to travel across the pond. The week-long celebration of crime writing took place every July. The festival attracted best-selling authors, agents, editors, and readers from all around the globe. Hal wouldn't admit it, but I was sure that the one thing holding him back from attending the book festival of his dreams was that he was worried someone in the crime writing world would be able to disprove his theory once and for all.

"Yes, it's time. I'm not getting any younger. I want to travel and experience the English countryside while my hips still work. Caroline has agreed to come, and I'd love to close the store for a week and have you and Fletcher come along. We can consider it a research trip. After all, you've already put on a festival of epic proportions here, which is only going to grow. We'll write it off in the name of competitive analysis." His eyes sparkled with excitement.

"Wow. Really? Count me in. I've never been out of the country. I would love to come, and I think we could learn a lot for our next Mystery Fest."

"Save the date for next summer. Put it on your calendar, and we'll begin making plans." He beamed with delight. "To Agatha's old haunting grounds—the Old Swan Hotel—we shall go."

"Does Fletcher know?"

"Does Fletcher know what?" Fletcher asked, strolling toward us from the servants' staircase with a box of books.

I waited for Hal to reply. I didn't want to be the one to tell him. This was Hal's big news.

"About the Harrogate Festival," Hal replied with a smile.

"Oh yeah." Fletcher set the box on the counter. "All of us taking a jaunt over to jolly old England. I've already told Hal I'm going to need a detour to 221B Baker Street, and I'm booking a nighttime tour of Sherlock's London. You want to join me?"

"Oh, uh. Maybe. I just found out that we're going, so give me a minute to wrap my head around it first."

"There's no rush. The festival is next July. We have ample time to plan," Hal said, giving me a knowing wink.

"I beg to differ. There's no time like the present to begin. I've started on an itinerary that I'll share in our group text," Fletcher said. "There's so much crime and murder tourism in England, I don't know how we'll pack it all in. We'll have to stick to a strict schedule."

Hal chuckled. "This trip is also meant to be fun."

"Fun? It's my ultimate dream. I'll get to walk the same cobblestone streets that Sir Arthur Conan Doyle walked when he penned Sherlock Holmes and Dr. Watson. Could there be anything better?"

I appreciated his enthusiasm. I also was very aware of Fletcher's deep obsession with Sherlock. I knew I would have to pace myself and put up some boundaries around how many shared activities we would do on the trip.

Someone banged on the door. We turned to see Rufus standing on the front porch, demanding to be let in.

Hal was closest to the door, so he opened it a crack. "We don't open for another twenty minutes."

Rufus ignored him and pushed the door open. "Where are they? Where are my film reels? I know they're in here somewhere and I'm not leaving until I get them back."

SIXTEEN

"Your film reels. Why would we have them?" Hal asked, giving me and Fletcher an incredulous stare.

Rufus squinted and started rummaging through the display in the front windows. "I know they're here. I want them back—now."

"Slow down." Hal spoke with a voice of calm reason. "Let's take a minute and talk this through. Why would you think your films would be in the bookstore?"

"It's the perfect hiding place," Rufus sneered. "You have so much junk packed onto the shelves. You could hide them in plain sight."

I took personal offense to that. The Secret Bookcase was meticulously organized. Every book and item in our inventory was cataloged, accounted for, and had its own place on our shelves.

Hal remained more centered. "Rufus, I understand that you're upset about the missing films and we'll do anything we can to help you recover them, but I assure you we don't have the films. If we did, we would have called you immediately to come get them. What possible reason would we have for taking them?"

Rufus paused briefly but then went back to digging through our display, paying no heed to the time and effort that had gone into putting the display together. "I don't know why you would be involved in this, but I heard from a reliable source that my films are here and I'm not leaving until we search every room."

A reliable source?

Who would have told Rufus that his films were at the bookstore?

"Where did you hear that?" Hal took the words right out of my mouth.

Rufus glared at him. "Someone I trust."

"Look, it's going to be difficult to help you if you don't give us more," Hal reasoned. "I've owned the Secret Bookcase for nearly forty years. What plausible reason would I—or any of my staff—have for stealing your films? We reached out to partner with you on this event. Why would we do anything to jeopardize a professional relationship?"

"I don't think you stole them." Rufus tossed a pink BASI-CALLY A DETECTIVE hoodie on the floor. "I didn't say that. I think you're either harboring them or the thief stashed them here for safekeeping, and I intend to get them first."

Harboring vintage films? That was a new one.

Hal held out his arms. "You can search the entire store. I promise you won't find your reels, but I would ask that you treat our merchandise with respect. Tossing things on the floor is absolutely uncalled for."

"Fine, but I'm not leaving until the films are in my hands. You'll have to drag me out of here kicking and screaming." Rufus took off toward the Conservatory.

"Should we follow him?" Fletcher whispered.

"I think it would be a good idea to *help* him." Hal emphasized "help." "Otherwise, we're going to spend the rest of the morning reorganizing the store."

"Good point." Fletcher motioned to the Conservatory. "Should I tag along with him?"

"No, why don't you two split up and look through the other rooms? I'll handle Rufus." Hal walked with a purpose into the attached bright and airy space we used for large events.

"Who would have told Rufus his films were stashed here?" Fletcher asked as we headed down the hallway.

"I have no idea. It doesn't make sense." I paused at the entrance to the Parlor. "I'm also stuck on how anyone could have gotten them into the store without one of us noticing. We saw the film canisters last night. It's not as if you could tuck one under your arm or in a book tote and stroll on in. They would be pretty hard to miss."

"Agreed." Fletcher chewed on the edge of his thumb. "Do you think it was Liam? Would he have told Rufus to come here?"

"Why do you ask that?" I flipped on the lights to the Parlor, which paid homage to Hercule Poirot with its Art Deco design. The room was painted in rich colors—velvet green and eggplant purple with touches of gold that fit the mood of the extensive collection of detective fiction and hard-boiled crime novels held within.

"Who else would throw us under the bus?" Fletcher scowled and smashed his lips together like he was rinsing with mouthwash. "Liam and Rufus are friends, aren't they? Isn't Liam the one who suggested we reach out to Rufus?"

"True, but why would Liam put us in the middle?"

"I don't know." Fletcher shrugged. "Because he's Liam Donovan."

Liam liked to be the smartest person in the room and had a tendency to belittle fluffy fiction, but I couldn't come up with a reason he would claim that we were involved in any way with Rufus's stolen reels.

"Yeah, maybe," I said to Fletcher. "You want to check the Sitting Room? I'll take a spin through the Parlor?"

He bobbed his head. "Time to break out our deerstalker caps."

I chuckled as he continued down the corridor. Traveling with him to Sherlock's homeland was either going to be incredible or maddening. Probably a bit of both.

I did a cursory check of the bookcases. Other than a few mis-shelved titles and spines facing the wrong way, there was no sign of Rufus's missing vintage films. Whoever had given him his information was misinformed.

Fletcher finished checking the Sitting Room and was across the hall in the Library, so I continued on to look through the Study with its cozy fireplace and antique desks where writing students tended to spend the afternoon typing away on their laptops with a mug of tea in hand. I found a notebook that someone had left behind, but no Hitchcock originals.

The last place to check was the Mary Westmacott Nook. It housed our collection of romance novels and paid tribute to the pen name Agatha used to write happy-ever-afters. Shockingly there was no sign of Rufus's vintage reels stashed amongst the Jane Austens or Danielle Steels.

This was a waste of time and energy.

The only other place to look would be outside on the Terrace. All of the stairwells with access to the upper floors were locked to the public, so unless Fletcher, Hal, or I had stolen the films, there was no chance they could be upstairs. I felt more than reasonably confident that we were all in the clear, so I guess I was left with the Terrace.

Outside didn't seem like a very clever hiding place, but since Rufus was so agitated, I decided to check just to say that we had covered every square inch of the estate.

I unlocked the door that led out to the patio and gardens. During regular business hours, customers were free to take a book and a cup of tea outside to the sun-drenched Terrace. Large potted palms and topiaries encircled the pressed terra-cotta stones. Benches in a U-shape provided extra seating, along with collections of Adirondack chairs interspersed between the greenery.

I checked the perimeter, peering into oversized terra-cotta pots and bending down to make sure Rufus's films weren't stashed beneath the benches.

Spoiler alert.

They weren't.

This was such a wild goose chase it made me wonder whether there was another reason for Rufus's insistence that we search the property. Could he be trying to distract attention away from something else?

Why hadn't he informed Dr. Caldwell? If he truly believed that his vintage collection was hidden away at the Secret Bookcase, wouldn't he have gone to the police first?

Something didn't add up.

I wasn't about to go inside when I noticed a flash of movement out of the corner of my eye.

Liam Donovan casually strolled through the garden pathway with his hands in his jean pockets and a sly smile on his face. "Morning, Annie. You're just who I was looking for."

"Why, so you could torment me more?" I blurted out. The sight of Liam immediately sent me into defensive mode. It was easier to be at odds with him than deal with my uncomfortable feelings. Fletcher's words came rushing back.

Why was Liam here?

Now?

The timing was fairly uncanny.

"Torment you? How am I tormenting you?" His smile faded. "And here I thought I was stopping to be nice."

I snipped off a yellowing leaf from one of the planters, buying a moment to compose myself. Liam's presence threw me off-balance. I became hyperaware of my body and how it wanted to pull toward him like a magnet. The chemistry between us was undeniable and there was a growing part of me that wanted to give in to it, but I needed to focus and keep my attention on the task at hand. "You sent Rufus to the bookstore, didn't you?"

"What?" Liam sounded genuinely perplexed. "For what?"

"He's inside right now." I motioned toward the glass doors behind us. "He's demanding that we search the entire store because he heard that whoever stole his reels hid them in the bookstore."

Liam stepped onto the Terrace. His well-worn jeans, T-shirt, and flip-flops matched his casual vibe. "That doesn't make sense. Where did he hear that?"

"My money is on you." I folded my arms across my chest.

Liam threw his head back and laughed. "Annie Murray, you're too much sometimes."

"What's that supposed to mean?"

"Why would I tell Rufus someone at the bookstore took his reels? That's ridiculous."

I had to admit he had me there, so I improvised. "Probably to irritate me."

"Is that really what you think of me?" He sounded like I'd injured him. "I own that I could have been kinder about my perspective on mystery novels, but I sort of thought that was our thing."

"Our thing?" I raised my eyebrows and tried to concentrate on anything but the way the light was hitting his eyes.

"Yeah, I thought you enjoyed the teasing." He nudged my waist playfully.

His bemusing smile was off-putting.

Why did I always end up feeling like the world was slightly off-center or spinning a little too fast whenever he was around?

"Except it's not teasing, Liam. You've made it crystal clear that you loathe the genre and would never stoop so low as to pick up anything with a skull on the spine."

"Damn, okay. I'm sorry." He held his hands up in surrender. "I took it too far, but I did not send Rufus to the bookstore. It's strange that he's here because that's why I came by."

"What do you mean?"

He reached into his back pocket and pulled out a film strip about two inches long. "Because of this."

I moved closer to inspect the film.

"Hold it up to the light," he said, handing it to me.

I did as directed and let out a little gasp when I realized what was on the strip. "That's Hitchcock's profile."

"I know." Liam's eyes raised, and he pressed his lips together. "I'm fairly sure that it's a snippet from one of Rufus's reels."

"Where did you get it?"

"I found it." He swiveled his head toward the grounds. "Next to a garbage can on the village square."

"Were you dumpster diving?" I chuckled, picturing Liam rolling up his jeans and wading through a pile of rubbish.

"God. No." He stuck out his tongue and hunched his shoulders like the thought made him sick. "I was on my way to the Stag Head, and I noticed something on the sidewalk. I assumed that someone missed the trash, but when I went to toss it, I realized what it was."

How had part of Rufus's film collection ended up near the trash?

"That's why I decided to come here first. I thought you would want to know."

I handed him back the strip. "Did you check the rest of the trash?"

"No, why?"

"For the reels," I said with more force than I intended. "We should go right now. Whoever stole them could have tossed them in the trash, but today is garbage and recycling. We have to beat the trucks."

Liam grabbed my hand to help me down the steps. A jolt of electricity shot through my body. "Let's go."

SEVENTEEN

We sprinted down the pressed gravel lane to the garbage can in question. I could hear the rumble of the trucks in the distance. We needed to hurry. Cedar Avenue was lined with benches, flowerpots, and wooden trash cans designed to blend in with the natural landscape.

The can sat adjacent to the Stag Head next to a mature oak tree.

"This is the scene of the crime." Liam ducked and pretended to check our surroundings as he carefully lifted the lid and peered inside.

"Are we really doing this?" I laughed out loud.

"The garbage truck is on the other side of the park. They'll be here soon." Liam cupped his hand to his ear. "We can't let potential evidence in a murder investigation get away. Do we have another choice?"

I couldn't believe that he was really up for this. "Okay, but do you have gloves at the pub?" I asked Liam. "We shouldn't touch the evidence if we find anything, in case there are fingerprints."

"Spoken like a true pro." Liam gave me a half bow. "I'm not thrilled with the idea of riffling through the trash bare-handed anyway. Wait here. I'll be back in a minute."

I felt silly, casually propping up against the trash can like I was enjoying the morning sun, but I didn't have another choice. We couldn't risk losing whatever potential evidence might be inside. Fortunately, there wasn't much traffic on the street and most people were occupied with dining or shopping and paid no attention to me.

An older woman who I recognized from our cozy mystery book club passed by on her way to the library and nodded hello. Mainly I kept my eyes peeled for any sight of Sam, Cora, Izzy, or Rufus. I didn't want to get caught red handed by one of my top suspects.

Liam returned shortly with two pairs of yellow kitchen scrubbing gloves that fortunately went up to my elbows.

"How are we going to explain ourselves if anyone asks what we're up to?" He tugged on the gloves, which fit his large hands perfectly.

"Let's say I accidentally dropped my bracelet in the can, and you're helping me look for it." I knew we should probably call Dr. Caldwell, but before I turned this into something bigger, I wanted to at least see if there was a chance the film canisters were in the garbage and the looming rumble of the garbage truck in the distance was like a ticking time bomb. If we were going to do this now was our chance.

"Is digging through the trash going to be enough to get you to forgive me for being an ass about mysteries?" Liam asked, lifting the lid.

An unpleasant odor wafted from the bin.

I covered my mouth with one hand.

This wasn't going to be fun. I hoped my coffee stayed down.

"I don't know, it depends on how dirty you get."

"How dirty do you want me to get?" Liam asked, dragging his teeth over his lower lip.

A flurry of fluttery sensations attacked my chest as a sudden flush of warmth spread up my neck.

Was he flirting while we were digging through *garbage*?

It brought new meaning to trashy romance novels.

I stifled a giggle and forced the jittery feeling away by stuffing my hands deeper into the bin.

"We should focus. The truck is sounding closer." I resisted the urge to plug my nose as I lifted old lunch containers and a puppy poop bag out of the trash. A yellowjacket buzzed past us, probably attracted to the smell of rotting meat.

"Oh God, this is gross." Liam gagged, carefully stacking piles of banana peels and fast-food bags on the sidewalk.

"If the films are on the bottom, they're probably ruined."

We stuck with it, piling rubbish as neatly as possible on the sidewalk. The film reels were nearly a foot in diameter. They would be hard to miss, but as we got closer to the bottom of nasty garbage, there was no sign of the retro collection.

"Nothing," Liam said with disappointment. "Is it weird that I was hoping we might find the reels?"

"Me too," I admitted.

"I guess we should put all of this back." Liam began returning the piles to the bin.

"I'm going to text Dr. Caldwell." I took off my gloves and tossed them in the trash. "She'll still want to see the film strip you found, but I doubt that she'll halt garbage collection. There's clearly nothing here."

Dr. Caldwell replied immediately, confirming what I thought.

> Tell Liam to bring me what he found ASAP.

"Can you take the film strip over to the theater?" I asked

Liam, showing him my screen. "I would do it, but she'll likely have follow-up questions since you found it."

"Yeah, no problem." He put the lid back on the can but didn't move. Instead, he anchored one hand on his waist and stared at me like there was something on my face.

I checked my hands to make sure they were clean. They were, although that wasn't going to stop me from giving them a good scrub once I got back to the bookstore.

"Thanks." I was used to him being antagonistic. It was off-putting to have him be so helpful. "I should get back to the bookstore. They're going to wonder what happened to me."

"Go ahead." His gaze was steady.

I got the sense he wanted to ask me something.

"I, uh, I want you to know that I'm..." He trailed off as the garbage truck rounded the corner and pulled up next to us. "Never mind. You go. I've got this."

I started to leave but changed my mind. "Thanks for helping, Liam."

Was it just me, or did his cheeks turn slightly pink? "Yeah, it's no big deal."

That was more like the Liam Donovan response I was used to. "By the way, we should probably keep this between us for the time being, at least until Dr. Caldwell says otherwise."

"Right. No problem."

The man was infuriating. For the briefest flash, I thought maybe we had shared a moment, but no.

I sighed and returned to the bookstore.

Hal and Rufus were deep in conversation near the register. Or maybe deep in debate. "Where did you come from, Annie?" Hal asked, looking grateful to see me.

"I decided to search the entire exterior, just in case." I figured that might appease Rufus.

"That's ludicrous." Rufus pounded his fist on the counter.

"No one would hide highly valuable films outside. Do you have any idea what kind of damage the elements might do to them?"

My adrenaline flared as I bit the inside of my cheek and forced a polite smile. It didn't take a film expert to realize that exposing the old reels to heat or dew would likely ruin them. "The good news is that they aren't outside."

"As I was saying, nor are they in the store," Hal added, scooping up a display of stickers and bookmarks that had gotten knocked over in Rufus's absurd search.

Rufus huffed and shook his finger at both of us. Spit spewed from his thin, narrow lips, spraying on the counter. Hal took a measured step backward to avoid the deluge. "This isn't the end. Do you understand? I'm going to the police. I'll have them get a warrant to search upstairs. If you're hiding my collection, I will find them, and I will press charges."

"Speaking with Dr. Caldwell sounds like a very reasonable next step." Hal was unflappable. "Now, we do need to finish preparations to open the store. I'm sure you can understand that." He pointed not very subtly to the door.

"I'll be back with the police and a warrant," Rufus threatened as he stomped off like a toddler who was being sent to bed.

"That was an unexpected plot twist," Hal said with a shake of the head. He returned the display to the end of the counter and began sorting through the stickers.

"Where's Fletcher?"

"He was doing a sweep of the Dig Room, not that he'll find anything there." Hal scratched his stubbly chin. "I have an odd sense about Rufus."

"Tell me more because I do, too." I squirted my hands with a generous amount of sanitizer that we kept at the drink station. Then I poured myself a cup of hot water and leafed through the packages of tea until I found a lemon mint.

"It's hard to articulate, but his reaction felt off, almost like a performance. It's as if he wanted to make a scene."

"I agree." I plunged the tea bag into the hot water. "Maybe he's trying to audition for Heather's next film."

Hal chuckled. "Could be."

I sipped my tea and flipped the sign on the door to OPEN.

Why would Rufus want to make a big scene accusing us of stealing or at least hiding his films? There had to be a connection with Martin's murder that I was missing.

Money?

Clout?

Rufus had mentioned that Martin was interested in purchasing his collection. Could their negotiations have gone poorly? Rufus had refused Martin's initial offer, but maybe Martin came back with a higher price.

Was it possible that Martin could have stolen the films?

What if Martin took the vintage reels? Rufus could have caught him in the act and killed him on the spot.

I frowned and chewed my lip. But the reels had been in the booth shortly before Martin was dead so that timing didn't line up.

I tried to approach the case from every lens. That was a tactic we'd been taught in school. What were the other possibilities? Could Martin have stashed away the films before he was killed? Could he have been the person who told Rufus the films were in the bookstore? Maybe he was intentionally trying to direct Rufus to the wrong place.

But what about the sliced section of film Liam found? As a film buff and collector, Martin wouldn't have destroyed the reel. He would have known that the reel would drop drastically in value if it weren't intact.

There was one other possibility to consider, which was that Rufus had stolen the films himself. He cut the section and left it near the garbage can for someone to find to prove that the reels were missing. The question was, why? What motive could he have for stealing his own collection?

To protect them?

Or for money?

I needed to follow up with Dr. Caldwell. Rufus likely insured his collection for a large sum. Could he have set up the crime in order to cash in on his policy?

EIGHTEEN

Customers breezed into the store all morning long. I didn't have a chance to dwell on Rufus because I was ringing up bookish tote bags and giving people hints as to how to open the secret bookcase in the Sitting Room. It was my favorite spot in the store. The room was designed to resemble Miss Marple's house in St. Mary Mead. I could imagine curling up in one of the cozy wingback chairs near the rounded windows with a cup of tea and having a little murderous chat with the astute fictional sleuth. We would dissect suspect behavior, body language, and motives while sketching timelines of everyone's whereabouts during the murder.

The Sitting Room was the first space Hal designed when he began renovations on the estate. In addition to decorating with early twentieth-century wallpaper, throw rugs, and craftsman-style furniture, he had installed a working secret bookcase, hence the name of the store.

The shelving unit looked unassuming, but hidden amongst its collection of mystery classics was a secret lever that unlocked, revealing a concealed room. Well, technically a glorified closet, but that was merely semantics. Whenever new customers discovered the lever hidden amongst the spines, they had a good chuckle at their detective skills (or lack there-of).There was nothing quite as rewarding as watching their faces light up when they finally found the lever though I still had to suppress a slight shiver, too, my thoughts drifting back to the body of a former college classmate I had found inside the tight space only a few months ago during Redwood Grove's first Mystery Fest. It was almost impossible to believe we were in the midst of another murder case again.

Late in the afternoon, when I went to help a customer find a copy of her childhood favorite—Judy Moody—for her son, I was surprised to see Izzy hanging out in the Dig Room.

Our children and middle-grade section was themed around Agatha Christie's *Death on the Nile*, complete with a sandbox filled with buried treasures. Archeological maps and blueprints of the pyramids hung from the walls. Binoculars, dig tools, antique compasses, and lanterns adorned the bookshelves.

I showed the customer where to find the nostalgic titles and approached Izzy. She was curled up in one of the miniature couches designed for our youngest guests, leafing through a Miss Marple picture book. Her shockingly bright hair reminded me of a peacock.

"That's one of our best sellers," I said to her.

She flipped the book and jolted upright. "You startled me."

"Sorry. I was just commenting on your book choice."

"This." She tossed the book on the kid-sized couch. "I was just killing time and getting a bit of inspiration."

"Are you thinking of doing a movie for kids?"

"God, no." She shuddered and ran her fingers through her spiky hair like she was trying to scrub the thought from her brain. "Working with child actors all day is my worst nightmare. No, thank you. I am considering adapting one of Agatha's novels and making it much, much darker, like full-blown horror. Sitting in here has me dreaming up scenes of creepy dolls that come to life and unearthing ancient bones that activate long-lost mummies."

I forced a tight smile, digging my thumb into my palm to suppress the urge to scrunch up my nose and make a face. How original.

She was simply mashing up old plots. A Christie horror sounded like a strong deviation from the original material, although I wasn't opposed to reinventing a classic. Even Hal, who was a true Christie-ophile, was a fan of some of the newer interpretations of her work.

Izzy stood and left the book on the edge of the couch. "Have you heard anything more about Martin's murder?"

I grabbed the book and returned it to its spot on the shelf that was mere fingertips away from Izzy. "Not much. What about you?"

She leaned close and whispered in my ear. "Have you heard what's going around about Cora?"

"No," I lied.

"It's juicy." Izzy pulled away and rubbed her hands together. She was clearly eager to pass on the gossip. "I won't go into all of the gory details, but let's just say she has some skeletons in her closet. Career-ending skeletons that she would have done anything not to let out. I do mean *anything*."

How had Izzy learned about Cora's past? Cora had insisted that no one knew. Was she wrong, or could there be another reason? If Izzy killed Martin, she could have read his review. Maybe she's the one who deleted the information about Cora. But why?

To blackmail Cora?

"You can't script this kind of drama," Izzy said. "First, Martin gets tossed off the balcony and plunges to his death. Now his young ingenue is about to make headlines for all of the wrong reasons. What's next? I'm on the edge of my seat, waiting with anticipation."

Her callous reaction to Martin's death and Cora's situation put me on the defensive. I wanted to see how she would react if I approached the conversation from an angle of empathy. "How are you doing? It must have been awful for you. Martin invited you for the weekend, right? I'm guessing the two of you must have been close."

"Oh, it's absolutely the worst." She threw her head back and pounded her hand against her heart. "I've been sick about it. Martin was one of a kind. I don't know if he'll ever be replaced in the industry."

"Had you known him a long time?"

"My entire career." She trolled the shelves while she answered, pulling out a title to give it a once over before returning it to its spot. "He's partially responsible for my success. He reviewed every one of my films and posted nothing but glowing reviews. His praise launched my debut into the top spot on opening weekend. I'm devastated that he's not with us any longer. It's a huge loss for film and for me personally." She tapped the side of her cheek like she was trying to hold in tears.

I didn't buy it.

Nothing about her response was sincere.

"We were going to work on a film together," she said, glancing at the movie poster of the 1978 version of *Death on the Nile*. "That ship has sailed now."

"Martin was going to direct?" This was a new piece of information. "I thought he was a reviewer. Is that common?"

"Not direct. Produce," she corrected. "He was set financially, and after years of judging movies from his cushy seat in the audience, he was ready to branch out and try something new. He was uniquely positioned to become one of the top producers. He had vast expertise, obviously. He was well-connected—every actor, director, and cinematographer knew Martin and did whatever they could to remain in good favor with him. And he had deep, deep pockets. He might have given Sam a run for his money.

"That's why he invited me this weekend," Izzy continued, barely aware that she was talking to me. It was like she was deep in her own internal monologue. "He hated Heather's film. He called me after watching an early screening and said it was the worst film he had seen in decades. I knew right away that was going to mean trouble for Heather and everyone else involved in the production. A bad review from Martin Parker is the kiss of death." She blew a kiss in the air.

"I don't understand. Why did he want you to come if he didn't like the movie?"

"Hated. He hated the movie," Izzy corrected me. "My job was to take notes on everything. He wanted us to analyze every aspect of the movie and the audience's reaction so we could do the exact opposite. He was curious about how theatergoers were going to respond to the film. As much as he hated it, I think he was also worried that it might resonate with younger audiences. He knew that Heather is savvy when it comes to marketing, and casting Cora, who has a huge social following, was a smart move. They've been doing tons of bloody teasers on social that are trending well. Even an event like this weekend. It's fresh. It's young. It breaks the old Hollywood mold and it scared Martin. He knew his career was on a downward arc. Modern audiences crowd-source their content and reviews. They don't care so much about what some old dude has to say about a movie."

This was exactly what I had tried to convey to Heather. Hearing it from a movie insider validated my perspective.

"Martin was a horror snob." Izzy leafed through a copy of a Hardy Boys novel. "He wasn't impressed with movies that sunk down to their viewers. He believed film should elevate and expand. He praised movies that pushed the envelope and challenged the norm. Not that he didn't understand the genre. He loved a good jump scare or blood splatter, but only in context. He felt like Heather had stooped too low. She went for the easy gags, the scare factor, which was so smart. It's exactly what her audience is hungry for. Martin preferred films that dissected the psychology behind killing. That's why he was such a huge Hitchcock fan."

I was glad she was revealing so much to me. And I was equally curious as to why she was being so forthcoming.

"What were you working on with him?"

"Huh? I'm sorry, what?" She stuttered and blinked hard like she was having difficulty understanding me.

"You mentioned that you and Martin were going to work on a project together. Is it your Agatha horror?"

She sputtered and put the book back on the shelf. "Uh, no. Uh, not exactly."

It didn't seem like a difficult question. Why had it rattled her so much?

"It doesn't matter anyway," she said with a dismissive flick of the wrist. "The film is dead in the water now. Martin was funding production. I'll either have to pitch it again and see if I can hook another producer, or I'll have to table it for a while." She glanced at a trio of gold watches on her arm. "Shoot. I lost track of time. I'm late. I should get going. Nice to speak with you."

With that, she darted out of the Dig Room and headed out the back door.

I had learned more than I had expected from our brief conversation. I wasn't sure what to make of the information, though. On one hand, if Martin was funding her next movie and had only written glowingly positive reviews about her previous films, what possible motive could she have for wanting him dead?

Yet, on the other hand, I didn't trust her.

She had been so lackadaisical about Martin's death. It was

only after I asked how she was doing that her tone changed. How did she know about Cora? And was she being truthful about the reason Martin invited her to the premiere? Questions swarmed my mind like the bees on the lavender in the gardens.

Had Izzy inadvertently helped Heather's case? I'm not sure that was her intention, but she had reinforced what I already knew to be true—*Midnight Alibi* didn't need Martin's stamp of approval. Heather was building a cult following, Cora was a social media star, and Martin's version of the good old boys' club in Hollywood was slowly slipping away.

The question I kept coming back to was what was Izzy's relationship with the stodgy reviewer? She was older than Cora by at least twenty years. Could Martin have made a similar proposition to her back in the early days of her career? Could they have been romantically linked? Or was there a chance that watching a new generation of young women like Cora refute vultures like Martin had awakened something within her?

I dragged my teeth on my bottom lip, tasting a hint of my pomegranate lip gloss as I thought it through. I needed to do a little research on my own. Martin's reviews were available online. There was one way to find out if Izzy had been his media darling (or something more)—to read them.

NINETEEN

After Izzy left, I took a quick break and went up to our shared office to see what I could learn about Martin's past takes on Izzy's films. Fletcher was on cash register duty, so I had the room to myself. I cracked open the creaky window, letting in fresh afternoon air. Since our office was on the second story of the estate, which was built in the late 1800s, it tended to get warm and stuffy in the peak heat of the day. Hal had once gotten a quote for installing air conditioning in the building that made him start sweating profusely and swearing under his breath. In the near decade I had worked for him, it was the only time I'd heard him use bad language. Needless to say, he shredded the quote and encouraged us to open windows and use fans if necessary.

Our mild climate in Redwood Grove rarely required the need for AC. The ocean breezes rolling in from the Pacific were a natural coolant. After propping open the window and drinking in the salty, woodsy air, I took a minute to tidy my desk.

New boxes of advanced reader copies awaited me, along with handwritten pictures and thank-you notes from a local third-grade elementary school class. We had arranged a special field trip to the bookstore for them, opening late on Tuesday so that they could explore the entire store. The visit was capped off by an appearance of Nate the Great. The long-running popular series was always a hit with students, and I hired a community college actor to dress up as the young sleuth.

I pinned the hand-drawn pictures and thank-you notes to my bulletin board. Unlike Fletcher's Sherlock-style murder board, cluttered with a dizzying amount of playbills and cover sketches, my heart-shaped board featured other notes from authors, a map of Redwood Grove, a flier from our inaugural Mystery Fest, and a picture of me and Pri. The built-in book-shelves on my side of the office housed my college criminology textbooks, *The Mystery Writers of America Cookbook*, stacks of advanced reader copies, and new orders waiting to be shelved.

I opened my laptop and pulled a packet of lemon drops from my top desk drawer. I sucked on the puckery hard candy and googled Izzy. She had been telling the truth, at least about Martin's glowing reviews of her work. I scanned seven reviews, and in each of them, Martin gushed about her cinematic genius, calling her the modern embodiment of Hitchcock himself and demanding that his readers rush to theaters to pack the house for opening weekend.

His words about Izzy's work read like poetry. He heaped lavish praise on her.

"Izzy is the contemporary incarnation of Alfred Hitchcock. Run, don't walk to the theater to witness her unparalleled story-telling on the big screen."

As I read through the reviews, I couldn't help but wonder if there was more to their relationship. Could Martin's love letters to Izzy's body of work point to something deeper? Was he in love with her? Did she know? Did she reciprocate his feelings?

Could he have been stalking her?

Or using his power and platform to keep her on the hook?

She came across as a free spirit, but that could be for show. Maybe her confidence was just an act. Perhaps her larger-than-life persona was masking hidden pain or past trauma.

I glanced at the clock on the wall, which hadn't worked for years, but I couldn't break the habit of checking to see if maybe today would be the day when one of us broke down and put new batteries in it. The clock on my laptop signaled that my break was almost over. I need to wrap things up and get to the Royal Playhouse soon to prepare for the afternoon showings. I bookmarked a few of the articles. I knew that Dr. Caldwell had her team reviewing every detail of each of the suspects' past, but I would make sure to mention it to her anyway.

Fletcher stood behind the register when I returned down-stairs. He wrapped an online order in book wrapping paper. "Annie, quick question. What time is the first film this after-noon? We've had a few people calling. I told them four, but I wasn't sure if it had been pushed back because of—well, you know, the murder."

"As far as I've heard, we're still a go for four. I spoke with Dr. Caldwell about it earlier, but I don't know what Heather is planning since Rufus's films are missing."

"Oh, I thought they were re-doing the screening of *Midnight Alibi*," Fletcher replied, tearing off a piece of tape. "That's what callers have been asking about anyway."

"That makes sense." I should have asked Heather about it earlier. I placed my finger on the seam in the wrapping paper so that Fletcher could secure it with the tape. He had the idea to gift wrap online orders in a custom Secret Bookcase wrapping paper. It was a brilliant suggestion. Customers loved the special extra touch of receiving wrapped books and it was great branding for the store.

"Is it going to be weird to watch it again?" Fletcher made a face. "I feel like I'll clench up in that flashing scene, expecting someone else to come flying off the balcony."

"Yeah. That's fair. I'm sure there's going to be some PTSD." The good news was that Dr. Caldwell and her team would be on-site. I couldn't imagine the killer striking again, not with the police and detective in the audience.

"Hal said you can head over to the theater whenever you're ready. We've got the store under control. He'll close, and I'll come help you during intermission."

"Sounds good." I grabbed my things. "See you there in a while."

I was glad for more fresh air and a chance to stretch my legs. It gave my brain a break from thinking about the case, which was exactly what I needed. One of the most unusual and wise pieces of advice Dr. Caldwell ever gave us in college was to give ourselves space.

"If you're feeling stuck, get outside. Move your body. Dance. Bake. Read. Paint. Do the thing that you love. Take a break. I can't tell you how many times I've had a breakthrough when I'm not sitting in front of my desk or reviewing case files," she had lectured our class, doing a little shimmy. "Detective work can be all-consuming. Don't let it drag you under. If you start with boundaries, you'll be much better able to balance the desire to drop everything. On my first case, I don't think I slept or ate for a week. I don't recommend that. It wasn't until my partner told me to go home and take a long hot shower or bath that I suddenly pinpointed a key connection between the killer and the victim. Would I have discerned that if I had continued living at my desk? Maybe. But it was certainly nicer to have an aha moment in the tub with a glass of Chardonnay."

I tried to embrace her philosophy as I took the long route through the village square to the theater. I couldn't wait to see Pri and ask her how the rest of her chat with Penny had gone. Martin's murder had pulled me out of my headspace about Scarlet. I wasn't sure if that was a good thing or not.

"Annie, hold up," a voice called.

I turned to see Sam struggling to catch up with me.

His gait was unsteady. He leaned heavily on his cane, keeping a death grip on it while fixing his eyes on the horizon.

I slowed down and waited for him.

Should I go to him?

His forward progress was tentative. He took an exaggerated step like he was nervous the ground might buckle beneath him at any moment.

"Are you on your way to the theater?" he asked, clutching the cane so tightly his knuckles turned white. He sucked air in through his nose in quick, succinct breaths.

"Are you okay?"

His cheeks were the deep red color of the roses in the park, and his neck bulged with tightness as he tried to regain his breath. "These old legs don't move so fast anymore. I guess I overdid it."

That was concerning given that he'd only jogged a quarter of a block. "Should you sit down for a minute?" I pointed to a bench across the street.

"Nah, I'll be fine." He slapped his thigh like he was trying to get blood flowing again. "I was hoping for a word with you as long as you don't mind a slow crawl to the theater."

"Not at all." I fell into step with him. I was struck by how commanding his presence was despite his limited mobility. Come to think of it, that rang true for everyone associated with the film. I guess there really was a Hollywood type. It made sense. In order to get ahead in such a competitive business, you probably had to take up space and bring bigger energy.

"You're probably wondering what I could possibly want to speak to you about." He was still working to steady his breathing. The soft thud of his cane making contact with the sidewalk emphasized his struggle.

"I'm all ears." I smiled.

He drank in air through his nose and exhaled slowly. "I

noticed you are close with the detective, and I wondered if you've heard if they're any closer to making an arrest."

I had to give him credit for being direct, but that wasn't what I had expected he was going to ask. "Not as far as I'm aware, no."

"Are you sure?" He sounded like he didn't believe me.

"Fairly sure."

He shuffled on the sidewalk, sending a small pebble out onto the street. I couldn't gauge whether his balance was off or if he was just that winded from his quick sprint. Either way, it made me wonder about his health. He wasn't that old—probably close to Hal's age, but he presented like someone much older and in poor health.

He covered his mouth as a rattly cough erupted from his lungs. "You want some advice, young lady? Don't take up smoking."

"Noted. I wasn't planning on smoking as a new hobby anyway." I winked and waited for his coughing fit to subside before continuing.

"You see, I'm coming to you because I'm worried about Heather. I've been around the block a few times as they say, and I can tell you're connected. You're in the know. I've seen you with the detective and she trusts you," Sam said, still breathless. "I have a feeling that she believes Heather killed Martin."

"What makes you say that?" I tried to stay open, but I couldn't ignore the prickly feeling spreading across my scalp. Sam had been watching me with Dr. Caldwell? When?

"It's obvious, isn't it? They've detained her. The evidence points to her. You must have heard about the tampering of the film?"

"You mean Rufus's vintage films?"

"No, *Midnight Alibi*." He stared at me with newfound interest. "Oh, you haven't heard then?"

I shook my head.

"*Midnight Alibi* was edited hours before Martin was killed. I have the time stamp to prove it."

I was unclear why he was sharing this with me, but I wasn't about to ask him to stop.

"The film was finished. It had already been distributed to theaters, but someone went in and recut it." He shifted his cane into his opposite hand. "Whoever changed it added the flashing sequences and took out at least three or four minutes of dialogue. I've been on the phone all morning with our distribution partners trying to figure out if it was just the copy for the screening last night or if we sent a bad version to everyone."

"What did they say?"

"Every copy we sent appears to be fine. No one else has any issues." He sounded resigned. "That's why I was hoping you might be able to speak with the detective."

"Why?" I waved to a group of familiar faces passing by on their way to the library.

"Well, there are only a few people who had access to the files. Heather is one of them." He sighed, using the cane like a probe as we stepped off the curb and crossed the street. "I'm concerned she tampered with the file in order to cause a distraction during the screening."

I fought the urge to frown and kept my expression neutral. He was basically admitting that he thought Heather had killed Martin. Why tell me? Why wouldn't he share his insights with Dr. Caldwell? It didn't add up.

"I hate to say it, but I think Heather might be involved, and since you and the detective are close, I thought you might be able to put in a good word."

A good word?

"Wait, are you saying that you think Heather killed Martin?" Why was he intentionally throwing Heather under the bus? It didn't make sense.

"I believe it was an accident." His body swayed slightly as

we stepped up onto the next curb. He cemented the cane on the ground.

I reached my hand out to help him up, but he refused with a silent shake of the head.

"I think she edited the film to throw Martin off."

"As in off the balcony?"

"No, no. I mean, I think she was trying a new tactic. She wanted to get his attention. He was planning to publish his review at the start of the screening. His mind was made up about the movie. I think Heather tweaked the film to stop him from doing that. She probably added in the flashing and strobing so that he wouldn't have any other choice. He never went anywhere without his laptop. I think she seated him upstairs on purpose so that she could steal his laptop and hold off the inevitable."

This was a brand-new theory. I wasn't sure how much of it I believed. Nor was I fully convinced that Sam was sharing this with me out of the goodness of his heart.

"I don't understand. Martin was a professional. He would have saved a copy in the cloud, right?"

"That's what I mean by the inevitable," Sam continued. "Heather wanted to buy herself—us—everyone involved in the film—some extra time. *Midnight Alibi* opened across theaters at midnight last night. If she could postpone Martin's review going live for a day or even a few hours, it would give initial audiences a chance to see the movie and make up their own minds."

I had to admit I was intrigued by his theory. Could the flashing film sequence have been a distraction? Had Heather and Martin gotten into a physical altercation while she was trying to steal his laptop?

He was contradicting himself, though. At dinner, he'd brushed off the idea that anyone needed to worry or give any thought to Martin's review. What had changed?

We passed the pizzeria. The smell of garlic and roasted red

peppers grilling in the wood-fired oven made my stomach rumble. I made up my mind to bring up the contradiction. I didn't have anything to lose. Sam had approached me, and I knew that Dr. Caldwell would appreciate any insight I might be able to pass on. "I got the impression that you weren't concerned about Martin's review at dinner the other night."

He stopped abruptly. "I'm not. I'm concerned that Heather was so consumed by making the film an overnight success that she couldn't hear that feedback. She is like a niece to me. If you could take it upon yourself to at least mention this to the police, I would greatly appreciate it."

"You should also tell them this, though. It could be a critical piece of information in the case."

"Oh, I already have." Sam coughed again. Then he cocked his head to the side and raised a bushy eyebrow. "They're aware."

Was he hinting at something? If he was, I wasn't picking up on his meaning.

"Who else would have had access to the files?" I asked, trying another tactic. "Would Rufus have been able to edit the film? He was upstairs in the booth for the duration of the screening."

"Rufus." Sam pulled back like he'd never considered the option. "I suppose he could have. That is, if he knows enough about current editing technology. I understand he's an expert in vintage reels, but I'm not aware of how extensive his skills are."

We made it to the theater. The marquee was lit up with red and white glowing bulbs and *Midnight Alibi* posters were plastered everywhere.

"I appreciate your help," Sam said, coming to halt and shifting the cane into his other hand. "I'm due to meet with Heather before screening number two, so I'll see you later."

Did that mean Dr. Caldwell had released her?

He used the door handle to steady himself as he tottered inside.

Was he in much worse shape than I realized at dinner? He had been seated for most of the night. I'd seen him come into the Stag Head with a cane, but his unsteady gait was much more pronounced now. I took a minute to gather my thoughts before going inside.

Did Sam have Heather's best interest at heart? Was he really looking out for her, or was he concerned that she was the killer and was trying to protect his own interests?

Who else had access to the original files? Sam's reaction to my question about Rufus threw him off guard. Was it possible that Rufus could have tampered with the film?

At this point, all of them were viable suspects. I had to remain focused and vigilant.

TWENTY

Immediately upon entering the theater, I noticed Heather pacing in the lobby, clutching her vape pen like a security blanket and yelling at the poor soul on the other end of the phone. Dr. Caldwell must have indeed let her go. I wondered if that meant she had officially cleared Heather as a suspect or if she had an ulterior plan. Maybe she wanted the entire cast and crew to reunite for the screening in order to observe them together.

"It's non-negotiable. I don't care who gets in the way. Run them over."

I froze, not wanting to eavesdrop, but she wasn't exactly being subtle.

"I'm dead serious. The film runs today. No questions. It's not up for debate. Have you seen last night's numbers? Ticket presales are off the charts today after news broke about Martin. Theaters are selling out. We are not pulling it. No way, understood?"

I looked around for Sam. He must have gone upstairs because the only other people in the lobby were the theater staff prepping concessions. I wondered how he managed the stairs with the cane.

Physicality was a key factor in Martin's murder. Whoever had killed him needed strength to throw him over the balcony. Or, if my other theory proved to be true and Martin hadn't been thrown from the upper level, they still would have needed strength to be able to drag Martin's body into the aisle.

"It's going to be a blockbuster weekend," Heather said, in tone that made it clear she was ending the conversation. "Get excited. Get enthused. We're about to have a megahit on our hands."

I waited until she hung up to announce my presence. "How's it going? It's good that you're here."

"Tell me about it. I thought I was going to be stuck in a jail cell for round two of our screening." She gnawed on her fingernail. "It would be better if I could vape, but aside from that, it's fine. Have you heard the news?"

"What news?" I assumed that she was referring to the investigation.

"*Midnight Alibi* hit the number one slot for viewings last night." She pumped her fist in the air twice. "I'm floating. It hasn't sunk in yet."

"Congratulations. You must feel really proud."

"That's not even the good news yet." She couldn't contain her smile. It completely changed her face, softening the hard angles and warming her eyes. "We're going to blow up for the rest of the weekend. I was on the phone with my distribution manager, and they want to add screens because so many shows have sold out."

"Was there any talk of postponing the film?" I asked in what I hoped was an innocent tone. "What did Dr. Caldwell say?"

"Dr. Caldwell doesn't say much. She left me with a bunch of warnings like I was a kid on detention. I'm not supposed to leave town, blah, blah, blah." She flicked her wrist. "Are you thinking we would have postponed because of Martin? No, this is Hollywood, where the show always goes on. Martin wasn't officially attached to the movie. I think the fact that he was killed at the premiere has boosted sales, but it's not only that. We're seeing Tom Cruise *Mission Impossible*-style numbers. It's unheard of. You don't see numbers like this for a small, indie-budget mystery. If this keeps up, we're going to start shattering records. *Midnight Alibi* is trending on social today. Trending. Can you believe that?"

I understood her enthusiasm. She had poured her heart and soul into making *Midnight Alibi*, but it was hard to ignore the macabre—her movie had benefited financially from Martin's death in more ways than one.

If Martin's review had been published, the film might have tanked. Now theaters were selling out because word had spread on the internet of Martin's unfortunate demise.

I couldn't entirely fault her for wanting to celebrate, but it also seemed in poor taste in light of the situation.

"Never in my wildest dreams did I think we'd be the number one film and trending opening weekend. Pinch me." She held out her arm.

I changed the subject. "So the screening is a go for sure this afternoon?"

"Yes, Sam is upstairs making sure that the files aren't corrupted this time. I don't know how that happened. It hasn't been an issue anywhere else, fortunately. I've personally called dozens of theaters to make sure there are no glitches. With the level of press coverage we're receiving, nothing can go wrong today. Everything needs to be perfect."

"Who had access to the files?" I asked.

"You mean aside from and Sam?" She paused and considered my question. "Izzy."

"Izzy?" I tried to conceal my surprise, but I'm sure Heather could pick up on the shock in my voice. "I thought she was your competitor. You made it sound like you two don't get along. Why would you let her have the files?"

She nodded. "We hate each other. I didn't give her the film. Sam did. Don't ask me why. I have no idea. I told him it was ludicrous, but he wouldn't listen." She shrugged. "He asked me to share the files with her at dinner. No, scratch that. 'Asked' is too tame. He basically told me that I didn't have a choice. Don't even get me started on it. I was pissed. He claimed that he wanted her to see my brilliance in how I cut the film together. I didn't buy it, but he controls the purse strings, so at the end of the day it's what Sam wants, goes."

This revelation made me even more curious about Sam and Izzy's relationship. Could they have teamed up to try and tank the movie? That logic worked for Izzy. It didn't make sense for Sam, though. His financial stake in the film should have made him eager to do anything to boost ticket sales.

A flicker of an idea flashed through my mind. Was there a chance he handed over the movie to Izzy in hopes that she would do something drastic? He'd been in the business longer than anyone else. If he saw the writing on the wall and knew that Martin's review was going to be published, could it have been a marketing ploy to create a different kind of buzz?

I needed to think about it more. "What about Rufus? Could he have tampered with the film?" I asked Heather, watching her carefully to gauge her response.

"How? He had one job—to play the movie." Heather scrunched her face. "He would have needed time and the right software. No, no. He couldn't have sliced my movie into shreds. Could he?"

"He was in the booth alone for a while," I replied, hoping that she would at least consider the possibility. "I just wonder if he could have deliberately altered the film." Rufus claimed to be an expert in current technology in addition to his expertise on vintage equipment. When Dr. Caldwell had questioned him shortly after the murder, he explained that he was in charge of loading the digital files and calibrating the projector and audio systems.

"Oh God. I never thought about that. He was in the booth for a good hour before the movie started. I guess he could have." Her eyes ping ponged from the concession stand to the door leading to the balcony. "Wait. Do you think he did? Why? Why would he ruin my movie?"

"I'm not accusing anyone. I'm trying to put together theories. That's all."

She smashed her lips together in a half snarl. "I'm going to have to keep my eye on him. He told me that he refused to leave his precious vintage films unattended, but what if you're right? What if he was working secretly for Martin? Maybe Martin paid him under the table to sabotage *Midnight Alibi*."

She had taken a much bigger leap than I imagined.

I hadn't meant to imply that I thought Martin and Rufus were secretly working together to ruin Heather, but that was two people who had now confirmed it was possible that Rufus could have tampered with the digital file.

How would Rufus have benefited from ruining the film? The only thing I could land on was that he had a secret agenda against modern Hollywood movies, but that was a huge stretch for a motive for murder, and he was equally versed in digital technology, so I scratched that idea off my mental list.

I hoped he would make an appearance for the premiere because I had some questions I wanted to ask him.

I didn't have time to perseverate because doors would be opening soon. I rearranged the book table. In addition to hardcovers and glossy screen adaptations of mysteries, I set out book totes, stickers, and a selection of our best-selling candles. I grabbed a lemonade from concessions and made sure our point-of-sale system was connected to Wi-Fi.

The minute the doors opened, people poured in. It was a

different crowd, younger, energetic, and costumed. Teens and twenty-somethings in graphic horror T-shirts, Freddy Krueger cosplay costumes, and *Scream* masks queued for snacks while snapping selfies and livestreaming. Word had spread, without a doubt. If this was indicative of other theaters throughout the country, Heather was going to have a megahit on her hands.

The energy was oddly enthusiastic as moviegoers ushered into their seats. It felt like déjà vu. Had it really only been less than twenty-four hours? So much had happened in a day.

Pri arrived right as the lights flickered and the warning bell to take our seats dinged.

"Annie, I have so much to tell you. You're not going to believe my day." Her cheeks glowed with color. "We were out at the Wentworth farm for almost two hours. It's so cool. Creepy. But cool."

"Tell me everything." I looped my arm through hers. We grabbed the last couple of seats in the very back row. That was fine with me. I didn't want to be anywhere near where Martin had fallen last night. "So Double Americano finally has a name and is considering moving here. This is basically the best day of your life. I'm so happy for you and happy to get to live vicariously through your love life. She already proposed. When's the wedding?"

"Penny. Penny and Pri, doesn't that have a nice ring to it?" She tapped her naked ring finger.

"I love that you're already getting way ahead of yourself and I will gladly go there with you. Can we host the wedding at the bookstore? Think about it—pre-reception outside on the Terrace with drinks and nibbles, the ceremony in the Conservatory, Hal can officiate. I'm seeing appetizers in each of the book rooms, dinner in the garden, followed by dancing under the stars."

"That's my literal dream. Maybe we should ditch this and go dress shopping." Pri pressed her hand to her waist to stop from laughing. "Okay, okay. I'll chill, but seriously, Annie, she could be *the one.*"

"Honestly, she seems great. She has a naturally calming energy and I get the sense that she's comfortable in her own skin," I said, squeezing Pri's arm. "I'm so happy you actually spoke to her."

"I did more than that. You'll be so proud of me, I barely stumbled over my words while we were touring the Wentworth estate."

"You did?" I let my mouth hang open in mock surprise. "I *am* so proud of you. Look at you, using complete sentences and your big girl words."

She nudged my elbow and scowled.

The final warning bell sounded. The movie would be starting any minute, and I felt a pang of regret; it was so enjoyable to chat with my best friend and focus on something normal again. Plus, I wanted all of the details about Penny.

"It lined up like divine intervention, Annie. She said she's driven by the Wentworth farm every time she visits Redwood Grove, but this morning for some reason she pulled into the driveway and took a picture of the for-sale sign. She was already going to call and make an appointment to walk through the house before she came to Cryptic, but she decided that she needed a strong Americano to give her the nudge to do it. This is why I think she could be my future. It's like the stars have laid out a path for us." Pri's knees jittered as she spoke. She couldn't contain her wide grin.

Before I could ask her more, the lights went out, and Heather stood in front of the screen. "Thank you all for coming out. I met some of you in the lobby and I am so impressed with your costumes and your energy."

Whoops and cheers broke out.

Heather took a minute to savor the praise, then she closed her eyes and pressed her hands together in gratitude. "As I'm sure you've heard, last night was an absolute tragedy. It touches my heart that you're here and you're eager to see the movie that we've all poured our blood, sweat, and tears into. Before we get to roll the film, I want to take a moment of silence for Martin Parker."

A hush fell over the auditorium.

Heather remained stoic with her eyes closed. She sniffed after a long minute and addressed the crowd again. "Thank you for that. Martin Parker was one of a kind. One of the greats who did so much to champion movies, including our little film that we're about to watch together tonight. I was fortunate enough to get to screen *Midnight Alibi* for Martin before his death, and he sent me a copy of his review. This hasn't gone public yet. I wanted to share it with you first. It seems like the most fitting way to honor his legacy to hear his words directly."

My eyes widened. "She's going to read his review?" I whispered. "It was scathing."

"Maybe she's leaning into the circus of it all," Pri suggested.

Heather cleared her throat. Her face was illuminated with an eerie blueish glow from her phone screen.

"*Midnight Alibi* is a tour de force of cinematic storytelling," Heather began.

I clasped my hand over my mouth. "That's not how Martin's review opened."

A person in the row in front of us turned around and shushed me.

"A masterpiece that defies all expectations," Heather continued. "The performances by this cast of newcomers are nothing short of transcendent. Cora Mitchell has cemented herself as one to watch. Her depth and authenticity rival that of some of Hollywood's most seasoned actresses. Dare I say, we might be watching the next Meryl Streep in action?"

Cora let out a loud gasp from the front row. She was obviously equally as surprised by Martin's sudden change of heart.

"Every frame is meticulously crafted by director Heather Hathaway, evoking a sense of wonder and horror that will leave you on the edge of your seat gasping to get off this dizzying ride of a modern thriller, yet distraught when it finally ends. The climax delivers a punch that will linger long after the credits roll. *Midnight Alibi* is an instant classic that will undoubtedly stand the test of time. This is powerful storytelling in the hands of true visionaries. Hitchcock has finally met his match."

"Holy smokes. That review is nothing like the one I read," I said to Pri, with my jaw still hanging open. "They are polar opposites."

"Do you think she made it up?" Pri asked, not bothering to keep her voice down. The woman in front of us turned around again and pressed a finger to her lips.

I leaned closer to Pri. "I am ninety-nine percent positive she wrote that review. She's trying to pass it off as Martin's now that he's dead." I shook my head. "It's a bold move, but I wouldn't put it past her. She was desperate to stop him from publishing his original review."

"Faking it is risky." Pri winced, lowering her voice to avoid being scolded again. "Super brazen, right?"

"Agreed."

Heather finished her speech by asking the cast and Sam to stand and be recognized. Cheers erupted as the actors took a bow.

"Look at what it's already done." I waved to the crowd, who were on their feet, applauding ferociously for a movie they hadn't yet seen. "It's like a rock concert. They're loving this."

The entire theater glowed like a nightclub from hundreds of phone screens recording the moment.

"How do you think Heather could pass off the review as Martin's?" Pri asked.

"If she took his laptop or gained access to his passwords, she could have logged into his email remotely, changed the document, and sent it to his editor." I reached for my book tote. "That gives me a thought, I wonder if either of the reviews have posted online yet."

While the audience continued to whoop and cheer, I scrolled through my phone, searching for proof that the review was live. "Oh my God, it's here, Pri." I held my screen for her to see. "I wonder if Dr. Caldwell knows."

"Without further ado, I give you *Midnight Alibi*," Heather said, silencing the crowd. Everyone took their seats.

My heart rate picked up as the opening credits began. I braced myself for the flashing sequences, but nothing came. The movie started without a hitch. There were no glitches or eye-piercing strobing lights. I wouldn't call it a cinematic masterpiece. It was a decent thriller with enough jump scares to keep my blood pumping. I was glad to finally get to see the conclusion since last night's showing had been cut short. But when the film ended, I was 100 percent certain Heather had written Martin's review herself. There was no chance he would have compared her to Hitchcock or called Cora the next Meryl Streep.

Heather had twisted his words in her favor. Did that mean she had killed him? I was leaning more and more toward yes.

TWENTY-ONE

As the crowd dispersed Pri and I remained in our seats. "I have to find Dr. Caldwell. I think Heather did it. To change Martin's review, that's next-level awful."

"Yeah, totally psycho, but not in the cool Hitchcock way," Pri agreed.

"Let's give everyone a minute to clear out the lobby. Tell me more about touring the Wentworth property with Penny."

"Did I really do that today? Tell me this isn't a dream I'm going to wake up from?" Pri strummed her fingers together. "The property is going to be a huge undertaking. The house needs a complete remodel. Apparently, one of the Wentworth cousins lived in it until the seventies. It's stuck in a time warp—shag carpet, mustard yellow appliances, and ugly brown cabinets in the kitchen, old electric, old plumbing. The grounds are just as rough. They're going to require some work. But it sounds like she can get it at a steal and she's so chill that if anyone can tackle it, it's her. You know how they say your crush or obsession will never live up to what you imagine them to be like in your head?"

"Do they say that?"

"Stay with me, Annie." Pri snapped twice. "Don't go down an analytical rabbit hole on me now."

I shook my head. "Never, I'm all ears, I swear." I made a little X over my chest. I truly wanted to hear everything about Pri's day, but her words brought Liam to my mind. Lately, I'd been imagining him more than I wanted to admit. However, I didn't have him on a pedestal. Quite the opposite. I'd spent so much time hating him, it was harder to see him in any other way.

"She's even better in real life than she's been in my dreams," Pri said, fanning her face. "She's so kind and easy to talk to and funny. Like, so funny. We ended up in one of the wings of the house, and she kept pretending like there was a ghost stalking us. Then the real estate agent startled us and, I kid you not, she jumped out in front of me and held her purse ready to strike. I lost it. I started cracking up, but it's also pretty romantic, don't you think? Her first instinct was to defend me."

"She sounds like a keeper. Did you get a sense of whether she's interested in the property?" I asked, watching the last few people trickle out of the theater.

"She's interested in the house for sure. She wants to put in an offer. She called her boss on the spot and began negotiating a plan to work remotely." Pri chomped on her bottom lip. "I just hope she's interested in me."

"Take it from a professional." I pressed my fingers to my chest. "She's interested."

"I love you, Annie, but how exactly are you a professional in this department?"

I gently flicked her wrist with my finger and thumb. "Hey, I'm trained to sleuth out secrets and lies. Love falls under the same category, and trust me, she's into you. Anyone in your orbit could see it."

"I hope you're right. If it all works out and her offer is accepted, she could be moving within the next month or so." Pri looked like she was an overinflated balloon about to burst. "Is this really happening? I know I'm getting way ahead of myself, but the fact that she's seriously considering moving here feels like a sign from the Universe, like a neon flashing sign."

Seeing Pri so happy made my heart swell.

"But on the other hand, I should probably play it much cooler. I'm coming on too strong. Should I act indifferent, maybe ghost her when she texts me?"

"No. Absolutely not." I cut her off. "Why would you do that? If you have feelings for her, you should go for it. You shouldn't hold back. If I learned anything after Scarlet died, it's that. We're not promised tomorrow. We have no idea what will happen next. Look at Martin. You could be flung off a balcony or run over by a truck on your way to work. Not that I want that to happen. My point is that it's better to take the risk."

A wry smile tugged at her cheeks. "That's incredibly wise advice, Annie Murray. I wonder if you've considered taking it yourself?"

I sputtered, taken aback by her intense eye contact. "I am. It's taken me a while, but I feel like hosting the Mystery Fest, and now this has been pushing me out of my comfort zone. The same goes for working with Dr. Caldwell. I'm reconnecting with my early passion for wanting to solve crime and seek justice."

"That's great. Although I wasn't necessarily talking about your professional life."

I knew exactly what—or who—she was referencing, but I wasn't ready to go there yet. "So, is there going to be a date? Did you ask her out?"

Pri looked like she wanted to say more, but she kept things light. "Yes, as a matter of fact, she's going to be back in town next weekend, and we're going out for a drink and dinner."

I squeezed her tight. "Oh my God. This is so exciting, and I get to live vicariously through your dating life. It's a win-win for both of us."

"Or you could pursue love, too," Pri challenged.

I felt my cheeks flushing and quickly shook my head. "Nah, it's more fun to just live through you." I linked my arm through hers. "Let's go see if we can find Dr. Caldwell."

We walked out of the theater together. The crowd was buzzing with post-show energy. Before I had a chance to scour the lobby for Dr. Caldwell or any of her team, Pri tightened her grip on my arms and squealed. "She's here. She's here."

"Dr. Caldwell?" I squinted and looked to my left and then right. How had I missed her?

"No, Penny." Pri lifted her arm and waved to Penny, who was leaning up against the concession stand. Penny caught her eye and strolled over to us.

"I thought you went back to the city." Pri dropped my arm and hugged Penny.

Penny returned the hug and shrugged as she pulled away. "I was going to, but I told my boss that something more important came up."

They were both smitten. It was so sweet to watch them flirt, but I didn't want to get in the way, so I patted Pri's arm. "I see someone I need to speak to about the case. Have fun." I wiggled my fingers in a goodbye wave and made my exit.

Knowing Pri, she would have tried to invite me out with them for drinks and dinner. I didn't want to be a third wheel, and I had been telling the truth about spotting someone I wanted to speak with. Heather surveyed the lobby, scanning the lingering crowd like a covert spy. Then she hurried upstairs to the balcony.

What was she doing?

Why was she going upstairs?

I followed her; after all, there were still at least a few super fans mingling in the lobby, comparing notes about the movie and admiring each other's costumes.

I paused at the bottom of the stairs.

I wasn't putting myself in danger. Was I?

No. There were plenty of people hanging out and my curiosity had gotten the better of me. Heather's impassioned speech about Martin's rave review made me confident that she had a hand in penning the piece that was published. Dr. Caldwell used to ask us to work through how every suspect in a case would benefit from the homicide, whether financially or emotionally. When it came to Martin's death, Heather arguably benefited the most.

When I reached the balcony, I watched her slip into the booth. Someone else was in there already, but I couldn't see who it was.

I knelt down and crawled between the first two rows of seats to try and get a better look.

Heather's hands flew as she spoke. I couldn't hear what she was saying, but from her animated gestures, she didn't appear happy.

If only I could get a glimpse at who was in the booth with her.

I crept up to the next row.

My heart raced with nerves.

How was I going to explain myself if I got caught?

I was looking for my purse?

I dropped an earring?

My contact fell out?

The last one wouldn't fly since I was wearing my glasses.

The muffled sound of a man's voice came through the box.

Was it Rufus?

I craned my neck so that I was level with the glass windows. If I wanted to see who Heather was talking to, I was going to have to risk it and stand up. My lecture to Pri about taking risks came back to bite me. This was a different kind of risk, though. It was calculated and necessary.

I carefully pushed up to my knees.

No luck.

I still couldn't see much.

This is one of the sucky things about being short.

I remained on my knees and stretched my chin higher, leaning to my left and then right.

Damn.

Heather was standing at exactly the wrong angle.

I didn't have another choice, so I stood up fully, exposing myself.

It wasn't Rufus in the booth with Heather. It was Sam. I recognized his white hair and beard immediately.

Sam caught my eye and gave me a look that made my entire body go cold.

I gulped and froze.

Should I pretend to be looking for something or someone? Should I run away? Should I make up a story that I was sent upstairs in search for them?

Possibilities spun in my brain.

Sam stopped Heather from speaking, placing a hand on her shoulder and pointing at me. She turned around and stared at me with wide eyes.

They said something to each other that I couldn't decipher and the next thing I knew, Heather's hand was on the doorknob. They were coming out of the booth.

What do I do?

What do I say?

Panic flooded my body.

I shouldn't have been so obvious. I should have stayed hidden.

But this was what I spent four years in college training for. This was the position I wanted to be in. I knew what to do. I could handle this.

I breathed in deeply to center myself.

I needed to defuse the situation as quickly as possible and the best way to do that was by telling a flat-out lie.

TWENTY-TWO

"Annie, what are you doing?" Heather asked innocently.

Sam stood behind her, like a protective force, gripping his cane and continuing to shoot daggers at me. What had I done to make him so angry?

"I was looking for you," I lied. "You're needed downstairs."

"For what?" Sam responded, stepping closer, making his body bigger with a wide stance.

Was he trying to intimidate me?

"The local press are hoping for a quote." I blurted out the first thing I could think of. I had seen the local reporter interviewing some of the cosplay kids earlier. Hopefully she was still hanging around.

"I already gave them a quote. I thought I spoke with every member of the press." Heather sounded confused. "But I'm happy to respond to any press, especially after the success of tonight." She started to move toward the stairs. "Where are they?"

"Over by concessions. I happened to see you come up this way and told the reporter I would come grab you." I was surprised by how easily the lies slipped through my lips.

"We'll finish this later, okay?" Heather asked Sam.

"Of course. Go. Go." He pointed to the stairwell with his cane. "Your public and adoring fans are waiting for you."

She left me alone with Sam.

My heartbeat throbbed in my head. I didn't like the feeling or the way Sam's eyes seemed to be burning through my skull.

"The press needed another quote, huh," he repeated, sounding skeptical.

"Yeah." I nodded, fully committed to maintaining the lie. "That was quite the review that Martin wrote. I wonder if that helped garner more interest."

"Could be." His unwavering eye contact made me uncomfortable.

"You must be thrilled. Getting praise like that from Martin and seeing sold-out theaters means the movie will be a hit." I needed to focus our conversation on something positive.

"It's already a hit. It's going to be a blockbuster. You can quote me right now that this will be our top-grossing film ever."

"Is that what you and Heather were talking about? Making plans to celebrate?"

"I'm not sure I need to share details of my *private* conversation with you." He tapped his cane against the floor.

Sam was blocking the aisle. In order to get out of the row, I would need to get around him. Something about his stance made me think he wasn't going to let me go that easily.

"I didn't mean that," I replied, hoping that my tone sounded calmer than I felt. "It must be so rewarding to receive accolades for your work. At dinner you were so reassuring with Cora that there was nothing to worry about when it came to Martin's words, and it turns out you were right. Hal always says that the gift of growing old is wisdom; well, that and not caring if anyone judges him for drinking a late-night snifter of brandy." I chuckled.

Sam didn't flinch.

"I know how much time and money you've poured into production," I said, while internally plotting different escape routes. I didn't think Sam would harm me. Why would he? But if I was wrong about that, I felt reasonably sure that I could outmaneuver him. Physically he was twice my size, but I'd seen him struggle to keep his balance, even with the help of the cane, on our walk to the theater earlier. If worse came to worse and he wouldn't let me past him, I could jump over the second row of seats and make a run for it.

"Do you?" He tipped his head and narrowed his eyebrows.

"Not technically. Just from our conversations." Why was he suddenly so antagonistic?

"You've been listening to everyone's conversations, haven't you?" His stiff posture and scathing tone made me feel like I was in trouble.

It was hard not to interpret his meaning. He was accusing me of eavesdropping, and he wasn't wrong. Heather might have bought my story. Sam wasn't.

How was I going to get out of this? I needed to try another tactic.

"Can I be honest with you?" I asked.

"By all means." He twisted a large gold knuckle ring on his middle finger and waited for me to continue.

"I followed Heather up here. I'm worried that she might be involved in Martin's murder." I took a chance. Sam might want to protect Heather, especially since her stock as a director was quickly rising, but I wasn't sure I had another choice. He wasn't budging, and he knew I was lying. My only way out was to be honest with him.

"Why?" His facial expression was passive, like he refused to give anything away or betray Heather.

"Martin's review." I gave him an imploring look. "You've been in the business longer than anyone here. You have to know that Martin didn't write that review."

He cleared his throat and rubbed the ring with his thumb. "What makes you say that?"

I couldn't tell him that Dr. Caldwell had shown me Martin's original review, but I could skirt around the truth. "Martin hated the movie. Everyone knew that. He made it crystal clear at dinner. It was obvious that he wasn't trying to sugarcoat how vile he thought the acting, directing, all of it were. I can't believe that he would have gone from completely and utterly bashing the movie to calling it one of the greatest films of all time."

"And you think Heather had something to do with—what? What exactly are you implying?"

Maybe this was a mistake.

Sam didn't sound like he appreciated my theory. Was he defending Heather because of *Midnight Alibi*'s success, or could he know something more?

"She could have changed the review. She could have gotten ahold of Martin's computer files and penned a very different version to share publicly."

"'Penned,' nice vocabulary you have." Sam tossed his head back and huffed. "I suppose that comes with working at a *bookstore*."

I bristled. The way he emphasized "bookstore" made it sound like a derogatory word.

I took a deep breath. "I know you don't want to think the worst of Heather. I realize that you've worked closely on the movie and you both have a lot riding on its success. I don't want to think the worst of her either. I've truly enjoyed getting to know her and I'm happy for her—and your—success, but you have to consider it. She had the most to gain with Martin out of the way."

"Exactly how do you suggest she gained access to his files?" Sam challenged, leaning slightly to one side. His cane was like an extension of his body; it moved with him.

"That I don't know," I admitted. "I'm still trying to figure that piece out." I didn't want to go into detail on my theory, especially if there was a chance he might share the information with Heather. Sam wasn't to be fully trusted, not yet.

"*You're* trying to figure it out." Sam lifted a single eyebrow. "You work at the bookstore, correct?"

I nodded.

"Young lady, I believe this is a matter for the police. If I were you, I would stick to selling books and leave this to the professionals." He hit the tip of his cane against the floor and stepped out of the way.

It was a not-so-subtle way of informing me that our conversation was finished.

"Enjoy the rest of the evening," I said with a smile as I brushed past him.

He caught my arm. "A word of caution: I'd be careful who you choose to speak to about Heather and your theory. There are a number of people who are very, very invested in *Midnight Alibi*'s trajectory to the top of the charts. Heather isn't the only one who would do anything for this film. If the wrong person were to hear that you're floating this idea out there, it could be dangerous."

He released me.

I went downstairs and tried to ignore my heart pounding against my chest and the damp sweat on my forehead.

Was Sam really looking out for me?

Or did he know that Heather had drastically altered the review?

Could Sam be in on it, too?

TWENTY-THREE

My conversation with Sam left me unsettled and on edge. I wasn't sure what to do next. Fletcher was packing up the book table. Since Rufus's films were still missing, the late-night Hitchcock showings had been canceled.

"How did sales go?" I asked.

"Not bad." Fletcher handed me the iPad. His eyes held a hint of mischief. "Take a look."

"'Not bad,' these are amazing numbers," I said, reviewing the end-of-day numbers. "We doubled last night's sales? Wow, I wasn't expecting that."

"Neither was I." He rubbed his hands together with excitement. "The buzz is legit. Everyone wanted a book for Heather and the actors to sign."

"But none of them have written books."

"I know. No one cared. People were buying up whatever they could to get autographed. A young guy dressed as Chucky had her sign his shirt. A couple of teens from the high school drama department had her sign their phones. Everyone is treating her and Cora like they're going to be the next Greta Gerwig and Margot Robbie. We only have that small box left."

He pointed to the tubs we used to cart everything to the theater.

I couldn't believe that *Midnight Alibi* had become an overnight sensation. "Hal is going to be so thrilled." I returned the iPad to the table.

"He already is. He stopped by on his way to dinner with Caroline." Fletcher snapped a lid on one of the tubs. "That reminds me, Liam asked me to tell you to stop by the Stag Head."

I froze for a second, wondering if Fletcher could see my heartbeat drumming on my chest at the mention of Liam's name. "Me? Why?"

"No idea. He left with Hal."

"Is Hal going to dinner at the Stag Head?"

Fletcher raised one hand in surrender. "Don't shoot the messenger, Annie. I'm just relaying what he said."

"Sorry. Yeah, it's not fair to put you in the middle. It's weird that Liam wants me to stop by." Maybe he had been doing more dumpster diving since I'd seen him last and found new evidence.

Fletcher lifted the first tub and placed it on the hand dolly. "I'm taking everything to the Secret Bookcase. Do you want me to come with you for protection? These bony arms know how to flip a page in a book faster than any other book slinger in the West."

I laughed. "That's very sweet and gallant of you, but I'll be fine."

"Don't let Liam talk you into listening to a lecture on Franklin Roosevelt and the WPA. He talked my ear off about the New Deal and its lasting impacts on westward migration, infrastructure, and land development."

"How did that come up?" I helped box up the last of the stickers and bookmarks.

"Don't ask me." Fletcher shook out the tablecloth and

folded it neatly. "I was telling him about the significant mark Sir Arthur Conan Doyle left on history, and in true Liam fashion, he found a way to compare the greatest fiction writer of all time to an American president."

"A four-term American president," I said. "And you better be careful saying about Conan Doyle being the greatest fictional writer around Hal. That could be grounds for firing."

"I don't have a death wish." Fletcher winked.

I left the last of the packing in his capable hands and stepped outside.

The sun hadn't yet set. The peachy sky glowed as I took my time walking to the Stag Head. People gathered at outdoor tables, enjoying our world-famous California wines and soaking up the late evening warmth.

Why did Liam want to speak with me?

Did it have something to do with Martin's murder?

Maybe he had gotten more information about the piece of film reel we had discovered. I felt like I was close to figuring it out, but there were still a few elusive, dangling threads that I couldn't wrap up.

I ran through my suspect list, letting the backdrop of the village fade as I strolled along Cedar Avenue.

Heather remained at the top of my list. I would bet the contents of my bank account on the fact that she altered the review. Her desperation to make the movie a success paid off, and she had Martin's unfortunate accident to thank for that.

Cora's past was a strong motivator. If Martin had outed her background, her career trajectory might look very different.

Izzy clearly had an ulterior motive for attending the premiere. Her and Martin's relationship was fuzzy. I was sure she was lying about something. Was it that she and Martin had been more than friends and colleagues? What if they'd had a fling and things took a nasty turn? Could she have killed him in a fit of revenge?

Sam contradicted himself. He dismissed Cora's and Heather's fears about a terrible review ruining *Midnight Alibi* and their reputations. Was it simply gaslighting? The puzzle pieces didn't fit because shortly after he'd pacified Cora, he stormed into the kitchen spouting off about wanting Martin dead. *His behavior just now was designed to intimidate me, but why?*

That left Rufus. *I didn't trust him. He was lying. I was sure about that. The question that tugged at my brain was what was he lying about?*

I made it to the pub and pushed the spinning rotation of questions into the back of my mind. The Stag Head was packed with people, I saw as I walked through the front doors, many of whom I recognized from the theater with their horror-inspired attire. A band was warming up in the back. A group of gamers commandeered two large tables where they were deeply entrenched in a battle of Risk. The booths and high-top tables were all full.

The scent of homemade chicken soup and fresh bread made me realize I was suddenly famished.

Liam poured drinks behind the bar. He caught my eye and waved me over. "Glad you could come by."

It was hard to hear him over the noise. "What do you need?"

"Do you want a drink? Food?" Liam shouted over the music.

My stomach rumbled in response. Dinner and a glass of wine sounded great, but Liam probably had an ulterior motive.

"Come on, I saved us a booth." He untied his apron, grabbed a bottle of wine and two glasses, and instructed his bartender to take over.

I followed him to the old-school booth with red vinyl fabric and dim lighting.

"Take a seat," he instructed, waiting for me to pick a side.

Then he sat across from me and uncorked the wine with one easy twist. He poured two glasses without speaking and handed one to me.

He took command of every situation. I hated to admit it, but there was something almost romantic about him taking charge. I took a long sip of wine, trying to buy myself time to try and get my emotions in check. My heart fluttered and my skin went clammy. Why did Liam always cause this kind of reaction?

"How's the wine?" He looked from the glass to me expectantly. "It's from a relatively new winemaker in Sonoma. They're a boutique vineyard and I think this Chardonnay rivals some of the best in the region."

"What if I don't like Chardonnay?"

He scowled and studied me for a minute too long, his dark eyes lingering on mine with an intensity that made my heart pound harder. "You only drink Chardonnay. I bought a case of this because I figured you would like it, and I wanted your opinion."

He bought a case of special Chardonnay for me?

That was one of the nicest things he'd ever done. Could Pri be right? Did Liam have feelings for me?

Don't go there, Annie.

He wants something from you.

"Well, what do you think?" Liam swirled his wine glass as he waited for my answer.

The wine was buttery and smooth, with a tart apricot finish. "It's lovely."

"You like it?" He stuck his nose in the glass and inhaled deeply. "I can smell the organic dirt and earth in this one. Sonoma is such a fertile growing area. It was long, long before white settlers came and stole the land from its native peoples."

Liam was a conundrum that I couldn't solve. His obsession with history made him come across like an alpha male, but he obviously had a deeper understanding of history's flawed past and a softer side that I was only just beginning to see.

"Are you hungry? I haven't eaten yet and it's chicken and dumpling night. Should I grab us a couple of bowls?"

Chicken and dumplings sounded amazing and smelled even better. Why did this suddenly feel like a first date?

My palms were sweaty. I clutched the stem of the wine glass, hoping he wouldn't notice.

"Um, I, uh." Why were words failing me?

"Annie, just say yes."

"Okay. Yeah, chicken and dumplings sound good."

He stood up. "I'll be right back. Don't go anywhere."

Where was I going to go?

I sipped my wine and gave myself a pep talk while I waited for Liam to return. There weren't many people who left me feeling as unsettled as Liam did. I hated to admit it, but there was some kind of an attraction. Liam was a bad match for me. We had very little in common, different lenses on life and the world in general, and most importantly, he despised mysteries. I couldn't be with someone who hated the thing I loved most. It was out of the question.

I needed to stuff my feelings down deep and stop letting Liam's mere presence rattle me.

"Hot from the oven, our signature chicken and dumplings, bread, and a fresh green salad." Liam set the steaming food in front of me.

My stomach rumbled in thanks.

"This looks amazing. Your chef is very talented. I meant to tell you that the other night."

"I taught him everything he knows."

"What?" I blew on my soup. I was tempted to dive right in, but heat bubbled from it like a volcano about to erupt.

"Nah, he's a good guy and a great chef, but everything on

the menu is my family recipe. I grew up in the kitchen." He unfolded his napkin and tucked it into his shirt like a little kid.

It was cute to see rugged, serious Liam wearing a napkin like a bib.

"You cook?" That was another piece of new news. I almost brought up the fact that I'd spent my formative years in my family restaurant, too, but decided against it. Some memories were better left in the past.

"Yeah. Why does your face look like that?" He picked up his fork and stabbed an heirloom tomato.

"I never pictured you cooking, I guess." I dipped my spoon into the hearty stew-like broth. "This is a family recipe?"

"This recipe is actually from my—" He chomped the juicy tomato. "Never mind, you don't want to hear about my family recipes. You're here to talk about the murder."

That was true, but I was equally intrigued by why he suddenly clammed up and shifted the conversation. Was it a touchy subject? He sounded bristly, almost pained. The briefest look had flashed across his face. It was a look I knew all too well. The look of grief.

Had Liam lost someone he cared for deeply as well?

Part of me wanted to try to pry open his crusty outer shell, but I could tell that he wasn't going to budge. His armor was up again.

"Did you learn anything new about the piece of film strip?" I asked, taking a timid bite of the chicken and dumplings. The soup was layered and rich with carrots, garlic, onion, and a trio of herbs. "Mmm, this is amazing. Am I tasting rosemary?"

"Can't share the secrets. I keep my recipes behind lock and key." He lifted his wine glass and winked. "I've learned not one but two very interesting things today. It pays to be a bartender. People tend to give up their secrets. They don't realize that we're always listening."

"Noted. I'll have to remember that the next time Pri and I are gossiping about our love lives."

"Your love lives?" Liam cleared his throat and gulped his wine. "I didn't realize either of you were dating."

"We're not. I mean, at least not officially. I was speaking in general terms."

"Oh, I see." Liam studied his plate with newfound interest.

Was he jealous? Did he think I was dating someone?

I didn't bother to clear up the misunderstanding if he did because we needed to focus on the case and who killed Martin. "What did you hear?"

He ripped off a hunk of his bread. "Izzy was here for a while. She was knocking back Jack and Cokes at the bar for a good couple of hours."

"She must have missed the movie, then. Come to think of it, I don't remember seeing her there." That was odd. Why had she skipped out on the screening?

"That's because she was right over there." Liam leaned around the corner of the booth and pointed to the end of the bar. "We got to talking, and she had a lot to say. Did you know that she wrote an original screenplay?"

"No." I took another bite of the soup, savoring its complexity as I bit into a buttery, tender piece of dumpling. "I know that she has directed a number of movies, all of which Martin loved, but I didn't know she was a writer, too. I chatted with her briefly at the bookstore and she mentioned that he was going to produce her new project, but she didn't say anything about writing it."

He used the edge of his napkin to dab his chin. "According to her, she wrote a new script for a thriller, and you'll never guess who bought it from her?"

"Sam?"

"No." He paused to take another bite of the crusty bread. "Try again."

"Not Heather. They are arch-enemies, and Heather doesn't have the kind of money it takes to produce a film," I thought out loud. "Wait, Martin. Was Martin going to buy her script?"

Liam nodded in recognition that I had pieced it together. "But he backed out at the last minute."

"So she could have been upset with him for not funding her film." I stirred my soup and thought about the implications.

"Oh, she's upset with him, but not just because he refused to fund her film." He was enjoying this.

"Why?"

"Because he stole her script." He carved his hands through his hair and watched my reaction.

"What?" I let my spoon drop into the bowl.

"Yep. According to Izzy, Martin stole her original script and was set to produce it on his own, with an entirely different cast, crew, and director."

TWENTY-FOUR

I tried to force my jaw to close. "What? If that's true, that gives Izzy a huge motive for wanting to kill Martin."

"Agreed." Liam took another bite of bread and brushed crumbs from his fingers.

"Okay, you weren't kidding about bartenders getting all of the good gossip."

"That's not all the gossip I heard today." Liam leaned back against the booth.

I had prided myself on being a help to Dr. Caldwell, given my background in criminology, but Liam was outmaneuvering me at every step. I was glad he was willing to share, but I wished I had done a better job of getting suspects to open up to me.

"What else did you hear?"

He sat up taller and looked around to make sure no one was listening. "This one is equally good and ties back into the film strip."

"Okay."

He was definitely enjoying having the upper hand.

"I overheard Rufus talking on the phone. He came in for a late lunch and took over this very booth, like it was his temporary office. He had a bunch of paperwork spread out and his laptop. I'm not fond of customers who linger. This is a restaurant, not a free co-working space."

"What about the gamers who hang out for hours?" I motioned in the direction of the gaming tables.

"That's different. They stay and spend money, ordering rounds of drinks, appetizers, you name it. Gaming works up an appetite. Rufus ordered a cup of soup and a glass of water and proceeded to take up the booth for almost two hours. I came over to tell him it was time to vacate the space. My staff tried a few subtle hints that didn't sink in. He was on the phone and didn't see me approaching from behind the booth. Guess who he was talking to?"

"Why are you making me guess about everything?"

"Because it's fun to see you out of your element."

"Out of my element?" What did that mean?

"Yep." He didn't elaborate.

"Anyway, I have no guess who Rufus was talking to, unless Martin is a ghost who has come back to haunt him."

That made Liam laugh.

Little lines etched the sides of his eyes. His laugh was deep and throaty. It made him look younger and made me feel like all of the nerves in my body were firing in rapid succession.

"No, he wasn't speaking to any sort of otherworldly apparitions as far as I know." Liam picked up his wine glass again. "He was talking to his insurance agent."

"About the missing films." That made sense. Rufus likely needed to file a claim with his insurance company.

"Yes, which I get sounds fairly tame, but here's the kicker. He bumped up his policy a few weeks ago. He was arguing with the agent about how much he would be owed, and he explained that he changed his policy after having a new appraisal done on the vintage reels and that they were now insured for two million dollars."

Woah. "Two million dollars," I repeated louder than I intended.

Liam held a finger to his lips. "Two million dollars. That's a nice payout, if you ask me." He raised his glass higher.

"So Rufus could have stolen the films himself in order to make a claim on his insurance policy."

"Yep. And pocket two million dollars in cash."

"I wonder how that might tie in with Martin's murder. Could Martin have learned about Rufus's plan? Maybe he caught Rufus hiding the films."

"Or tearing off a piece of the film strip," Liam added, scooping a hunk of tender chicken onto his spoon.

"Right. And, in the heat of the moment, Rufus killed him to keep him quiet." I hated to admit it, but reviewing the case with Liam was strangely rewarding. We seemed to read each other's minds and come to the same conclusions.

"What do you think the odds are that the reels are safely hidden away somewhere and the scrap of film that I found by the garbage can was his way of planting evidence."

"Proof for the insurance company that they were stolen," I said.

"You know what this means?"

"We have to find the films—now." I was already on my feet.

"Right now? What about dinner?" He motioned to his half-eaten bowl.

"Liam, if we can find the films first and prove that Rufus stole them for the insurance money, we could help close the case." I grabbed my book tote and reached inside for my wallet. "What do I owe you?"

"Nothing. It's on the house."

"Thanks." I didn't have time to argue. We had to find the vintage reels.

"Give me a minute to make sure my staff have everything under control." Liam picked up our dishes.

I followed behind him with my wine glass, finishing the last few sips for courage. Where would Rufus have stashed the films? They had to be somewhere in or around the Secret Bookcase. It's the only thing that made sense.

I put myself in Rufus's shoes. He would have been desperate to hide the canisters as soon as possible. If he had taken them directly from the Royal Playhouse Theater, he could have torn off the piece and left it by the garbage can on purpose to throw the police off the trail.

I had been highly suspicious of his behavior when he showed up at the bookstore and accused us of harboring his prized possessions. But I had to give him credit. It was a distraction. A ploy.

"Where are we going?" Liam asked, handing me a doggie bag of my leftovers. "I put in a couple of our cannoli. You can have them later."

"Thanks." His sweet acts were as confusing as the murder investigation.

"Where to?"

"The bookstore." I raced to the door with Liam lagging at my heels.

"Why the bookstore?" he asked as we jogged on the sidewalk until we got to the gate at the end of the lane.

Liam yanked on the heavy iron bars. "It's locked."

"I have a key." I dangled the key and tossed it to him. "It's weird, though. Hal never locks the gate at night."

Maybe he changed his mind after realizing that there was a killer among us.

We hurried on the gravel drive, our feet kicking up little pebbles. The spring bunting and twinkle lights that stretched across the pathway fluttered in the light breeze. We only turned the tiny gold lights on when the store was open, but LED lights illuminated the ground.

I wished I had worn tennis shoes. My Mary Jane clog

sandals kept slipping as I raced to keep up with Liam. I also wished I had brought along a cardigan. The air held a slight chill as the sun dipped behind the estate, giving the impression that it was backlit.

The soft glow of the sunset made the mansion seem even more gilded, but as we made it to the front, I noticed that the interior of the manor house was plunged in darkness. Not a single light was on upstairs or on the main floor. Even the two coach lights mounted on either side of the front door were off. Hal always kept the historical lights on. He loved their charm and would tease that we never knew if a horse-drawn carriage might arrive in the middle of the night delivering a mysterious guest or urgent message.

"It's weird that everything's dark." I checked my watch. "It's only eight. I can't imagine Hal's already in bed."

"Maybe this is a dead end." Liam craned his neck toward the shingled peaked roofline. "You're right, it looks pretty quiet in there."

"Or maybe Rufus is inside as we speak." I glanced down the pathway toward the Terrace and gardens in hopes that maybe I might spot movement, but the grounds were still. "He could have locked the gate behind him to buy himself a few extra minutes. It locks from this side so all he would have to do is unlock it again on his way out."

"Should we call the police? This is feeling out of my comfort zone." Liam drew his eyebrows together in concern.

"Great minds think alike," I blurted out before I realized what I was saying.

His eyes twinkled under the dusky evening sun.

"I'm calling Dr. Caldwell now." I grabbed my phone. The call went straight to voicemail, so I left her a detailed message and sent her a text just in case. "Okay, she's in the loop. I vote we proceed with caution."

"You're really something, Annie Murray." Liam grew still.

He stared intently at me like he was trying to decide if I was delusional or brilliant.

We didn't have time to waste. I reached into my book bag and dangled the key to the bookstore in front of him. "Let's do this."

I unlocked the door and marched up the stairs with an air of authority I didn't feel internally. My knees were wobbly, and my breath caught in my chest, but we had to do this. If Rufus destroyed the films, it would make it so much harder, if not impossible, to prove that he was the killer. We had a motive. Now we needed tangible evidence.

"Should we leave the lights off?" I asked Liam in a whisper. "If Rufus is here, we don't want to let him know that we're on to him."

"Yeah, that's probably a good idea." Liam flipped on his phone flashlight.

"This way." I motioned to the Conservatory. "This is where they went first."

"You think he smuggled the films into the store under the guise that you all had stolen them and then stashed them for safekeeping?" Liam moved with intention, taking slow measured steps.

"It sounds a little outlandish, but it's the only explanation I have at the moment, so let's go with it." I skirted around the display tables and tea and coffee station.

"Okay, I'm with you. Lead the way," he replied without a hint of hesitation.

He was. Liam was like a bodyguard. He kept his body within inches of mine. I could smell hints of garlic intermixed with his aftershave as we rounded the cash register and moved toward the ballroom. The aroma was intoxicating and extremely distracting.

Stop it, Annie.

This isn't a date.

You're looking for evidence that could be connected to a murder.

That thought instantly sobered me.

We didn't have any protection, aside from each other, and if the films were connected to Martin's death, we could be putting ourselves in harm's way.

I needed to concentrate on one thing, and one thing only— finding Rufus's films.

The cavernous room felt cold and oppressive. It was bathed in a pool of moonlight. The large arched windows along the far wall, which during the day provided warm, natural light, now reminded me of spectral mirrors, casting long shadows on the floor.

We typically used the space for large events with rows of chairs set out in front of the stage, but they had been put away. The vastness of the room made it feel overwhelming empty. Every creak of the floorboard or rustle of the curtains made Liam and I both stop in our tracks.

He used his flashlight app to scan the first section of bookshelves.

"Any ideas on where Rufus could have hidden them?" Liam asked, keeping his voice low and his phone directed at the shelves.

"No." I sighed, wondering the same thing.

At that moment, a loud crash thudded at the far end of the room.

We both jumped.

Liam put his arm out in front of me. "Don't move."

Someone had knocked down a bookcase at the back of the ballroom, and they were heading straight for us.

TWENTY-FIVE

My throat seized shut. I couldn't swallow; it was like I had a huge wad of gum lodged in my windpipe.

Liam blocked me with his body. "Who's there?"

Heavy footsteps thudded one after the other, reverberating on the hardwood floors.

"The police are on their way," Liam said, holding his phone in the direction of the person. "You're not going to get away with this."

The person had almost caught up to us. They were tall and dressed in black and lumbering toward us like they were prepared to attack.

"I'm warning you," Liam said in a firm tone, making his body bigger by planting his feet wide. "There are two of us and a squad of police cars about to arrive."

I glanced around. We weren't near enough to the bookshelves for me to grab a bookend or a heavy anthology to use as a weapon.

I wound the strap of my book tote tightly around my wrist. If nothing else, I could try to get in a good swing at our attacker's head.

They came into view.

My hunch had been right, but I wished it hadn't. Rufus was barreling toward us with a decorative sword he had ripped off the wall in his hand.

"Get out of my way." He waved the sword in a slicing motion, swiping at the air.

Liam ducked and nudged me backward. "Rufus, you're not getting away with murder. Like I said, the police will be here any minute."

I hoped that was true.

What if Dr. Caldwell hadn't listened to my message yet?

There was no guarantee that help was on its way. For the moment, it was me, Liam, and a sword-wielding killer.

Rufus skidded to a stop. "What are you talking about?"

"We know you did it," Liam replied, puffing out his chest.

Think, Annie.

There has to be something you can do.

If Liam kept Rufus talking and distracted, maybe, just maybe, I would be able to make an emergency call.

"Did what?" Rufus secured his grip on the sword.

"It's over, okay." Liam tried to meet Rufus at his level with a more calming tone. "We know you killed Martin. We know why. We've informed the police. As I already mentioned, they are on their way here now. So, let's end this without anyone else getting hurt. It will be much better for you in the long run."

I watched Rufus blink rapidly like he was trying to process Liam's words. He reminded me of a villain from a kids' cartoon with his oversized black coat and hunched shoulders.

This was my chance. I lifted my phone ever so slightly so I could see the screen and pressed the emergency call button.

The sword slipped in Rufus's hand as he stood at an impasse. He regained his grasp and narrowed his beady eyes on Liam. "What the hell are you talking about? I didn't kill anyone."

I could hear the operator on the other end of the line asking questions. I couldn't risk answering, but I turned the phone so that, hopefully, they could pick up on the background conversation and send a team.

"Rufus, it's over." Liam kept me shielded but motioned with his hands for Rufus to lower the sword. "Drop your weapon and this can all end now before you're in even more trouble."

"What are you talking about?" Rufus repeated, not lowering the sword. "I didn't kill Martin. I didn't kill anyone."

"Then what are you doing here?" Liam caught my eye to signal me to stay behind him. This was one time when I wasn't going to argue with his inclination to want to protect me.

The operator's voice crackled on the phone. Rufus's eyes darted to me. I clicked it off and stuffed it behind my back. Liam reached for my arm and squeezed it three times like he was trying to signal to me with Morse code. I wasn't versed in the old wartime communication, but I caught his drift right away and tried to make my expression as innocent as possible.

Rufus stared me down like I was the criminal. "What are you doing? What's behind your back?"

"Nothing," I lied. My palms felt damp. I clutched the phone as tight as I could, willing it not to slip out of my hand. "Why did you knock over the shelf?"

"To scare you off. I didn't want to be seen. I don't know how you found me. I thought I was careful. No one was supposed to be here tonight."

"You're not supposed to be here," I retorted. "This is private property. I work here and have a key. How did you get in?"

Rufus finally let the sword fall. It rattled on the hardwood floor with a metallic thud, making me startle. "I stole a key when I was here earlier."

"Why?"

"I needed somewhere to store my movie reels until I could

find a more permanent hiding place for them," he admitted, sounding almost defeated.

The fact that he released the sword brought me some relief. It was a good sign that, if nothing else, at least Liam and I had the upper hand now. Rufus's singular focus on his reels made me more inclined to believe him. It would explain his behavior and it tied into our working theory that he had stolen his own collection.

"Wait, so they aren't here now?" I was momentarily distracted by the dark chandeliers hanging above us. Their crystals caught slivers of light and scattered them like ghostly apparitions throughout the room.

"Now they are, but they weren't when I claimed that one of you took them." He kicked the sword with his foot, sending it spinning. "I knew I needed a way in late at night, and I didn't want to break in or do any damage that would put too much heat on me, so I made up the story, and while you all were distracted looking for my reels, I swiped the key from the cash register drawer. My plan was to come back tonight, hide the canisters underneath one of the shelves, and buy myself a little time for things to cool down before I came back for them."

"So you admit that you faked the robbery?" Liam asked. "You took your own films."

Rufus nodded.

"For the insurance money?" I kept my death grip on my phone.

He shook his head. "You don't understand. I've got some huge debts that I need to pay off. It's not even a real crime. No one got hurt. The insurance companies are the real criminals anyway. They take our money and do nothing. I was going to cash in on my policy. As long as no one found the films, I was in the clear. I needed them in the bookstore until I could safely transport them to a storage unit I rented. Eventually I was going to sell them in the underground market, but not for a while."

"And double dip," Liam said with disgust. "Insurance fraud and murder are going to be two rough charges for you to shake, especially since you seem to have little empathy for the fact that someone did indeed get very hurt by your little charade."

"No, no." Rufus shook his head violently. "No one got hurt. I don't know why you two are talking about me killing Martin. I admit that I staged the break-in at the theater, but I swear on my life that I did not kill. I didn't even know him. Why would I kill him?"

"Because he caught you in the act," I suggested.

"You've got that wrong." Rufus tapped the edge of the sword with his toe. "I didn't kill him. I wasn't anywhere near him when he died. I wasn't even in the theater."

I could hear the sound of sirens approaching. My shoulders relaxed a little, but I stayed close to Liam.

That was a huge relief, but we needed to keep him talking until the police arrived.

"Where were you?" I asked, trying not to get distracted by the scent of Liam's aftershave or the shadows drifting across the ceiling. None of us had moved from our spots. It was like we were chess pieces glued in place, plotting three moves ahead.

"I snuck out right as *Midnight Alibi* started." Rufus fixated his beady eyes on the mural on the wall behind the stage like he was suddenly enraptured by the Baroque artwork. "It was my one chance to smuggle the reels out of the theater without being seen. Everyone was focused on watching the movie. I snuck out the side exit and was going to stash the films at the Stag Head. I found the perfect spot the night before, but on my way to the pub, I bumped into a police officer on my way. I panicked. I had to change my plan on the fly and get back to the theater before anyone noticed that I was gone, so I double-wrapped them in plastic garbage bags and dumped them in the garbage can. When I got back to the theater, Martin was already dead and it was chaos so I slipped back upstairs unnoticed."

"We found a ripped section of film by the garbage can," I said. I could see the flashing lights of the police cars on the front windows of the lobby. Liam shot me a quick thumbs-up to signal that he'd noticed them, too.

I didn't think we were in any danger now, but I wasn't going to take any chances until they were actually in the building.

"Yeah, I ripped a little piece of it getting them back out of the cans later that night." He spoke directly to me, never once so much as glancing at Liam. "Martin's murder was good for me. I figured I had a little more time than I had anticipated before the police might come search my house since everyone would be focused on finding his killer. I didn't want to risk ruining them in the garbage, so I took them back to my house and hid them in my garage, then I came here and stole the key. Tonight I was going to hide them and come back for them in a few days to put them in a more permanent storage spot."

Everything he was telling us made me believe him. Rufus had definitely engaged in a criminal act, but now I wasn't so convinced that he was a killer.

TWENTY-SIX

I had to shield my eyes from Dr. Caldwell and her team of police officers' blinding lights as they stormed the ballroom. "No one move. Hands up where I can see them," she commanded. Despite her petite stature, she had no problem controlling any situation. I wouldn't want to mess with her.

Rufus reluctantly raised one hand, almost like he was giving a long-lost friend a half-hearted greeting.

"Both hands in the air—now," Dr. Caldwell yelled, directing her team to flank on either side of her.

I watched in awe as her team surrounded Rufus in one meticulously coordinated move. Before I could blink, his hands were cuffed behind his back, and the sword was in the possession of one of the officers.

"I confess that I stole my films, but I didn't touch Martin." Rufus pleaded his case. "I was telling them the same thing. I wasn't going to hurt anyone."

Dr. Caldwell ignored him and turned to me. "Annie, can you turn on the overhead lights, please?"

"Of course." I was glad to shine as much light as possible on this situation. It took a minute for my eyes to adjust after I flipped on the crystal chandeliers. I waited nearby with Liam while Dr. Caldwell asked Rufus a series of questions about the missing films and his whereabouts the night of the murder. Rufus begrudgingly complied with all of her questions and requests for more information.

"Uh, hello. Am I missing out on a party?" A voice interrupted the interrogation.

We turned to see Hal lingering in the archway between the Conservatory and the Foyer.

Hal was safe. Thank goodness.

A flood of relief washed over my body, but I also wondered where he'd been. He couldn't have been upstairs this entire time, could he?

"Do come in." Dr. Caldwell curled her finger to invite Hal closer. "Apologies. You were next on my list to call, but I've been a bit wrapped up."

A look of understanding passed across Hal's face as his eyes danced between Rufus, us, and the collapsed bookshelves.

"I was just about to say that we'll continue our questioning at the station." Dr. Caldwell motioned to one of her team. They proceeded to usher Rufus out of the room.

"What's going on?" Hal's gaze drifted again from the broken shelves and then to Dr. Caldwell. "Please tell me that no one was hurt."

"Perhaps a few of your books." She walked in that direction. "Come with me. Let's assess the damage. I'm assuming you'll want to file a damage report."

Hal ran his fingers through his hair like he was trying to make sense of what he was seeing. "I'm not tracking. What happened?"

Dr. Caldwell pressed her hands together and took a small sniff of air in through her nose. "Sorry. I tend to move at a rapid pace and I'm sure it would be most helpful for you to have a clear understanding of what's occurred in your place of business." She went on to explain that Rufus broke in (with a key he had stolen from the bookstore) and his intention to use the store as his hiding spot.

"Wait, but no one was hurt?" Hal looked at me and then Liam with concern.

"We're fine," I assured him.

"That's a relief." Hal placed his hand on his chest.

"I'm not sure the same can be said for some of these titles." Dr. Caldwell knelt to pick up a book. Its cover was smashed in, and the edges folded up.

Hal shook his hands. "I don't care about the books. The books can be replaced. People can't. When I got home from dinner and saw all of the flashing lights, my heart stopped. I thought something happened to Annie or Fletcher."

"I thought the same thing about you." I moved closer to him and squeezed his arm. "You know, speaking of Fletcher, I'm surprised that Fletcher didn't bump into Rufus."

"Why?" Dr. Caldwell pushed her glasses up the bridge of her nose.

"He was coming here to drop off the books after the event." I hadn't seen any tubs by the front door, but then again, it was dark, and I had been focused on tracking down evidence that I thought was tied to Martin's killer.

"Has anyone heard from him since?" Dr. Caldwell asked.

I didn't like Dr. Caldwell's tone or the implication. "No, but I figured he went home. It's late."

"Can you check in with him, please?" She made strong eye contact with me.

I couldn't tell if I was picking up on her intensity or if I was overreacting. "Let me check the Foyer while I call him. If he was here, the tubs would be in the front." I called his number, which went straight to voicemail. There were no tubs in the Foyer or behind the register. Fletcher wouldn't have stayed to put everything away on his own. Maybe he changed his mind and went home instead.

"No answer," I said to Dr. Caldwell. "I texted him, too."

"Okay, keep me posted."

"Do you think that Rufus killed Martin?" Liam asked.

Dr. Caldwell's lips pursed into a small circle like she was preparing to whistle. "I have further questioning to do with him at the station. It's too soon to say. Nothing is off the table at this point."

"Should we check on Fletcher?" Hal asked.

"We can do that," Liam said. "I'm taking Annie home anyway. We can stop by his place."

Taking me home? We hadn't discussed that.

"Good." Hal let out a sigh of relief. "I don't want anyone walking around the village square after dark. Not after this." He motioned to the bookshelves.

"Don't touch anything tonight," Dr. Caldwell interjected. "I apologize for the inconvenience, but one of my team will take photos to document the damage. We'll try to be quick and out of your hair soon so you can continue with the rest of your evening."

"If by evening, you mean making myself a hot cup of chamomile and going to bed, then yes." Hal smiled. "It's been a long day."

I was worried about him. He wasn't getting any younger. I knew he was putting on a brave face for us, but I could tell that he was upset, as he should be. It was unsettling to think that Rufus had broken in and had intended to use the bookstore as a hiding space. "Hal, Fletcher and I will take care of this in the morning. Don't worry about any of it. Go make some tea and get some rest."

Dr. Caldwell nodded approvingly. "Good plan. I need to get Rufus to the station. I'll leave two of my officers to document and help you file a report. Everyone, please remain aware. I don't believe that there's an immediate threat of danger, but until we have a suspect in custody, I will not rest."

That I believed; I was sure Dr. Caldwell was operating on a combination of coffee, tea, and little to no sleep.

"Thank you for seeing Annie home," Hal said to Liam, like a parent to a boyfriend after a date.

I felt my face begin to flush. "I'm an adult woman, and I'm standing right here," I said with annoyance.

"This has nothing to do with gender or how capable you are." Hal cleared his throat and scowled. "I don't want anyone out on their own tonight. Look what happened here. I was at dinner with Caroline for less than two hours, and I returned home to this."

That was a fair point.

"You be sure to lock up once the police are done," Liam said to Hal.

Hal gave him a half nod.

We left, retracing our steps. Liam was quiet as we walked down the lane under the lamplight. He scanned the surrounding darkness like he was anticipating an attacker to jump out at any minute.

"Do you think Rufus did it?" I asked after we had gone about half a block.

"He's not the guy." He shook his head and frowned. "It would be great if he were. Closed case as they say, but Rufus isn't a killer. He's unscrupulous, that's for sure."

"I'm inclined to agree with you, but like Dr. Caldwell said, until she's made an arrest, everyone has to remain a suspect. That's how the process works. She has to take him in for questioning and make sure she establishes a firm timeline for his whereabouts during the murder. She'll need to re-check witness statements and reports to see if anyone can corroborate his story, and they'll pull cell data to geotarget his movements."

"Technically speaking, fine. You're the expert on the criminal justice system," Liam said in what I could only interpret as a complimentary tone. "But I don't buy it. Not Rufus. The guy was shaken. He needed cash. Killing Martin didn't help his financial bottom line. There's no motive."

"Unless Martin caught him. He could be lying about leaving the theater when he did."

"True, but the rest of his story lines up."

"Yeah, I agree. I was thinking the same thing—the garbage, his bizarre claim that one of us stole the films, breaking in tonight..." I trailed off for a minute. We came to the end of the driveway.

"What?" Liam glanced in both directions before we crossed Cedar Avenue.

"Huh?"

"You were going to say something else, but you stopped." He waited for me to step onto the sidewalk first. "Do you have a theory?"

"I don't know." I felt like there was an idea nudging at my brain, but I couldn't fully form the thought.

"Give it a minute. Stop thinking, and it will come to you."

How did Liam know I was in my head?

"Do you know where Fletcher lives?" he asked.

"Yeah, this way." I pointed across the street to Oceanside Park, but before I could turn in that direction, I ran smack into Cora.

"Annie, sorry." Cora threw her hand over her mouth. "I didn't even see you. Izzy and I were deep in conversation, and I wasn't paying attention."

"No worries." I smiled at her and Izzy.

"Where are you two off to?" Cora's doe-like eyes drifted from me to Liam. "Clubbing? Pub hopping? Izzy and I will crash your party. We're trying to find where the action is tonight because we're ready to celebrate."

I waved my hand to the nearly deserted sidewalks. "I'm

afraid Redwood Grove doesn't have much of a nightlife scene. State of Mind Public House does karaoke on Saturday nights, and the Stag Head is open for another hour or so, right, Liam?"

Liam checked the time on his vintage leather watch. It was no surprise that he preferred an analog timepiece. "We're open until eleven. You've got plenty of time for a celebratory cocktail or two."

Izzy scrunched her mouth and shrugged. "We were hoping for something a bit more lively, but a cocktail will have to do. We'll do it up big when we're back in LA," she said to Cora.

I glanced at Liam to see how he would react. Obviously, his weekly poker games at the Stag Head paid off because his face revealed nothing but a fixed, polite smile.

"Are you celebrating *Midnight Alibi*'s record-breaking box office opening?" I asked. It was strange that the two of them had paired up. Wouldn't it make more sense for Cora to celebrate with Heather?

They shared a brief look. Then Cora clapped twice and rubbed hands together. "Can I tell them?"

Izzy grinned widely. Her smile transformed her face. "Go ahead. The news will be out soon."

"Izzy has cast me in the leading role in two new films," Cora squealed. "Can you believe it? Back-to-back leading roles. I'm flying high. It's such a dream to get to work with you."

Izzy was more subdued, but her eyes twinkled with delight. "To think I briefly thought maybe our sweet, young Cora had a hand in Martin's murder." She ruffled Cora's head like a big sister.

Liam cleared his throat. Was he as confused as me?

"I'm not following," I said to Cora, rubbing my arms to stay warm. Stars flickered on above the ridgeline of redwoods in the distance. "Are you talking about the remake of *Death on the Nile* that you were going to do with Martin?"

Izzy wrapped her silky purple shawl that matched her hair

around her shoulders. "Yes, that's a go, as is my new screenplay that Martin stole from me. My phone has been blowing up today. I sent out a few feelers after Cora and I had a long chat and cleared the air about both of our pasts. She's a hot commodity and a breakout star. Now is the time to bottle that magic while it's hot. Everything is being greenlighted with Cora's name attached to the projects."

"Sounds lucrative," Liam said with a touch of skepticism.

I didn't blame him. Izzy had thrown Cora under the bus earlier. It was hard not to imagine that she was taking advantage of Cora's sudden success for her own gain.

"That's Hollywood." Izzy patted Cora's arm. "What do you say, cocktails on me?"

"You bet." Cora couldn't contain her enthusiasm. Her entire body twitched and shimmied like she was warming up for an important scene. "Do you want to join us?"

"Thanks for the offer, but we're on our way to see a friend." I didn't mention anything about Rufus or Fletcher because I wasn't sure what this new revelation meant for the case.

"Congrats," Liam said with a curt nod as a way to close the conversation.

We left them and crossed toward the park.

Cora and Izzy were going to partner on two new projects. They were both benefiting from Martin's death. Could that mean they had also partnered on his murder?

TWENTY-SEVEN

"Well, what do you make of that?" Liam asked.

"Good for them, but also it's convenient that with Martin out of the way, suddenly Izzy's projects are being greenlit."

"Because of Cora," he added pointedly.

Amber streetlamps and moonlight guided our path through the rose garden. Never would I have imagined that I'd be walking through a romantic, moonlit garden with Liam Donovan. Not that this was romantic. The concept was romantic. We were on a mission to find Fletcher.

"Exactly. Cora's stock rose overnight. Izzy is savvy and has been in the business long enough to realize she has a chance to capitalize on Cora's instant stardom by casting her in future films, thereby ensuring that the projects will receive financial backing. Does that cast more suspicion on Izzy? I mean now that she can claim her screenplay back as her own also gives her a strong motive. Could she—"

Liam cut me off and grabbed my hand suddenly. "Hold up."

"What?" I glanced around us. Ancient wisteria crept over the wooden pavilion to our left and sleepy roses napped in neat rows to our right.

"Play it cool. Walk closer to me and don't turn around. I think we're being followed."

"Someone is following us?" I whispered to Liam.

"Yes. Look straight ahead. Act normal. I'm going to put my arm around you, okay? Let's pretend like I'm walking you home from a great date."

"A great date, yeah. Best date of my life. I'm practically all aflutter like I'm living out my own Jane Austen fantasy."

He wrapped a muscular arm around my shoulder. The same fuzzy feeling I'd experienced earlier buzzed through my body.

I threw my head back and chuckled like I was having the time of my life and he'd said something hilarious.

"No need to overdo it, Annie," Liam muttered, keeping his arm securely around me.

I leaned against him. "This is how I would act on the best date of my life."

He swallowed hard. "The best date of your life. I knew I was dashingly handsome and a real Renaissance man. Your modern Mr. Darcy, perhaps? I'm flattered by your attention and affection."

Liam was an Austen fan?

No chance.

He was definitely making fun of me.

I wanted to punch him but had to keep up the act. "Can you tell if they're still behind us?"

"Yep. Tell me where we're going. Are we still heading in the right direction?"

"Fletcher's apartment is by the Grand Hotel." I didn't want to gesture and give our stalker a clue which way we were headed. "Should we abort? Should I call Dr. Caldwell?" This was getting to be a habit.

"Let's stay the course for a minute."

My cheeks burned with heat. I wasn't sure if it was

entirely from the danger or if it was being this close to Liam again. I needed to concentrate and think logically about each of the suspects. It couldn't be Rufus. He was at the police station with Dr. Caldwell. That left Cora, Heather, Sam, and Izzy.

I felt relatively confident that I could rule out Cora. The fact that she had approached me about her secret of her own accord gave her more credibility.

I wanted to believe Izzy's explanation about her screenplay and *Death on the Nile* reimagining. Martin's attachment to her projects made sense. I wasn't sure her motives were entirely selfless when it came to hiring Cora as the lead, even knowing the truth about Cora's background. But the fact that both women were benefiting financially from the critic's death did give them a motive for killing him. However, I couldn't work out the logistics of how they could have pulled it off. Unless my theory that something other than Martin's body had been tossed off the balcony proved true. The more I thought about it, the less plausible it seemed. I felt like I was overcomplicating things. Dr. Caldwell had told us time and time again that the simplest answer was most likely correct.

That left Heather and Sam. Heather had been top of my list since the beginning, but I believed her. I couldn't articulate why. It was a gut feeling.

There was no chance that Sam could physically keep up with us. Nor would he be much of a threat to either of us unless he had a gun. But even so his demeanor at the theater had left me unsettled. I'd been bothered by what was bugging me about our interaction... Then it hit me.

"Oh my God, that's it," I said to Liam. "I think Sam is the one following us. I think he's the killer."

"The guy with the cane?"

"That's what I've been missing. That's what I overlooked. I should have known. It's so obvious. I learned that early on in my criminology courses and I ignored the most obvious detail in this real criminal case."

"What's the most obvious?"

"His cane. He doesn't need the cane. It's a prop."

"A prop? How do you know?"

"When he picked it up at the theater. He used his other hand and I could tell there was something off about it."

Liam secured his grasp on my shoulder and picked up the pace. It was hard to keep up with his long strides, but I did my best, and before I knew it, we came out of the gardens and turned on the street toward Fletcher's. We were only a few houses away. Fletcher was smart and quick-witted; I doubted that he was in any serious danger, but I was still anxious to make sure he was okay.

"It was too light. He lifted it like it was a toy. That's because I think it is a toy—well, at least a prop for the stage. He was pretending to be frail like he had to rely on the cane. It was all part of his act. He killed Martin. He changed the review. It's been him all along."

"You really think so?"

"I'm positive."

Before I could say more, a woman's voice calling from behind interrupted us. "Liam, Liam, I've been trying to catch up to you. We need you at the pub. There's been a fire."

We turned to see one of Liam's waitstaff, still in her apron, running to catch us.

"A fire?" Liam gasped. "Is it bad?"

She caught her breath and thrust her thumb behind her. "In the kitchen. Chef says he needs you."

Liam hesitated, scanning our surroundings, which were quiet and calm, like any other night in Redwood Grove. Moonlight spilled onto the sidewalk and the scent of brewing bedtime tea drifted out of the windows of the cozy bungalows nearby. "Uh, I need to take Annie—"

This time I cut him off. "No, go, Liam. You literally have a fire to put out." I motioned to the Grand Hotel, which was less than fifty yards away. "Fletcher's place is right on the other side of the hotel. I'll check on him and call Dr. Caldwell about the other thing on my way."

He didn't budge.

"Go." I pushed him toward his staff member.

He opened and closed his mouth like he was trying to find the right words. "Okay, but check in and let me know that you're okay."

"I will," I promised. "Now, go put out a fire."

I chuckled to myself as I continued along the street. Liam and I were quite the pair. We managed to convince ourselves we were being followed by Martin's killer when in actuality it was his poor waitstaff trying flag him down.

As I walked, even under the cover of darkness the wisteria along the railings at the edge of the park smelled ambrosial. I reached into my pocket and pulled out my phone to text Dr. Caldwell. I needed to tell her I was checking on Fletcher and about my breakthrough about Sam.

My body still buzzed from the rush of thinking we'd been tailed.

I concentrated on my feet as I texted while I walked, knowing it probably wasn't the smartest idea, especially in the dark. I have a tendency to sway toward the clumsy side of things. I could picture myself faceplanting, but I didn't want to waste any more time getting to Fletcher's.

After I hit "send," I started to tuck my phone away, but as I did, I heard the sound of thudding footsteps behind me and the woosh of something swinging in the air.

The next thing I knew, I was on the ground.

Was I imagining things again?

Had I tripped?

Pain shot up my left arm, to my shoulder and all the way to my forehead. I touched the tender spot.

Did I get hit or was the pain from the fall?

I couldn't tell.

Everything was blurry and fuzzy.

I rolled onto my side, keeping my injured arm as close to my body as I could. The pain was intense. It made me want to vomit.

I must have been hit.

I squinted to focus, trying to ignore the tiny spots trying to take over my field of vision. The French-inspired Grand Hotel looked blurry, like I was seeing through splotched, dirty glasses.

How hard had I been hit?

Suddenly, a figure came into blurry focus.

I let out a scream, which sounded strangely as if it was coming from somewhere else.

I screamed again as the figure stepped closer, and I finally saw my attacker's face.

"Sam?"

He held the cane like a baseball player, swinging it up behind him ready to strike, like he was desperate to get a hit.

I shielded my head and yelled for help.

Someone had to be nearby.

Please let them hear me.

I considered my options. I could try to make a run for it, but my head was spinning. I wasn't sure I could stand on my own, let alone run.

Sam didn't say a word, which made him all the more terrifying. He slid his hands higher on the cane preparing to smack me again.

I dragged myself away from him on the pavement, not caring about the grazing to the skin on my arms. I had to get out of here. I had to do something.

"Help!" I screamed with every ounce of air left in my lungs.

Where was my phone?

I must have dropped it when I fell.

Then the cane made contact with my back in one harsh blow. Pain radiated in both directions—up and down my spine.

This was bad.

Sam was winning and I was starting to fade.

My vision flickered in and out like the stars above.

This is not how I imagined my life would end.

Is that what Scarlet thought, too?

"Hey, get away from her—now!" Liam's voice cut through the buzzing sound in my brain.

Was it an illusion?

No.

Liam wrestled the cane free from Sam's hands and snapped it in half. Then he tackled Sam and held him to the ground. He tossed me his phone. "Call Dr. Caldwell."

I didn't hesitate, but I didn't call Dr. Caldwell directly. Liam appeared to have the upper hand, but he couldn't hold Sam down forever. If Dr. Caldwell was busy questioning Rufus, she might not be able to take my call.

I dialed 911 and explained that we needed the police—immediately.

It felt like déjà vu.

"Tell them we need medical assistance, too," Liam added, keeping a tight grasp on Sam's wrists.

Sam hadn't uttered so much as a single syllable.

"Is he hurt?" I held my hand over the receiver.

"No, you are." His voice caught. "I'm so sorry, Annie. I heard the screams and ran back as fast as I could."

"Am I hurt?"

The dispatcher asked me dozens of questions while we waited for the authorities to arrive. It didn't take long. I thanked my lucky stars, not for the first time, for the benefits of living in a small town. I'd barely had a chance to explain the strange turn of events before the police arrived on the scene.

Liam handed Sam over to the police and knelt beside me on the sidewalk. "Can someone take a look at her?"

"I'm fine," I protested, but the sky appeared to be spinning like the stars were rotating at warp speed.

A paramedic led me through a series of tests, checking that I could track their finger and shining a painfully bright light in my eyes. "We're going to bring you in to run a few more labs and probably keep you overnight as a precaution."

"I don't need to go to the hospital. It's just a bump." I raised my hand to try and touch the most painful spot on the base of my skull, but I couldn't do it.

"It's not up for debate, you're going," Liam said; his voice was thick with emotion. "I can't believe I left you."

"You had to go—the fire..." I trailed off. How much time had passed? Had Liam made it to the Stag Head and come back for me? Everything was jumbled and messy, like I'd dumped a thousand-piece puzzle on the ground and was trying to put it back together.

"What about Professor Plum?" I asked Liam.

He frowned for a moment. "Is he your boyfriend?"

"If my boyfriend has four legs and a tendency to purr, yes."

"Your cat, right. At least your sense of humor is still intact. That's a good sign. I'll feed your cat." He reached out his hand. "Give me your keys."

"To my house?"

"How else would I feed him?"

I wasn't sure how I felt about Liam Donovan being in my cottage, but I couldn't abandon Professor Plum.

"Tell me what I need to do," Liam said, taking notes on his phone while I explained Professor Plum's eating routine and where he could find the cat food.

The paramedics helped me to my feet. At least I could

maintain some sense of dignity by walking to the ambulance instead of getting carted off on a gurney.

"I'll check in with you at the hospital after I feed Professor Plum and make some calls to let everyone know you're in good hands."

Who was he going to call?

I didn't have a chance to ask because the paramedics helped me into the ambulance and took my vital signs. At the hospital, a doctor gave me a complete exam and deemed me well enough not to have to get an MRI or CAT scan.

They gave me some medication for the pain that made me drowsy.

I spent the rest of the night drifting in and out of restless sleep as nurses constantly rotated into my hospital room to check my blood pressure and adjust my IV.

Even though it wasn't my best night of sleep, I could at least take solace in the fact that Martin's killer had been caught. My tired brain was buzzing with questions about Sam, but they could wait for another day.

TWENTY-EIGHT

The next morning, I woke to a colorful display of flowers and balloons. My tiny hospital room looked like it had been overtaken by roses, tulips, and get-well-soon Mylar balloons.

A nurse brought me breakfast. "Are you ready for visitors? Because you have quite the crowd out there."

"I do?"

She nodded. "It's like brunch out in the lobby."

"Send them in." I propped up my pillow and sat up taller in bed, balancing the tray with a fruit cup, toaster waffle, and something resembling soggy scrambled eggs on my lap.

Hal, Fletcher, Pri, and Penny flooded in carrying more gifts.

Pri took the tray off my lap and handed me a latte and a pastry bag from Cryptic. "Nope, girl. I can't let you eat that. You're our local hero. You can't have gummy eggs and stale waffles. I made you my concussion special."

"Concussion special?" I took a whiff of the latte. It smelled spicy, like cinnamon and nutmeg. "Is this a Christmas coffee in the middle of summer?"

"No. It's basically health food. It's a golden turmeric latte with lots of warming spices." She sat at the edge of my bed and massaged my feet. "It's good for circulation. It will keep your blood flowing."

"Health coffee, that's a new one." Penny winked at her and set a bouquet next to my bed.

"Trust me on this one." Pri patted my feet. "I'm a professional."

I smiled, but it made my head hurt.

"How are you feeling, Annie?" Hal brought me a stack of my favorite books—the newest Janice Hallett and two new debut novels. "You look like your cheeks have some color, but I don't like that bandage on your head."

"Okay, a little sore, but better." I peeked into the pastry bag to discover a cherry almond croissant, my favorite.

"You're going to spoil me." I sipped the coffee cautiously, not sure how my stomach would react.

"You took a blow for the team," Fletcher said, staying near the foot of the bed. "We're just glad you're okay. Me in particular because I hear you got attacked looking for me."

"That's not your fault." I removed the flaky croissant from the bag. "I'm glad you're okay. We got worried when you never showed at the bookstore."

"I did, though. I explained to Liam and Hal, I went in through the back gate last night. I cut through the park and dropped the stuff off in the Dig Room. I must have missed Rufus, or maybe he was already up in the front of the bookstore while I was there, but I left and went home to watch reruns of *Monk*."

"That's a relief." I broke off a piece of the croissant, getting crumbs everywhere. "Did Sam confess?"

Hal shook his head. "Not as far as I've heard, but Dr. Caldwell said she has a solid case against him."

Everyone filled me on how many people had crowded around the police station last night and how Rufus had confessed to stealing the tapes and agreed to pay for damages at the Secret Bookcase. He would replace every title dinged up in the fall as well as pay for new bookshelves.

"That's enough for me," Hal said with a shrug. "I don't need to make things worse for him. He's done that himself, and as long as our books and people are safe and sound, then the world is right with me."

"What about Heather, Cora, and Izzy?" I adjusted the pillow so it wasn't touching the bruise on my back where Sam had hit me with his cane.

"They sent you a lovely gift from Artifacts. They swung by the store to check on you after they heard the news and asked if I could recommend a shop in town." A slight blush crept up his cheeks. "I suggested Caroline's shop. She put together candles, tea, a new robe, and a blanket. Liam took it to your place when he went to feed Professor Plum this morning. It will be waiting for you when you get home."

"They're on their way back to LA. I sent them off highly caffeinated," Pri added. "Just so you know we're all invited to the premiere of *Death on the Nile* when it releases."

Everyone let out a collection groan.

"Too soon? Too soon?" Pri winked.

It felt good to laugh despite the fact that my head felt like shattered glass.

The conversation shifted to plans for the day. Everyone hung out for a while, keeping my spirits up. I looked around at my friend group and felt lucky. When I had first moved to Redwood Grove, I never would have imagined being surrounded by so much love.

The nurse came in to start my release paperwork and shooed everyone out.

"I don't want to see you at the bookstore until those bandages come off, understood?" Hal tenderly kissed the top of my head.

I fought back tears. It was incredible to know that they were my found family. Seeing death and dysfunction close up these past few days made me all the more grateful.

After the nurse finished checking my vitals, another soft knock sounded on the door. Dr. Caldwell peered into the room, holding a bouquet of lilies. She didn't look like she'd slept much and was wearing the same suit I'd seen her in yesterday. "It's good to see you sitting up and with color in your cheeks. Liam told me you were pretty shaken up last night, understandably so."

"Did Sam hit me?" I asked. "Everything is so blurry. Liam and I thought we were being followed, but then we realized it was one of his staff and then everything after that feels surreal, but it was Sam who knocked me over, right?"

She nodded. "There is one person at fault for all of this, and he happens to be behind bars at the moment. I have witnesses that have come forward identifying Sam as the figure in the trench coat assisting the drunk person in the balcony. It's unclear to me why he disposed of the coat so carelessly. My guess is that he ran out of time and panicked after he threw Sam over the railing. The good news is that I have a feeling when the forensic report comes back on the coat, we'll have concreted evidence linking him to the murder. I intend to build a rock-solid case against him that will keep him there permanently."

"But he hasn't confessed?"

"I don't need a confession. We have a digital trail of everything he's done, including re-writing Martin's review."

"So it was him." I reached to my bedside table and took a bite of the croissant. "Was Martin already dead or did the fall kill him?"

"The fall was the cause of death, but I appreciate that you explored other possibilities and followed your intuition."

"I felt like something was off about Sam, but I couldn't put my finger on it. The cane was his alibi. It's kind of brilliant. I wrote him off for a long time because I didn't think he had the strength to do it."

"You are not alone in that assessment. I believed the same. It wasn't until the digital evidence came through that I began to realize my mistake. Take a look at this." She approached the bed and handed me her phone. "He changed the entire thing and submitted it to Martin's editor under Martin's email account. We've been looking into his financial records as well. It seems that Sam may have been a relatively successful producer, but he's terrible at hiding evidence. His paper trail is longer than the Pacific Crest Trail. I'm not worried in the slightest about landing a conviction. If he happens to confess before the trial, that's icing on the cake, but it's not necessary."

"That's good news." I reviewed the documents, happy that she trusted me with confidential information and that we finally had the right person behind bars.

"Listen, Annie, your sole job at the moment is to recover and heal. When you're up for it, I'd like to continue our discussion about your future. You've shown real resolve and dedication with this case, and it's thanks in part to your efforts that this investigation progressed so quickly and we have Sam in custody."

I breathed in slowly, allowing her words to sink in and resonate. After being attacked last night, the idea should have been unthinkable, but to my surprise I knew immediately the opposite was true. If I had been even a tiny part of bringing Martin's killer to justice, how could I say no?

"Think about it, will you?" She pushed her glasses down and beamed at me before clasping my hand in a rare show of affection. "You were made for this work, Annie."

I must have drifted off to sleep again because the soft sound of a man's voice stirred me from a strange dream that involved a

Hitchcock impersonator baking croissants at the Secret Bookcase.

I opened my eyes to see Liam in the doorway holding a soup container and a bundle of sunflowers. "Did I wake you?"

"Not really." I brushed my hair off my shoulders and stretched. It was a good thing there wasn't a mirror in the room. I couldn't imagine how I must look.

"How are you doing?" he asked softly, hanging near the foot of the bed. "I'm so sorry about last night. It's my fault. I never should have left you."

"What? No. It's Sam's fault. You're not responsible for my well-being. I'm an adult."

He made room for the sunflowers next to the other bouquets. "I should have trusted my gut, though. I knew someone was following us."

"Yes, your staff member." I tried to raise my eyebrows, but it hurt too much. I hid a wince. "How's the restaurant by the way?"

"Fine. It was a small grease fire and thankfully the chef got it under control." He lifted the container. "I made you my famous chicken soup recipe."

"*You* made me soup?"

Why did my heart have to tick like a bomb waiting to explode as he came closer?

He lifted the lid and produced a spoon from his pocket. "This is my specialty. It will have you feeling better in no time."

I wasn't hungry, but it smelled divine, and Liam Donovan had taken the time to make me his special soup. How could I refuse?

I took the container and spoon from him, and he watched as I took a mouthful, toying with the top button on his shirt.

"It's seriously delicious. Thank you. I can't believe you made me soup."

"It's the least I could do. I've been so worried about you."

His eyes held a sense of longing that made my already weak limbs feel weaker.

"I'm okay," I said truthfully, taking another taste of the soup. It was layered with herbs and veggies and had a hint of citrus finish, like he'd squeezed in fresh lemon juice at the last minute. "And for the record, I owe you. You got there right in time. I was about to pass out."

"I should have gotten there sooner. I never should have left you." He sat on the edge of the bed and tenderly brushed a strand of hair from my eye. "Does it hurt?"

"My head's a little throbby and my back's sore, but hey, we took down a killer last night, so who cares about a few bumps and bruises?" I reached out my fist.

He bumped his against mine. "You realize most people would be falling apart? You're pretty amazing, Murray."

"What can I say? Crime fighting is in my DNA."

A dimple appeared on the side of his cheek when he smiled. But then his face turned serious. "There's something I have to show you." He reached into his pocket. "Annie, you're going to be upset with me."

"Why?"

"Shouldn't you say 'why now'? You're always upset with me."

"True." I winked, which made my face hurt.

"I was petting Professor Plum last night. By the way, he thinks he's a dog or something. He greeted me at the door and had a full-fledged meow conversation with me while I fed him. Anyway, I hung out with him for a little while before I went to give my report of the events to Dr. Caldwell, and when I was stroking him, I accidentally broke his collar." He opened his palm. "I'm sorry."

"No, it's no big deal. I've been meaning to get him a new one." I was relieved. After everything we'd been through, I had expected something much worse than a broken cat collar.

"Whew, I was really worried. I'm heading straight to the pet store from here to get him a new one." He paused like he wanted to say more, but the nurse appeared in the door and cleared her throat. "Come by the pub. I owe you a real dinner soon. In the meantime, finish that soup."

I watched him stroll out of the stark white room. It was time to admit that Pri was right. Liam Donovan was officially under my skin and not in a bad way. We were entering dangerous territory, dancing on the edge of a love/hate relationship that was shifting further and further away from hate. I didn't know what it meant yet, but I did know that this experience had tethered us together and I was going to have to confront my growing attraction to him soon.

I held Professor Plum's collar in my hand, feeling my last connection to Scarlet slipping through my fingertips. But then I noticed it. Why had I never seen it before?

A tiny hidden pocket on the inside of Professor Plum's collar.

A secret pocket.

I gulped as I used my fingernails to reach into the pocket and pull out a computer chip. There was only one person on the planet who could have put the chip there—Scarlet.

A LETTER FROM THE AUTHOR

My deepest thanks for following along on Annie's journey with *A Murder at the Movies*. I hope this story brought you a moment of escape. If you want to hear more about new books, what's next for Annie, bonus content, and more, you can sign up for my newsletter.

www.stormpublishing.co/ellie-alexander

I would be beyond grateful if you would consider leaving an honest review for this book. Reviews help so much. Even a short review can make all the difference in encouraging a new reader to discover my books. Thank you so much!

Thanks again for being part of this amazing journey with me, and I hope you'll stay in touch—I have so many more stories and projects in the works.

Happy reading,

Ellie

www.elliealexander.co

facebook.com/elliealexanderauthor
instagram.com/ellie_alexander
tiktok.com/@elliealexanderauthor

ACKNOWLEDGMENTS

As with *The Body in the Bookstore*, I have to send huge bundles of thanks to the team at Storm and my editor, Vicky Blunden. It's been such a delight to truly collaborate together. I so appreciate your insight, guidance, and partnership with this series.

Writers spend a lot (some might say too much) time alone in our heads, talking to imaginary characters and making up fictional worlds. That makes it all the better to have real-world connections with readers. My crew includes Lizzie Bailey, Flo Cho, Courtny Drydale, Lily Gill, Jennifer Lewis, and Kat Webb. Thank you for reading early drafts, brainstorming title ideas, offering your input on Annie and Redwood Grove, and your ongoing support.

To Mary Jane O'Rourke, thank you for our brainspotting sessions, which sparked so many ideas for this series and what's to come.

To inhabit Redwood Grove, I took inspiration from actual places, including the stunning gardens and estate at Filoli, the sweet downtown of Los Altos, and the Midpeninsula Regional Open Space in California. While venturing out to take copious notes and pictures, Gordy, Luke, and Olivia tagged along (as they always do) to help me get out of my head and into Annie's.

Made in the USA
Las Vegas, NV
07 July 2024